A STAB AT LIFE

RICHARD KING

A STAB AT LIFE

Baraka
Books

Montréal

ISBN 978-1-77186-206-6 pbk; 978-1-77186-217-2 epub; 978-1-77186-218-9 pdf

Cover by Richard Carreau
Book Design by Folio infographie
Editing by Elise Moser and Robin Philpot
Proofreading by Barbara Rudnicka

Legal Deposit, 2nd quarter 2020
Bibliothèque et Archives nationales du Québec
Library and Archives Canada

Published by Baraka Books of Montreal

Printed and bound in Quebec

Trade Distribution & Returns
Canada – UTP Distribution: UTPdistribution.com

United States and World
Independent Publishers Group: IPGbook.com

We acknowledge the support from the Société de développement des entreprises culturelles (SODEC) and the Government of Quebec tax credit for book publishing administered by SODEC.

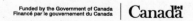

Dedicated to the memory of Margaret Noseworthy, 1942 – 1981.

CHAPTER ONE

"Put the gun down, dude."

Constable Gilles Bellechasse looked forward to an easy shift on that warm evening in May. Spring weather did a lot to inhibit the kind of mischief that would require police attention. Gilles was however to look back on that evening as the catalyst that would lead to his transformation from idealistic cop to more seasoned detective. He was partnered with Nicole Bélanger, and their job was to patrol a sprawling neighbourhood in Montreal's west end that was one of the most diverse in Canada both culturally and linguistically. Of course, English- and French-speaking Quebecers were an important part of the mix as well.

The patrol area, Côte-des-Neiges, included the Université de Montréal, and the students living in the *quartier* represented every French-speaking country in the world. The spiritual mix was diverse too, but there was little religious discord. Muslim and Jew, Protestant and Catholic, Hindu, Buddhist and the rest, all got along and lived in peaceful co-existence.

Gilles and Nicole had very similar attitudes to policing. Like Nicole, he was a cop who was a social worker at heart, and would rather resolve disputes than make an arrest. Plus Gilles didn't make snide remarks about women on the police force or tell sexist jokes. This meant that he and Nicole could focus on doing their jobs for the eight hours they spent together.

If Gilles had a shortcoming, it was his tendency to put the job ahead of what Nicole thought of as his personal needs. Gilles insisted they take their supper break between 5:30 and 6:00 p.m., reasoning they were likely to be needed from six o'clock on. Domestic disturbances often started at the dinner table. Drivers who stayed too long at one of the many bars and pubs that dotted their area could have an accident driving home.

Both Gilles and Nicole brought food from home, so after buying a couple of coffees at the Starbucks on Côte-des-Neiges, they headed for their favourite spot to take a break. Kennedy Park was one of the larger parks in the area, taking up the equivalent of four city blocks. There was a parking spot by a copse of trees and shrubs they liked and where they could enjoy a quiet thirty minutes before the activity of the night began.

They parked and Gilles reached for his sandwich and the books and manuals for the exam he would have to pass in order to be promoted to the Major Crimes Division. Nicole admired Gilles's ambition but she preferred to read a novel during her breaks. She fished around in her bag for her book and realized that she had forgotten it at home. There was no hope of getting Gilles to take his nose out of his books, so she sighed and gazed out the window at the activity in the park. Looking through the trees, she could easily see what was going on from the squad car though the car was hidden from the view of those in the park.

"Pas de livre ce soir, Nicole?" Gilles mumbled, to which she grunted a no.

Nicole spotted a couple of guys on one of the benches behind the trees. One was Asian and the other white. They looked to be in their early twenties and were sitting man-spread style, making it impossible for anyone else to sit there.

They were dressed in high-tops, basketball shorts and muscle tees, and they had a couple of large bags from the nearby McDonald's. Each guy held a burger in one hand, dipping into one of the bags with the other to pull out fries. From time to time some other young person would stop by and have a short conversation with the guys, shaking hands in the choreographed style of their generation, then walking around the bench and taking something out of another McDonald's bag as they left.

"Gilles," Nicole said, nudging her partner, "Regarde."

"Qu'est-ce qui se passe?"

"Those guys are dealing. Probably pot." With a jut of her chin, Nicole indicated the two men on the bench.

Gilles tossed his books into the back seat to focus on the two guys. Another customer approached, had a brief conversation, did the handshake which served as a cover for the passing of money, walked around the bench, took something out of the McDonald's bag, and walked off.

"Tabernac," Gilles exclaimed, "right under our noses. That's insulting – and illegal." Gilles paused for a moment and added with a smile, "It wouldn't be happening if our genius government hadn't raised the age for buying the stuff legally."

"They can't see us," Nicole pointed out.

"Well, we can see them. Let's go."

They radioed in to say they were about to investigate a couple of drug dealers and that arrests were likely to follow. Gilles and Nicole got out of the car and walked into the park.

They didn't barge through the bushes, which would have alerted the dealers, but walked around the copse that hid their car and approached the two guys from behind. Gilles circled left and Nicole right so that they appeared in front of the suspects, blocking any possibility of their running away.

"What are you guys up to?" Gilles asked conversationally.

"Just enjoying a nice evening in the park, Officer," the tall well-muscled Asian guy said. He looked like he was relaxing after a basketball game. Or would have if he had had a basketball.

"What's in the bag?" Nicole asked. Her tone of voice was a little more aggressive than Gilles's.

The less athletic-looking white guy held the bag out to Nicole and said, "Fries. Want some?"

"Don't be a smartass. What's in the other bag?"

The skinny white guy ran his fingers through his long dark hair and stared at Gilles and Nicole but didn't say anything for a couple of beats. "What's it to you?" he sneered. "We're having a burger in the park. Got a problem with that?"

Gilles put his foot on the bench next to the Asian guy and said, "Yeah, I do. Now let's see what's in the other bag."

The Asian guy tried to get up but was blocked by Gilles. The white guy was able to slip past Nicole and said in a loud voice, "Leave us the fuck alone. This is harassment."

A second or two later, half a dozen other young guys formed a semicircle around them.

Gilles asked for backup on the radio attached to his vest, but he didn't move away. "I'm not asking again," he said calmly and reached for the bag. The Asian guy shifted to his left, using his hip to push the bag just out of Gilles's reach.

The white guy tried to walk past Nicole but she put her hand on his chest and pushed him back onto the bench. As she did this, one of the guys standing to Gilles's right pulled a gun. Nicole saw it before Gilles did. "Pistolet!" she shouted and pulled her gun.

Gilles turned toward the guy with the gun, backed up a step or two and pulled his Glock out of its holster. He stood at the apex of a triangle with the Asian guy and the kid with the gun the two points on its base. He was facing the seated Asian but by turning his head slightly to the left he had the kid with the gun in full view. The kid was standing with his legs apart with the gun at shoulder height pointed at Gilles's chest.

"Put it down!" Gilles commanded, "And get on the ground." Without taking his eyes off the kid, he continued, "The rest of you, down on the ground. Don't be idiots."

Seven of the eight people slowly began to obey Gilles's order. The kid with the gun appeared too terrified by his own stupid bravado to move.

"Do as he says. Put the gun down, dude. You're making things worse," the Asian guy said. "You're a fuckin' asshole!"

The kid heeded his friend's advice and slowly started to lower the gun, but as he did it went off. The bullet caught Gilles at the waist, the only unprotected area of his upper body where his bulletproof vest exposed a couple of inches of midsection when he had his arms raised to point his gun.

Gilles collapsed to the ground.

Nicole shouted, "Gilles!" and dropped to one knee to attend to her partner. The kids took off running, leaving the bag of drugs behind.

Gilles was bleeding out and Nicole knew she didn't have time to retrieve the car's first aid kit. She covered Gilles's wound with her right hand and with her left pressed the "talk" button on her radio. "Officer shot. Send an ambulance," she shouted, and gave her location.

Seconds later, the park was flooded with cops. A moment or two after that an Urgences-santé ambulance appeared on the scene. It must have been very close by.

Most of the cops spread out, looking for the suspects. Nicole was aware of the activity, but her attention was on Gilles.

Nicole had managed to slow the flow of blood. One of the cops brought a first aid kit and she did her best to further stanch the bleeding. The Urgences-santé emergency medical technician tore Gilles's shirt away and applied a pressure bandage directly to the wound. A second EMT pulled the gurney out of the ambulance and rushed over with it. The first EMT slipped his hands into Gilles's armpits, the second one got between Gilles's legs and gripped him under the knees. They counted to three in unison, swiftly and carefully lifting him onto the gurney. They pushed it into the ambulance. One of the EMTs jumped into the back and Nicole got in the front with the driver. No more than five minutes had passed before they were on their way to the Gursky Memorial Hospital. The driver radioed ahead to report that he was en route with a gunshot wound, a cop, in his truck.

The siren tore through the quiet residential street that led to the ambulance bay. Under normal circumstances the ambulance drivers cut the siren when they turned onto the last block-and-a-half to the hospital. There was very little traffic on that street and the siren was not a necessity. This evening was an exception. Time is of the essence for gunshot victims and the driver did not want to have to slow down for even a second.

The driver slowed just enough to make a smooth turn into the ambulance bay. Annie Linton, the nurse on triage duty, and Athanasios "Tom" Andreadis, the senior orderly on duty, were waiting with a gurney. The driver got out and took three quick steps to the back of the ambulance. He yanked the back door open, pulled the gurney from the back of the ambulance, and with the help of the second EMT carefully brought the wheeled legs down. Nicole jumped out of the ambulance ready to help if needed. Annie took command of the transfer and motioned for Tom to place the hospital gurney next to the one from the ambulance. Tom steadied the gurney and Annie called, "On my count, one, two . . . " She stopped when she noticed that the pressure bandage had come loose and blood was spurting from his wound. "Gently," she called out, "lower him gently. His bandage came off."

The EMTs lowered Gilles back onto the gurney and one of them reached into the ambulance without taking his eyes off the patient. He felt around for the pressure bandages, grabbed a couple and tossed them to Annie. She caught them in her left hand, tossed all but one of them onto the still-empty gurney, and tore open the one she held with her teeth. She applied it to the wound and the bleeding stopped.

Again, she called out, "On my count, one, two, three!" The EMTs lifted Gilles's body and with Tom's help placed him on the gurney.

Annie and Tom, with Nicole close behind them, wheeled the gurney into the triage area.

Nicole ran alongside the gurney keeping a comforting hand on Gilles's shoulder. He opened his eyes and tried to turn his head to see where he was being taken. "Ne bouge pas," she said and smiled encouragingly. Gilles stared at her and smiled wanly.

"Where's the surgical resident?" Annie demanded. "I called the surgical floor when I got the call about a gunshot wound."

Annie got a blood pressure cuff on Gilles's arm. His blood pressure was low but steady. The bandage was doing its job.

Tom picked up the phone on the nurse's desk and was about to page the surgical resident again when Christine Fraser, the surgeon on duty, walked quickly into the triage room. Annie gave her what information she had and Nicole Bélanger confirmed that her partner had been shot once. Fraser examined the wound and reapplied the pressure bandage. She took the phone from Tom, punched in some numbers and told the person who answered, "I'm bringing a gun shot wound up for surgery. Which OR is open?" She listened for a moment, then turned to Tom and said, "OR three." Tom pushed the gurney to the bank of elevators. Dr. Fraser kept pace with him, her hand on the patient. "We've got this," she told the wounded cop, "you'll be fine."

Once Gilles was on his way to the operating room, Annie turned her attention to Nicole. She sat her down and gave her a wipe to clean the blood off her hands. Annie checked Nicole's blood pressure and other vitals. Amazingly, Nicole did not show any symptoms of shock. Her pulse was elevated, but that was not surprising given what she'd been through.

"Tell me what happened," Annie said to Nicole.

As they walked to the registration area, Annie took Nicole's hand and gave it a comforting squeeze. "It could have been worse, a lot worse. You got him here in time and Dr. Fraser will get him fixed up."

Nicole took a deep breath and said, "Thank you. I appreciate everything you've done."

Annie smiled. "Now I have to ask you to talk to one of our clerks, to get your partner's information." Annie motioned for Nicole to sit down next to the registration desk. "This is Steve. He needs you to give him as much as you can so we get . . . " Annie paused. She realized that she didn't know her patient's name.

"Gilles, Gilles Bellechasse," Nicole volunteered.

" . . . Gilles's personal information into the system."

Nicole sat down next to Steve's desk and answered as many of his questions as she could.

By the time Nicole had finished with Steve, the waiting room had filled with cops.

Nicole approached the senior officer, Lieutenant Lefebvre, and asked, "Est-ce que vous avez trouvé quelque chose? The gun? The little shit who did this?"

"No, nothing."

"Shit!" Nicole exclaimed.

"First things first," Lieutenant Lefebvre said. "How's Gilles?"

"He's in the operating room now. The nurse told me he'll be fine."

"Thank God."

Lieutenant Lefebvre turned to the group of cops milling about in the waiting room and loudly declared, "Écoutez-moi. Gilles is being operated on. He's going to be okay. I'll stay here with Nicole. The rest of you, canvass the neighbourhood and bring me the little fucker who did this."

The cops slowly dispersed, heading back out to the streets to find the perpetrator. News of the shooting had spread rapidly; for the first time in years, every young male in the neighbourhood was home in time for dinner.

Annie approached Nicole and Lieutenant Lefebvre and told them they'd probably be happier waiting for news in the waiting room on the surgical floor. Before they left the ER with Tom, who brought them up to the waiting room, Nicole gave Annie a long hug and said, "Merci pour tout. Bless you."

When Tom returned from the surgical floor for the second time that evening, Annie asked him, "Any word?"

"No," Tom replied, "not yet. You know, I've lived in this neighbourhood for over thirty years. My kids grew up playing in that park. There never used to be any trouble. Now look." Tom shrugged to express his feeling that the neighbourhood had changed and not for the better.

"Yeah," Annie agreed and called for the next patient. Nothing stopped the flow of patients into the ER of the Gursky Memorial Hospital.

CHAPTER TWO

"You may not remember me."

Gilles was released from the hospital a week later and was told he'd be on medical leave for at least the following two months. He knew he had to follow the doctor's orders but he hated the feeling of doing nothing. He took advantage of the time off to prepare for the exams that would get him off patrol and into the Major Crimes Division.

He studied hard and sat the exam in June, three months earlier than he would've been able to had he not been wounded. He passed the exam with top marks and was promoted to the Major Crimes Division when he returned to work in July.

While he recuperated and studied, he thought about the pretty nurse who had taken charge of him at the hospital. His memories of the evening were fuzzy because he'd slipped in and out of consciousness. But Nicole had filled in the important details about the nurse who'd discovered he was losing blood and stanched the flow before handing him off to the doctor who performed the surgery.

The nurse's name, Nicole informed him, was Annie Linton. Gilles decided he would drop by the hospital to thank her as soon as he was able.

Now that he had recovered from his wound and the exam was behind him, Gilles stopped by a florist for a large, colourful bouquet and made his way to the Gursky Memorial Hospital. It was only when he arrived at three in the afternoon that he realized he'd assumed Annie would be on duty. There was the distinct possibility she was working another shift or she had the day off. He went to the information window in Emergency and asked the clerk if Annie Linton was at work. Luckily, she was. She'd been assigned to work in one of the department's wards and the woman working at the information desk paged her and asked her to come to the registration area. She didn't mention there was a good-looking guy waiting there with a bouquet of flowers.

Gilles paced while he waited. Annie walked toward the registration area and couldn't help but notice a man pacing in the area, holding a large bunch of flowers. She felt she'd seen the man somewhere before but couldn't place him. He was tall with an athletic build. He was dressed in casual clothes but carried himself with a military bearing. His brown hair needed a trim but she had to admit as she got closer that it looked good the way it curled over his ears. When she was close enough to see his face, she lost interest in his hair and was taken by his sharp blue eyes. Then she realized who he was. He was the cop who'd come in with a bullet wound a couple of months before. Annie didn't handle that many gunshot wounds so she remembered the few bullet-wound victims she'd triaged. She slowed her pace for the last few steps, a little flustered as she realized that he was the reason she'd been called to Reception and that he'd likely come to thank her for what she'd done. Annie worked for the pleasure of helping those who needed it. She didn't expect special thanks for doing the job she loved. Doing it well was its own reward. She could count on one hand the number of times a patient had come back to thank her, and never had anyone brought flowers. Of course, she realized, the man could be visiting someone else and only wanted to see Annie because he was at the hospital for that other reason.

Gilles stopped pacing when he noticed Annie walking toward him. His memory was vague but he recognized her as soon as he saw her in her scrubs. She was short, no more than five feet two inches, and she had mahogany brown hair in a ponytail. Her eyes were grey-blue and her smile, which was a permanent part of her demeanor, was warm and comforting. There was something about Annie that Gilles and everyone who met her found attractive. It was more than the fact that she was very pretty; her compassionate soul shone through. As she approached, Gilles noticed that her scrubs were a little too large for her frame and he could not tell what kind of body they hid.

The glass doors slid open automatically. She stopped for a moment as she crossed the threshold into the public area of the emergency department. Gilles strode over to her, his normally serious face graced with a smile almost the equal of hers.

"You may not remember me," he said. "I'm the cop whose life you saved a couple of months ago."

Annie looked up at Gilles and said, "Yes, of course I remember you. I'm so glad you've recovered."

"Thank you," Gilles replied and held out the flowers. "These are for you. A very small way of telling you how much I appreciate what you did for me."

By this time, word of Annie's visitor had spread through the emergency department and nurses, doctors, and orderlies who were not otherwise occupied had gathered in the reception area to witness Annie's meeting with the good-looking fellow.

Annie accepted the flowers and blushed. "Oh my, they're beautiful. Thank you. They're not necessary. But thank you, again."

Gilles smiled. He was used to being in charge, but he hadn't considered what he would do once he had thanked Annie and given her the flowers. He was tongue-tied, and at that moment he looked over Annie's shoulder and saw the nurses and orderlies watching and smiling at them.

Gilles chuckled and said, "Taber . . . " He paused before he finished the word and then continued. "I didn't mean to attract attention."

Annie turned toward her colleagues, blushed again and shooed them with the back of her hand, but none of them moved.

Gilles looked around and saw they were only about five paces from the door to the drop-off area. He took Annie by the elbow and said, "Can we step outside for a minute or two?"

Annie nodded and allowed herself to be guided out of the building. Just before they passed through the double door, Annie leaned back slightly so that she was looking at her colleagues behind Gilles's back and mouthed, "Go away."

No one moved.

Gilles gazed down at Annie, looking straight into her eyes. "I heard from my partner that your quick thinking saved a bad situation from becoming a disaster. I want you to know I'm thankful for what you did."

Annie looked up at Gilles, holding his gaze, and replied, "I appreciate this. It's very thoughtful of you." She lifted the flowers slightly to indicate that she meant his words and the gift.

Gilles's original plan was to drop by the hospital, talk to Annie for a couple of minutes to thank her, and give her the flowers. But now, standing in front of the emergency department on a hot summer afternoon in July he was overcome with the desire to spend more time with her.

"This may be out of line," he said, "but I'd like to take you out to dinner some evening."

Annie didn't immediately answer and he worried that he'd overstepped some kind of boundary. He knew that if he'd been on duty and Annie had been in some way involved in a case he was working on, it would be totally inappropriate to ask her out. But he was off duty, on personal time. He hoped he hadn't insulted her.

Annie had been hit on so many times at work, usually by doctors and guys visiting a patient that her defenses rose when the question was posed. She took a deep breath to clear her head and realized that there was really no reason not to accept the invitation. "That would be nice," she said.

Gilles breathed a sigh of relief. "When would be a good time for you?" he asked.

"I work for the rest of this week but I'm off on Sunday and for a couple of days after that. Then I'm on evenings again for a week," Annie told him.

"Well, how about Sunday, then?" Gilles asked.

"Sunday," Annie repeated. "Yeah, that would be perfect."

"Where can I pick you up?"

"I'd write down my address but my hands are full," Annie said with a smile.

Gilles took his phone out of his pocket and said, "I'll put it in my cellphone."

Annie gave him her address and said, "Is seven okay?"

"Perfect," Gilles replied. He bent forward to give Annie the traditional Montreal double-cheek kiss goodbye, but the fact that she was holding the flowers prevented him from doing it. He was only mildly embarrassed by his attempt. Montrealers move from casual acquaintance to friendship pretty quickly and the city's tradition of a kiss on each cheek would not be considered inappropriate in a situation where the presentation of flowers resulted in a dinner date.

Annie smiled again and said, "I'll see you Sunday at seven."

"I'm looking forward to it," Gilles replied.

He waited for Annie to return to the emergency department before he left. Once back in the reception area Annie had to face her friends. The patients in the waiting room were surprised by the cheers and whistles that greeted Annie as she came through the glass doors. Tom Andreadis, short with a perfectly round head that he kept shaved to white stubble, said, "Funny that he didn't bring any flowers for me."

"Way to go, Annie," said one of the nurses who'd witnessed Annie's meeting with Gilles.

"You guys! Instead of not minding your own business, help me find a vase for these."

Tom went into the storage area behind the triage desk and returned with a plastic stand-up portable plastic urinal that in another context would look like a cheap vase and asked, "Will this do?"

"It will have to," Annie replied and took it from him. She carried it and the flowers to the ward where she was working. She filled the urinal with water, put the flowers in it and placed it on the unit manager's desk.

She was just about to get back to work when her friend Ursula, also an ER nurse, approached her and said, "Spill, girlfriend. I want the story, all of it." She used the Jamaican accent of her parents for emphasis.

They agreed to take their break together so Annie could fill her in.

On that Tuesday in July, Gilles walked out of the Gursky feeling very pleased. May and June had been stress-filled months during which he'd regained his strength and studied for the sergeant's exam. He found that he tired easily and barely left his condo. He thus missed out on the beautiful spring weather. Also, he did not see his daughter as often as he would have liked.

Emilie Bellechasse, Gilles's fifteen-year-old daughter, lived with her mother in Longueuil, a suburb on Montreal's South Shore. Gilles lived in the city. Following his divorce from Yvonne he'd purchased a condo near a metro station so it'd be easy for Emilie to visit. He was also close to the Jacques Cartier Bridge to make it easy for his ex to drive into Montreal to pick Emilie up or drop her off. Gilles had hoped that would make the separation easier on her.

Cops work nights and weekends, and this meant that he wasn't always available when Emilie needed him. It was tough enough for married cops to maintain a normal family life; it was ten times harder for those who were divorced. Gilles hoped that his promotion to Major Crimes would give him a more stable work schedule and that he could be more available to his daughter. He had five full days before he had to report for work and he intended to use much of it to do things with Emilie.

There was a message from his ex on the landline. Gilles sighed and called her. Yvonne only called when there was a problem.

"Yvonne, âllo," Gilles said when she answered.

"Finalement," she said by way of a greeting. She informed him that the principal at Emilie's high school wanted to meet them. Emilie was skipping classes and her marks weren't good.

"C'est important, Gilles," Yvonne stated forcefully, as if Gilles hadn't understood the situation. "When can you meet with Monsieur Gingras?"

"Demain ou jeudi ou vendredi soir," Gilles responded. "I'll be back at work on Monday."

"Of course, your precious work," Yvonne shot back.

"Oui, my precious work," Gilles said, sarcastically. "Set something up and I'll be there. Now can I speak to Emilie?" He left the phrase "for Christ's sake" unsaid. He preferred to call his daughter on her cellphone but felt an obligation to talk to his ex-wife about their child at least once a week.

Yvonne did not respond but dropped the phone on something hard, probably the counter in the kitchen, and called, "Emilie, ton père est au téléphone."

"Bonjour, Pa."

"Bonjour, Lapin, ça va?" Gilles did not wait for an answer. "I'm free all weekend. Can we spend some time together? We can do anything you like. We can even go to the country if you like. I don't have to be back until Sunday afternoon."

"I have a party on Friday night so I'll want to sleep in on Saturday. Can we do something in the afternoon? I'll come to the city."

"Sure thing, darling. We can just hang out if you like and go to dinner. You'll probably want to spend Saturday night with your friends, not your old man."

"Okay, Pa, I'll call you on Saturday. Bye."

"Bye-bye, Lapin, see you Saturday."

Emilie ended the call before her mother could get back on the line.

Gilles spent the rest of the week catching up on household chores, shopping for the kind of food his daughter was likely to want. The meeting his ex set up with the school principal occupied most of the late afternoon on Thursday. He hung out with friends at a sports bar that night.

Gilles spent Friday reviewing the procedures he would need to know for his new job in Major Crimes and spent a quiet evening at home watching TV. Knowing that he'd probably end up doing a lot of running around with Emilie the next day, he decided to have an early night and was in bed by ten.

CHAPTER THREE

"J'ai un laissez-passer," Gilles explained and showed his badge.

The cellphone woke Gilles up at two in the morning. He looked at the display but only saw a blur, his eyes still unfocused with sleep. It was not unusual for cops to get phone calls in the middle of the night, but Gilles was a heavy sleeper and it took him awhile to get his brain up to speed.

"Allo," he said groggily.

"Gilles!" His ex-wife's shriek brought him to full consciousness.

"What is it, Yvonne? It's two in the morning."

"It's Emilie." Those two words sent a jolt of fear through Gilles and brought him to his feet. He walked to the chair where he had left his clothes the night before and, holding the phone with one hand, he searched for his trousers with the other. "What's wrong? Is she ill? I'll be there as fast as I can. Does she need an ambulance?"

"No, you idiot," Yvonne yelled. "She's not ill. She's not here!"

Gilles didn't have to ask any more questions. He was too much a cop and a father. He understood perfectly what his ex-wife meant. This was not the first time their rebellious daughter had broken curfew, but it appeared to be the first time that Yvonne hadn't been able to track Emilie down.

When Emilie had disobeyed one of her parents' rules on other occasions, Yvonne hadn't called Gilles right away but had waited until a day when she felt it would be easier to play on his guilt and make Gilles feel like a failure as a father. Yvonne and Gilles were in fundamental agreement on the subject of their daughter's upbringing and the rules they expected her to follow. But there were times when Yvonne felt overwhelmed in her role as the custodial parent. Because Gilles's job meant that he had to work shifts she felt he did not spend enough time enforcing their rules with Emilie. And this circled back, in Yvonne's mind, to the reason for their divorce.

"Have you called her? Have you called her friends?" he asked.

"Yes, of course, what do you take me for?"

Gilles knew better than to get into an argument. He wanted facts so he could make sure his daughter was safe. "Do you know where she is?"

Gilles could hear Yvonne's breathing in the brief silence before she answered, "She's at some kind of club. Her friend Monique got home an hour ago, but Emilie stayed. I spoke to Monique's mom and to Monique."

"What club?"

"It's got a funny name, Cuisses, something like that. It sounds like a strip club," Yvonne reported.

Gilles repeated the name to himself to see if he could make sense of it. Cuisses is the French word for thighs and Yvonne was right, it did sound like a strip club. But Gilles had never heard of a strip club by that name and Montreal cops were up to date on the strip clubs in the city. He repeated the name to himself several more times until he realized that the name of the club wasn't Cuisses but Q'Z, pronounced "cues." It was a bar, dance club and pool hall rolled into one large place on two floors of an old warehouse in the Saint-Henri district.

"It's not Cuisses," Gilles told Yvonne, "it's a place called Q'Z, a club in Saint-Henri."

"Well then, that's where she is, and she has no business being there. At least I hope she's there and not gone off with someone." Yvonne started to cry. "She's only fifteen."

"Yvonne," Gilles said calmly, "I know where the club is. I'll find her. Don't worry. I'll call when I have her with me."

"Please," Yvonne said and ended the call.

Gilles got dressed in a hurry and, badge in hand, he was in his car and on the way to Q'Z in less than ten minutes. He thought of bringing his gun but decided against it. He was off duty, and he was more than prepared to flash his badge, if necessary, to get his daughter. But flashing his gun was something else entirely. If his commanding officer learned Gilles had used his badge to rescue his daughter there would be no repercussions. All the cops had families, after all. But if he was armed, well, that was a different story, and the brass would be unlikely to look the other way.

During the day it would have taken Gilles close to thirty minutes to get to the corner of Saint-Rémi and Acorn. At two in the morning it barely took fifteen minutes. Of course, he didn't obey the speed limit. In the time it took him to get there he wondered why Emilie hadn't called if she was in some kind of trouble. They had a deal. No matter what the situation, if Emilie needed help she could call and he'd come and get her, no questions asked. Of course, once she was safe, they would probably have a conversation, but there would be no recriminations or punishment if she called her dad.

He pulled up in front of the warehouse and walked to the main entrance. There were two large guys standing at the door. They were wearing black T-shirts with Q'Z emblazoned across the front in gold letters. The T-shirts showed off the doormen's biceps to advantage. The word Sécurité was written on the back of the T-shirts in large letters. Both men were wearing headsets with mics. Gilles ignored the guys at the door and reached for the handle to pull the door open. One of the doormen pushed against the door, preventing Gilles from opening it.

"Désolé, Monsieur. The club is full," he said with fake *politesse.*

"J'ai un laissez-passer," Gilles said, flashing his badge.

The guy with his hand on the door backed up a pace or two and reached up to his microphone and moved it in front of his mouth. He was about to speak to someone inside. Gilles put his hand up to the mic and closed his fist around it. "This is not a raid," he explained. "I'm looking for someone and I don't want to be announced. Get it?"

The doorman nodded.

"If I get the sense you've talked to your boss or whoever, I'll come back with a squad and a wagon, and I'll tell your boss it's because of you. Do I make myself clear?"

"Oui, chef," the doorman answered and backed away from the door, allowing Gilles access to the club.

Gilles entered and his senses were assaulted by the music. He not only heard it but he felt it vibrate up his legs and into his brain. Colourful beams of light rotated and flashed around the room, more or less in synch with the music. The room was enormous. A bar ran across the wall to the right of the entrance. The bar was more than twenty feet long and there were five bartenders working at it. The DJ station was opposite the entrance and Gilles could see the DJ, wearing a headset and working the turntables. Gilles could make out tables and booths along the back wall. Most of the space was taken up by a packed dance floor. From where Gilles stood it looked like the crowd was a large amoebic mass moving to the music.

The pool tables, Gilles knew, were on the second floor. He could see the winding staircase to his left. He moved cautiously into the room, giving his eyes a chance to adjust to the semi-darkness. It looked like there were two hundred people on the dance floor, and Gilles hoped he'd be able to spot Emilie without having to work his way through the crowd. Gilles believed he could find his daughter anywhere, no matter how big the crowd, no matter how daunting the circumstances. He was about to see if this was true.

His eyes focused and he scanned the crowd. A path opened up and he saw Emilie dancing with a guy who'd pulled her close, both his hands on her ass. Gilles strode up to the dancing couple. He came up behind the guy and gripped his right shoulder with his left hand.

"Hey, fuck," the guy said and turned to Gilles, "what the fuck?"

Emilie looked up and saw her father, "Christ, Dad," she asked. "What are you doing here?"

"I could ask you the same question."

Emilie's dancing partner was obviously not paying attention to her exchange with Gilles because he growled, "Fuck off, buddy, we're dancing."

"Not anymore," Gilles said. He removed his hand from the guy's shoulder and reached for his badge. He flashed it at the fellow and took Emilie by the hand to lead her away. She resisted at first but when she saw her dance partner back off she realized that she was best off leaving with her father.

Once outside, Gilles stopped to talk to the doormen. "I want you to remember my daughter," he told them. "She's fifteen years old, and once you scrub the makeup off her face and dress her properly, she looks it. If I find out you've let her—or for that matter her friends—in again I can promise you it will be the last time anyone gets into the club. Get it?"

The doormen nodded dumbly, happy that nothing worse had happened than a father rescuing his daughter.

Gilles got Emilie settled in the car and they drove to his condo. She sulked the whole way. While en route Gilles called Yvonne and told her that Emilie was safe and would be spending Saturday with him as planned. And, Gilles told Yvonne, he and their daughter would be having a conversation.

Annie woke up late on Saturday morning. It was her first weekend off in six weeks. Even though she felt rested she burrowed into the covers and closed her eyes, hoping to fall asleep for another hour just for the pure luxury of it. She gave up after five or ten minutes, sighed and got out of bed. She slept naked but kept a set of old scrubs close by. She slipped into them, made her bed and went into the living room of her upper duplex on Park Row East in western NDG, Notre-Dame-de-Grâce. The sun was streaming through the windows and she could see people with dogs and kids enjoying Saturday morning in the park opposite her flat.

"You up, mom?" Her daughter Pamela called from the dining room.

Annie turned and went to her daughter, who was doing homework. Annie bent over her daughter and gave her a hug. "Morning, sweetie," she said. "Homework on a beautiful day like today? You're a star."

"Mom . . . " Pamela responded but didn't complete the sentence.

Annie went into the kitchen and called out, "I'm making coffee, want some?"

"Yeah, please."

Annie prepared herself some fruit and yogurt. She handed a cup to Pamela, took a sip from hers, and sat down to breakfast.

"Studying?" she asked.

"Yeah, anatomy."

Annie marvelled at her daughter's determination. She was a pre-med student at McGill University and she put her commitment to become a doctor ahead of everything else. Pamela had received permission from the medical faculty to take an Anatomy and Cell Biology course over the summer. Annie sometimes worried that her nineteen-year-old daughter was denying herself a social life, but Pam consistently placed near the top of her class and worked hard to maintain that status.

"So guess what?" Annie asked.

Pamela gave Annie a long look, the kind of look only a daughter can give her mother. "Muuuum!" Pamela said, drawing out the word in a sing-song voice.

"Oh, all right, spoil my fun," Annie replied with a smile and then said nothing.

"Well, are you going to tell me or what?"

"Okay. But only because you insist. I have a date tomorrow. For dinner."

"Oh, Mum, that's terrific."

Pamela got up and gave her mother a hug while Annie was still seated. Annie craned her neck and kissed her daughter on the cheek.

"So, getting back in the game, eh?" Pamela asked. Annie had accepted Gilles's invitation because she thought it would be fun and interesting to meet someone new, not because she felt the need for a man in her life.

"C'mon, Mum, tell me more!"

"Well, I guess you could say I met him at work." Annie fiddled with her coffee cup. Now that she was telling her daughter the story she didn't know exactly how to describe how she and Gilles had met.

"A doctor? Surely not a patient!"

"Yeah, a patient. A former patient actually," Annie explained.

Pamela's eyes widened and she said, "I thought that was against the rules, a code of behaviour or something."

Annie smiled at her daughter and answered, "It's true that nurses get hit on all the time and we learn quickly not to take these things seriously. This was different, though. The guy's a cop. He got shot and came in a couple of months ago when I was working in triage. I got him patched up and up to surgery. I doubt he stayed in the hospital for very long."

"So how did this date thing happen?" Pamela asked, "If you haven't seen him in a couple of months."

"He came in a few days ago to thank me. He was very sweet and he brought me flowers. In the process of thanking me, he asked me out. Very hard to refuse a good-looking guy with flowers," Annie said.

"Yeah, especially if he has a gun!"

Annie spent Saturday evening watching a movie with her sister Rosemary and Rosemary's husband at their house. Pamela went out with friends.

Sunday was truly a day of rest for Annie. She spent the day in her scrubs reading the Saturday newspaper, catching up on email and her Facebook page. She even found time for a nap, which was unusual.

Late in the day, she showered and dressed for her date and was ready when Gilles rang her doorbell promptly at seven.

Annie liked the way Gilles was dressed in dark-wash jeans, dark brown Ecco loafers with white soles and a neatly pressed yellow Ralph Lauren Oxford cotton shirt. He was clean-shaven and his thick brown hair was parted on the left a stray lock falling over his forehead on the right.

The other thing Annie noticed about Gilles, and this was important to her, was he was a considerate walker. Gilles was over six feet tall and Annie was just five foot two. He adjusted his pace to hers. Annie disliked people, men in particular, who charged ahead and forced her to walk at an uncomfortable pace in order to keep up. First dates that started that way didn't usually lead to a second.

It was only a short walk from Annie's door to where his car was parked on Sherbrooke Street. Gilles opened the passenger door for her and held it while she slipped into the seat of his dark blue Honda Accord. Annie appreciated this small act of politesse, which according to her friends who dated more than she did, was all too rare.

Once Gilles was settled in the driver's seat and heading east along Sherbrooke he explained where he'd made dinner reservations. "I thought we would go to a restaurant in Saint-Henri. It's called Le Rougeot. It's named after a belle époque restaurant in Paris. Have you heard of it?"

Annie turned slightly in her seat and said, "No. But I've read that new and interesting restaurants are opening in Saint-Henri almost weekly."

"Oui, you're right," Gilles said with a smile.

At the restaurant, Gilles and Annie perused their menus in silence. Annie was uncharacteristically nervous. She wanted to know what had motivated Gilles to become a cop, but wasn't certain that she should start their date with such a personal question.

Gilles was either less nervous or more foolhardy, because he asked Annie, "What made you decide to become a nurse?"

Annie smiled and thought, well, you can't beat that for bluntness. She was charmed that Gilles was so direct. He looked her in the eyes and waited for her answer.

Before she could respond the waiter arrived with the wine. Once that was poured and tasted, Annie took a long sip and told Gilles that as a child she had developed a serious lung infection and spent a long time at the Children's Hospital. As she recuperated she decided that she wanted to be just like the nurses who cared for her. Annie paused and took another sip of wine. "Not an exciting story, but that's it in a nutshell."

"That's wonderful," Gilles said.

"Now it's your turn," Annie said. "What made you decide to become a cop?"

"My story is not all that inspiring. My father was a cop and so was my grandfather, so my career was kind of preordained. Maybe if I'd had older brothers who joined the force there would've been less pressure to go into the family business and my life would have taken a different turn. But there you are."

The waiter delivered their food and they took a minute to begin eating before resuming their conversation.

"Do you have brothers and sisters?" Annie asked.

"Yes, two sisters, one younger, one older."

They were quiet for a moment, each wondering how many personal questions to ask this early on a first date.

Annie broke the silence and asked, "Did you join the force right after college?"

"Not quite." Gilles paused to take another mouthful of smoked venison. Annie had ordered the Arctic char. "I guess I had a bit of rebellion in me because I took a year to study in France. In Paris, at the Sorbonne."

"Amazing. I have to say that that was the last thing I expected to hear from a cop."

Gilles smiled. "Really, are we that conventional?"

Annie blushed and then giggled a little nervously. "No, of course not. Well, yes, I'm sorry, I don't mean to be judge-

36

mental, but how many of your fellow officers have been to the Sorbonne?"

"Well now that you ask, so far as I know, none."

The plates had been cleared away. The dessert menus lay untouched near the edge of the table. "What was it like, living in Paris?"

"Well, I loved it; it's a great place to be a student. But I found the Sorbonne a little disappointing. I expected the courses to be more rigorous. I heard that things kind of fell apart academically after the student riots of 1968."

"But the point is, you had a great opportunity, right?" Annie asked. She finished the wine in her glass and Gilles poured some more for her from the second bottle they'd ordered.

"Oh, without question. I'm not complaining. I had a great year. I would have stayed longer, believe me, but I had made deal with my father—a year in Paris, then back to Montreal to finish my bac and then off to the police academy at Nicolet.

How about dessert?" he asked.

"I couldn't," Annie replied. "But I could go for a coffee."

"So could I." Gilles signalled the waiter and they ordered two cappuccinos.

As they drank their coffees the conversation turned to the subject of children and Annie and Gilles traded stories about their daughters.

It was just past ten o'clock when they left the restaurant. "I lost track of the time," Annie said. "It went by so fast."

"I had a lovely evening. I don't remember when I've enjoyed being with someone so much."

Gilles walked Annie to her door. "I had a wonderful evening. I hope it's the first of many. I'll call you very soon."

Annie agreed, "Me too. Thank you. You have my cell number and I always have my phone with me, even at work. If I can't talk, I'll call you back. Promise."

"And I promise to call," Gilles said. He and Annie two-cheeked with a little more feeling than normal. Annie went upstairs to her flat and Gilles drove home.

Gilles didn't want to seem pushy by setting up a second date while on the first, but neither did he want to leave things for too long. He called Annie on Tuesday and they made plans to go out on the following Friday.

CHAPTER FOUR

"Crap, that's gotta be deep."

Mikel Esperanza liked to get to his corner of Kennedy Park a little before noon when the weather was nice. Lunch hour was a very busy time in illicit drug dealing. High school students were free for forty-five minutes or so, plus there were all those others who also enjoyed grabbing a bite and replenishing their supply of marijuana in the park. On this sunny day late in September, Mikel was late. His younger brother Ferdy had forgotten his lunch and Mikel had to walk it over to Ferdy's school. It was just after one in the afternoon when Mik walked through the park, heading to his preferred spot—the corner of the park hidden from the street on one side by shrubs and trees and away from the playground and sporting areas. The perfect spot for doing a little discreet drug dealing. Mik hoped that some of his clients would be waiting for him, but as he approached the park bench he used as his base of operations he saw that there was no one there. He swung his backpack off his shoulders and rested it on the bench. He kept his inventory in a McDonald's bag. Because his attention was focused on getting ready for business, he didn't notice a figure wearing an extra-large hooded black sweatshirt approach him from behind. He first realized that he was not alone when he was stabbed. Mik shouted, "Hey, fuck!" and tried to pull away. His assailant held Mik by the neck as he pulled his shiv up and to the left. Mik crumpled to the ground. The attacker cut through the trees and onto the street. As soon as Mik hit the ground he started to scream for help. A couple of high school students who had decided the day was too nice to spend in class, the better to buy some weed and enjoy an afternoon goofing off, arrived on the scene less than a minute later and found Mik lying in a growing pool of blood.

"Holy fuck," said the first student, "what happened, dude?"

The second student was a little less stupid and said, "Idiot. The guy's been stabbed." He knelt beside Mik and tried to talk to him. Mik's answer was unintelligible. The kneeling student reached for his cellphone and called 911 for an ambulance. In spite of the fact that the operator told him to wait for the ambulance to arrive, the students took off running. The less stupid of the two grabbed Mik's backpack with the McDonald's bag still in it.

On that same sunny Tuesday in the third week of September, Annie was working the afternoon and evening portion of a double shift in triage, her preferred service. As usual, Tom Andreadis was the orderly on duty. Probably because the weather was unseasonably warm, and people preferred to be outdoors enjoying the day, the patient load in the emergency department was light. Annie had noticed many years earlier that on nice days people stayed away from that service.

She and Tom, who had just come on duty, were chatting at the triage station; they were trying to decide which of them would go to get coffees, when Tom, motioning toward the closed-circuit television set with a nod of his head, said, "Ambulance."

Annie looked at the TV and saw the ambulance pull into the garage and watched as the driver leapt out and rushed to the back door. Ambulance drivers usually moved quickly but ran only when they believed that the risk of death was imminent.

Annie quickly got to her feet and started moving toward the second triage area, the larger one closer to the ambulance bay, pulling on latex gloves as she walked. The room was big enough to accommodate a gurney, two EMTs, the triage nurse and an orderly. It was also more private than the triage station used for walk-in patients. "Come with me!" she commanded and Tom followed her to the triage room, arriving just ahead of the EMTs and the gurney bearing the patient.

"What've we got?" Annie asked. The patient was a young Filipino man who looked to be in his early twenties. Annie observed that the young man was pale and was having trouble breathing. Before the EMT had a chance to answer Annie had taken the patient's wrist to check for a pulse and found it weak. "Stabbing victim," the EMT informed her. "Stomach."

The EMTs unbuckled the belts holding the patient to the gurney and Annie pulled the blanket covering the patient down to expose the wound. Annie and Tom saw a blood-soaked bandage on the right side of the man's lower abdomen.

"Christ," Tom muttered.

"Get me some bandages and call the surgical resident," Annie ordered. She gently applied pressure to the wound to see if she could stanch the bleeding. It didn't work. She pulled up the bandage and applied the new one in a way that temporarily closed the wound, a clean slice that looked like it had been done with a fast sideways motion of a very sharp instrument. The wound angled upward from the lower right to the upper left and stopped several inches to the left and above the patient's belly button.

Annie placed an oxygen mask on the patient as two other nurses and a doctor came rushing into the triage area to assist her. "I've got it," Annie exclaimed. "But check for other wounds."

"Nothing on my side," shouted Lynne, one of the nurses who had come to Annie's aid. She had examined the right side of the young man. "Good on the lower extremities," said Ursula, the other of the two nurses assisting. Annie had a blood pressure cuff on the patient and was waiting for the read as the ER doctor felt around the patient's neck and head. "Clear here," he shouted adding to the cacophony of information.

"I'm barely getting a read on the pressure," Annie called just as the surgical resident, Christine Fraser, rushed in. Annie was relieved to see her as she had the reputation of being the best surgeon to have in an emergency. She was the doctor who had worked on Gilles when he was brought in.

"Stabbing," Annie stated, as Fraser approached the patient. She looked at the wound and said, "Crap, that's gotta be deep. Let's go."

They lifted the patient and transferred him to a new gurney; Annie rushed to the victim's right side to check the wound. The new bandages were soaked with blood. "Bleeding out," she called to Dr. Fraser.

"Do what you can. We've got to move," Dr. Fraser shouted back at her. She was in the lead, pulling the gurney, with Tom pushing from the rear as they headed out of the triage area. Annie kept pace with them, trying all the while to put some pressure on the wound to staunch the bleeding.

A squad car arrived within minutes of the ambulance and secured the crime scene in the park.

◉

Captain Henri Lacroix was in his office at the Major Crimes Division headquarters in the east end of Montreal. The division was quartered on the second floor of an office building above a shopping centre, Place Versailles, which made it invisible to the general public. His square office held the inexpensive furnishings provided by a city that did not spend money on things that could not be seen. He looked up from the report he was reading and gazed through the window in the wall opposite his desk, which looked out on the squad room. Most of the detectives were in groups of two and sometimes three, going over files. The captain was certain that their conversations had more to do with sports and their personal lives than with whatever cases the files were concerned with. One of the detectives, Gaston Lemieux, was seated at his desk reading something on his computer screen. Another of the cops, the newest member of the squad, Gilles Bellechasse, looked lost, not knowing which group to attach himself to.

Captain Lacroix was half out of his chair, about to head into the squad room to ensure that the cops under his command were working to clear cases, when his computer emitted a long beep and his printer started printing a document. Henri Lacroix sat down and twisted in his chair so that he was facing his printer, on a table to his left. He pulled the sheet out of the tray, read it and got to his feet. He strode into the squad room and with the report in his left hand called for his crew's attention. "Il y a eu un coup de couteau," he stated, referring to the page in his hand, and gave the location of the park where the stabbing had taken place. "The victim has been taken to the Gursky Memorial Hospital. You two" — he pointed at Albert Cadieux and Stephanie Giroux—"get to the park. A squad car has secured the scene. Keep it secure

until the forensic team takes over and then start a canvass."
Lacroix paused for a minute and stared at Cadieux and
Giroux until they got moving. He turned to Lemieux and
said, "Get over to the hospital and find out what you can.
The victim has been taken into surgery."

Gaston got to his feet and said, "Oui, chef." He headed to
the door that led to the reception area and the elevators. Before
he reached the door Gilles asked, "Can I ride with Lemieux?
My girlfriend is a nurse in the emergency department at the
Gursky. I know most of the people on staff there." This was an
overstatement but Gilles was certain that he would be able to
make a positive contribution to the investigation.

"OK, Gaston?" Lacroix asked in deference to Lemieux's
seniority and the fact that he was the best cop in the unit.

"Yeah, fine," Lemieux answered. Gilles took a couple of
quick steps to catch up as Lemieux walked out of the squad
room, "Merci, chef," he said as the door closed behind him.

On the drive over to the hospital Gaston Lemieux explained
to Gilles that he expected him to follow his orders, show initia-
tive, and most important, not expect Gaston to repeat himself.

The EMT who had been in the back of the ambulance with
the patient said, "I found his wallet. Here." He handed a bat-
tered cloth wallet with a Velcro closer to, Steve, the clerk who
was working the registration desk inside the triage area, and
said, "This is from the stabbing that just came in."

He opened the wallet and looked for the patient's
Medicare card, the *carte soleil*, so he could do the admissions
paperwork. He found the plastic card, as well as several slips
of paper with telephone numbers written on them along with
identifying initials. There were also some old receipts and an
old high school ID card.

The patient's name was Mikel Esperanza, twenty-three years old.

The registration clerk finished the paperwork for Esperanza and walked the chart over to the main registration area with the intention of leaving the chart for Annie or Dr. Fraser. Four uniformed cops rushed into the waiting room of the emergency department and looked around, apparently for the stabbing victim. The registration clerk walked out to talk to them. "Looking for the stab?" he asked. "*Oui,*" one of the cops answered. "Where is he?"

"The OR."

"Where is that?" the cop asked.

"First floor," Steve replied, indicating the bank of elevators with his head.

The cops knew that a couple of detectives were on their way so they waited near the door.

A couple of minutes after the uniforms arrived, Gaston and Gilles strode into the ER. Gaston had a brief discussion with the cops, then turned to Gilles and said, "The victim is in the OR. It's on the first floor. Can you find it?"

"Yeah," Gilles replied and the two men headed to the elevators.

◎

Annie, Dr. Fraser, and Tom wheeled Esperanza into a pre-op room. "I'm going to scrub and change. I'll send someone to get him," Dr. Fraser announced and left the room.

Annie and Tom knew that they could not go into a sterile area. Annie moved to the head of the gurney and placed her fingers on the patient's carotid artery to check his pulse. Nothing. Annie pulled an eyelid up and recognized the blank stare of death.

"Dr. Fraser," she called. "I think we lost him." Annie did not wait for Dr. Fraser to get back into the room. She started chest compressions. Dr. Fraser came in and used her stethoscope to check for signs of life. Annie continued the chest compressions while Dr. Fraser examined Esperanza. Dr. Fraser looked at her watch and said, "I'm calling it. It's three forty-five. You can stop, Annie."

Annie moved away from the patient. As there was no chart with Esperanza, Dr. Fraser pulled a pad and pen out of a pocket and wrote the date and time on a slip of paper, tore it off, and slipped it under his shoulder.

"Where's the chart?" she asked.

"They're making it up in the ER," Annie explained.

Dr. Fraser was about to say something when Gaston and Gilles knocked on the door and, without waiting for an answer, walked into the room. Annie had just pulled the sheet over the head of the body.

Gilles and Gaston identified themselves and approached the body on the gurney. Annie said, "Hi," to Gilles but didn't offer a more personal greeting. Gilles and Annie had never before been in a professional setting together and had not worked out how to handle themselves in such a situation.

Dr. Fraser introduced herself to the two cops. She walked around the gurney and shook hands with both men. "I'm sorry to have to tell you, your victim died of his wounds. I just called it."

Gaston reached into the inside pocket of his blue blazer and pulled out his cellphone. As he punched in a telephone number he asked, "Do you have the paperwork? The medical examiner will want to see it."

"No," Dr. Fraser began to explain but was interrupted by Gaston speaking into his phone.

"I'm at the Gursky Memorial, first floor. Send a wagon and the examiner. Stabbing victim." Gaston disconnected and turned to Dr. Fraser. "I'm sorry," he said. "I have to start the investigation process and that will require a death certificate and a report from the medical examiner."

"As I was saying," Dr. Fraser said, "We didn't wait for the chart but got the patient, the victim, up here as quickly as possible."

"I'll call down," Annie said and pulled the hospital phone out of the pocket of her scrubs. Annie punched in a series of numbers and said, "Steve? Can you have the chart for Esperanza sent up? And be sure to include a blank death certificate."

"I'd like to have a look at the victim," Gaston said, "while we wait for the medical examiner."

Annie looked to Dr. Fraser who said, "Absolutely. I'm sure you don't have to be told not to touch him."

Annie pulled down the sheet to the victim's shoulders and Gilles gasped and exclaimed, "Oh my god!"

"Is something wrong?" Gaston asked. He was aware that this was Gilles's first homicide and that it took new detectives some time not to be upset by their first contact with a corpse.

"No—I mean yes," Gilles said, making no effort to keep the excitement out of his voice. "He's one of the kids who were in the park when I got shot."

At that moment, the door opened and an orderly came in with the chart. Dr. Fraser flipped it open, made some notes, and pulled the slip of paper with the time of death from under Esperanza's shoulder and slipped it into the pocket on the inner cover of the chart. She flipped through the pages until she found what she was looking for, wrote her notes and filled in the death certificate.

Gaston turned to Gilles and asked, "What do you know about this kid?"

"Nothing really," Gilles replied. "I was questioning him about drug dealing, which is what he was doing, and before I got very far I was shot."

"Was he the shooter?" Gaston asked.

"No," Gilles said. "It was someone else. One of his buddies."

Gaston reached into his inner blazer pocket and pulled out a notebook and a pen. While he wrote he said, "So this may be a drug-related homicide, possible gang implications." He asked Dr. Fraser for the victim's name and other personal information. Dr. Fraser read the details from the chart and Gaston recorded it in his notebook. "Is there next-of-kin information?" he asked.

"There is," Dr. Fraser explained. "But it's from his file. He's been here before for minor injuries. It may not be current." She read the name and phone number from the chart to Gaston.

Gaston returned the notebook and pen to his pocket and said, "Okay. Here are the next steps. Sergeant Bellechasse and I will wait for the medical examiner to arrive, and when he does, I'm going to turn the victim over to him. Sergeant Bellechasse will remain until the medical examiner removes the body. When the ME arrives, I'm off to the crime scene." He turned to Gilles and said, "Meet me there when the examiner is done." He pulled the sheet back over the head of the body.

"Annie, Nurse Linton that is, will remain here. I don't think I'm needed but if the ME needs me, An . . . Nurse Linton can have me paged," Dr. Fraser stated.

"Thanks for your assistance," Gaston said.

Gaston and Dr. Fraser left the room together. Gaston headed for the elevators and Dr. Fraser went in the other direction, to somewhere on the surgical floor.

"Is this your first one?" Annie asked, referring to the dead body on the gurney. "No, hardly," Gilles replied as they sat down. "Why do you ask?"

Annie smiled at her boyfriend and said, "Well, you went white. I thought you were going to faint."

"Yeah, well I haven't become hardened to them yet so I felt a bit *mal à l'aise*, queasy," Gilles replied, "but I didn't want to embarrass myself in front of Gaston Lemieux. He's the top guy in the squad."

"Are you feeling better?" Annie asked.

"Yeah, thanks. Do you ever get used to it? Death, I mean."

"Kind of," Annie replied. "I've been a nurse for more than twenty years and in that time, of course, I've lost patients. So I know that it's part of life. So I can deal with it. But I haven't allowed myself to become blasé about it, not even in the cases where the patient was old and at the end of a long life. And I feel awful when a young person dies." Annie turned away from Gilles and looked at the body on the gurney. "Especially if the victim is around the age of my daughter," she continued. "We both know how the parents are going to feel."

"Absolument," Gilles said. "I know how I would feel."

Annie was about to say something when she heard the door open behind her. She and Gilles got to their feet when Dr. Charles Lapointe walked into the room. "Bonjour," he said with a formal little nod of his head. "Je suis Dr. Lapointe, le médecin légiste. Je cherche Gaston Lemieux."

"I'm Sergeant Bellechasse. Detective Sergeant Lemieux left for the crime scene. Annie, Nurse Linton, and I have been here the whole time."

Gilles knew that it was important to establish that the victim of a crime had not been left unattended, that any evidence that an examination of the body would produce had not been tampered with.

Dr. Charles Lapointe was a tall thin man who taught in the medical faculty at the Université de Montréal and worked as the medical examiner for the police on a part-time basis.

He dressed in the formal style of a doctor who began his practice in the mid-twentieth century. He wore a grey three-piece suit with a bow tie. He also sported a white lab coat. His horn-rimmed glasses emphasized his intelligent eyes. He wore his grey hair short. He carried a well-worn doctor's bag made of black leather. It looked to be almost as old as the doctor himself.

"Pleased to meet you," Dr. Lapointe said and extended his hand.

"Likewise," Gilles replied and shook the doctor's hand.

Dr. Lapointe then turned to Annie and shook her hand as well and said, "I'm pleased to meet you as well, Nurse Linton. Let's take a look, shall we?" The trio walked over to the body.

Dr. Lapointe and Annie pulled on latex gloves. Gilles stood a pace or two behind them so as not to get in their way. Dr. Lapointe placed his medical bag on a small shelf attached to the wall, six or so inches from the gurney. Annie pulled the sheet away from the body.

"Young," Dr. Lapointe stated. "Sad, sad and stupid, a real waste. I'll do a full exam at the office. I just want to get a preliminary look here."

Annie nodded and Dr. Lapointe lifted the victim's shirt to get a look at the fatal wound. He and Annie bent over the body to get a clear look at it. "Have you seen many knife wounds, Nurse Linton?" Dr. Lapointe asked.

"A few, not many," Annie responded.

"I've seen too many," Dr. Lapointe commented. "Do you notice something unique about this one?"

Annie examined the knife wound without touching it and traced its trajectory along the victim's stomach. "Well, it's a mess. The entry looks to be at the lower right of the victim's abdomen and slicing slightly upward to the left. I'm guessing that the perpetrator made some fast jabbing motions as they moved the weapon upward. The evidence suggests that the stabber was right-handed and the wound cut through the victim's appendix, his colon, and maybe even his liver."

Dr. Lapointe turned to Annie and said, "Well done, Nurse Linton. Very observant. You could have a career in criminal pathology." Dr. Lapointe made the last comment with a smile.

"No thanks," Annie said. "I prefer that my patients can get out of bed."

"I take it that this is not the gurney that he was brought in on," Dr. Lapointe said.

"Is that important?" Gilles asked. "He was brought in by ambulance."

"No, just an observation," Dr. Lapointe said. "There's not a lot of blood on this gurney."

"Oh," Gilles said, not understanding the point Dr. Lapointe was making.

"The area of the wound is very vascular," Annie added helpfully. "There would have been a lot of blood."

Dr. Lapointe treated Annie to another smile of approval. He recovered the victim with the sheet and said, "I'm done here." He walked to the door and motioned to the two technicians from the medical examiner's office who were waiting down the hall with a gurney of their own. They came into the room and transferred Mikel Esperanza's body to it. They wheeled it out of the room.

Dr. Lapointe followed them but stopped at the door and turned to Gilles and Annie. "Give my regards to Detective Sergeant Lemieux and tell him that I'll have a full report for him in a day or so. But Nurse Linton has provided the important information he'll need for the moment."

"Merci docteur," Gilles said. Dr. Lapointe left the pre-op room and accompanied the technicians to the elevator.

"You got all that from just one look at the wound?" Gilles asked Annie.

"Yeah, kind of obvious when you think about it," she replied.

"I'm impressed," Gilles said. "Well, I suppose I had better get to the crime scene, where I expect there to be a lot of blood."

"And I've got to get back to work," Annie said.

The couple walked out of the pre-op room—not holding hands, that would have been inappropriate—but walking close enough together so that their hands touched.

CHAPTER FIVE

"We have some bad news."

As they passed through the waiting room in the emergency department, Gilles noticed a uniformed cop pacing in front of the large windows that looked out onto the street. Annie returned to her post in the triage section and Gilles approached the cop. "Are you waiting for me?" he asked.

"Oui, le sergent-detective Lemieux m'a demandé d'attendre."

"Give me a second," Gilles said. He'd noticed Tom working in the triage area; he walked over and asked him, "Were you the one who helped with the victim?"

Tom and Gilles had a nodding acquaintance, having spent a bit of time chatting on the days when Gilles picked Annie up at the hospital. "Yeah. Me and Annie," Tom replied.

"Did he say anything?"

"No, nothing. He was in pretty bad shape," Tom told Gilles.

"That's what I thought," Gilles said. "But I was hoping that I was wrong."

"Was he one of the troublemakers who've taken over the park," Tom asked, "or was he a victim of the troublemakers?"

"Let's not jump to any conclusions. . ." Gilles said, "yet. I can say that we're going to work to get to the bottom of things."

Gilles bade Tom goodbye and walked out of the triage area.

"Okay, I'm done here. Let's go," he said to the waiting uniformed cops.

The drive to the park took barely five minutes. Gilles thanked the cop for the lift as he got out of the car. He walked over to where Gaston Lemieux was talking to a group of cops, some in uniform, some in plain clothes. Gilles joined the group in time to hear Gaston's final comment. "I've given you the details of the crime, the murder, now it's up to you to canvass the neighbourhood to get as much information as you can. Thank you."

With that, the group of cops broke up into teams of two and headed off to the homes and apartment buildings they had been assigned, to see if they could find anyone who might be a witness to a murder. Gilles approached Gaston and reported, "Dr. Lapointe has taken the body to his office for a thorough examination. He sends his regards, by the way. He'll get in touch with you as soon as he has a report to deliver."

Gaston smiled and said, "Thank you. Yes, I've known Dr. Lapointe since I was a child. He and my father were at university together. Did he make any comments in the way of a preliminary report?"

"Yes," Gilles replied. "Actually it was Annie, Nurse Linton, who determined the nature of the stabbing. But the doctor agreed."

"And . . . " Gaston prompted.

"She described the wound as a mess. She thinks there was a kind of sawing motion as the attacker drew the weapon up towards the vic's midriff. She and the doctor concluded that the knife or whatever was used was very, very sharp. There would have been a lot of blood."

Gaston turned to show Gilles the crime scene. The murder had taken place on or near the bench where Gilles had first confronted the victim all those months ago. It was likely that this corner of the park was Esperanza's turf. Gilles walked up to the bench and saw that it and the ground under it and in front of it were covered in dry or drying blood.

"Chrisse," he exclaimed. "He must have lost most of his blood."

"It wouldn't surprise me," Gaston agreed.

Gilles took a moment to look around the park in order to place the murder area in a larger context, to see how the perpetrator might have approached the victim. The park itself was quite large, covering an area that was the equivalent of four blocks in length and two in width. There was an area diagonally opposite the scene of the murder, at the point in the park furthest away from it, which was a fenced-in children's play section. A soccer pitch occupied another area of the park, and a third area was dedicated to picnic tables and barbeques. There was a series of pathways lined with benches connecting the various sections of the park and there was plenty of room for people to bring their lawn chairs and blankets to sit and read, chat, or just plain enjoy being out of doors. The spot where the murder occurred was the only semi-concealed part of the park but it was open enough so that anyone could approach it from any other part of the park. It seemed to Gilles that the only way to approach this area without being seen would be from the street through the trees—in other words, exactly as Gilles had approached the area on the day he was shot. Upon close inspection of the shrubs and trees Gilles noticed that there were several with bent and broken branches, some black sweatshirt fluff attached to one of them. Gilles called to one of the forensic techs and told him to photograph the broken branches and bag the coton ouaté.

Gilles could not get close enough to the crime scene to give it a thorough examination as the team from the forensics division had it closed off with yellow police tape and they were combing the scene for evidence. Another set of feet tromping over a crime scene, even covered with protective booties, would not be helpful.

"Do you want me to assist in the canvass?" Gilles asked.

"No, we've got that covered. You and I have the unfortunate duty of paying a visit to the victim's family to tell them what happened," Gaston responded.

Gilles had never had to bring news of a death to a victim's family, but he knew from his conversations with other cops that it was one of the most unpleasant duties they had to perform. Like everyone else, cops had families, and they could easily identify with the sadness and misery that news of the death of a loved one brought.

"I took note of his address at the hospital," Gilles said. He pulled a notebook from his inside jacket pocket, flipped it open and showed it to Gaston. "But you know, I suspect his family already knows. Look around. There's not a soul in the park. I'll bet that the news travelled through the neighbourhood and everyone stayed away."

"Good point," Gaston agreed. "The park was deserted when I got here. That's in itself unusual on a nice day like today. In any event, we have to talk to the family."

Gaston and Gilles walked to the car and set off for the Esperanza home, located in an apartment building on Plamondon Avenue. The building where the Esperanza family lived had been constructed, like all the other apartment buildings on the block, just after the Second World War. Building materials were in short supply and the buildings were cheaply constructed as basic, inexpensive accommodation. The buildings were all four or five floor walk-ups and the area had attracted the working poor from its inception. All the buildings were red-brick affairs without architectural flourish or elevators. The original tenants, working-class English- and French-Canadians, had improved their financial lot sufficiently so that they could move to the suburbs surrounding the city, and the buildings on Plamondon and its neighbouring streets had been given over to families of immigrants primarily from the subcontinent of Asia and the Philippines.

Gaston parked a short distance from the building that housed the Esperanzas. He and Gilles walked to the building and up the stairs to an apartment on the third floor. In response to what Gilles hoped was a respectful knock on the front door—after all, they were calling on a family who were in mourning, or soon would be—a young boy of about twelve years of age opened the door.

Gilles introduced himself and Gaston and asked if the lad's mother was at home. The boy silently stood away from the door, indicating that the two men should enter. They followed the boy down a short corridor to a living room where a middle-aged and a young woman sat side by side on a sofa. They had obviously been crying.

Gaston cleared his throat and said in a soft voice, "Madame Esperanza, I'm Detective Sergeant Gaston Lemieux of the Montreal Police. This is Sergeant Gilles Bellechasse. I think you know why we're here."

Mrs. Esperanza remained seated but looked up at Gilles and Gaston with red-rimmed, soft brown eyes. "I know it's about my son, it's about Mikel."

"Yes, Madame, I'm afraid it is. We have some bad news, I'm very sorry to say," Gaston informed the woman.

A loud wail escaped from deep within Mrs. Esperanza's chest. "No, no, no," she sobbed and turned her head into the younger woman's chest. The young woman pulled her close and tried to comfort her. She looked up at the two cops and, doing her best to suppress her grief, said, "I'm Sandra

Esperanza, Mikel's sister. Is Mikel, is Mikel . . . ?" She could not complete her sentence.

The young boy joined his mother and sister on the sofa. The living room was not large and the sofa, along with a couple of stuffed chairs and a large television set, took up most of the space. There was a coffee table separating the sofa from the two chairs. Gaston had been on many visits such as this one and they never failed to make him aware of the awesome burden of this part of his job. He did his best to deliver the bad news with respect for the survivors and the victim – even in cases where the victim was a criminal with a long record of arrests. This was the first time Gilles had had to bring news of death to a family, and he couldn't help imagining how he would feel if he had to hear news of this nature about Emilie.

"May we sit down?" Gaston asked softly.

"Yes, please," Sandra replied.

Gilles and Gaston each sat in one of the chairs facing the family, and Gilles asked, "May I ask what you heard?"

Gaston would have taken a different approach. He would have, in as comforting a way as possible, told them of the death of their son and brother. He liked the approach that Gilles was taking, getting the family to talk. It would make the bad news just a little bit easier to take. Sandra, who looked to be in her mid-twenties, dressed in jeans and a purple shirt over a black tank top, sat up straight and said, "We heard that there had been a stabbing and that Mikel was hurt, taken to a hospital in an ambulance. We've been calling but no one would tell us anything. Please . . . " she said, again leaving the sentence unfinished.

Gaston looked at Sandra and then at Mrs. Esperanza. "There was a stabbing and I'm sorry to have to tell you that Mikel died as a result of his wounds."

Sandra bowed her head and the two policemen could see her tears slide silently downs her cheeks, landing on her shirt. The young boy also began to cry and hid his face in his hands. Mrs. Esperanza put her arms around both her children. Gaston noticed a box of Kleenex on the lower shelf of the coffee table top. He picked it up and got to his feet to hand it to Mrs. Esperanza.

She removed her arm from around her son's shoulder, accepted the box and thanked Gaston. "When can we see him?" she asked.

"Not for a day or two," Gaston replied. "A *post mortem* has to be done by our medical examiner."

"We know this is a very hard time for you and your family and we're sure you would rather we weren't here, but we have to ask you some questions," Gilles said.

Sandra got to her feet and ran the fingers of both hands through her black hair, pushing it away from her face. "Really? Really, you have to do that now?"

"Yes, I'm sorry we do," Gilles said. "We can do it in another room if you like." He indicated the young boy with a nod of his head. The child was trying to gain control of himself. He had stopped crying but was sniffling and was sitting close to his mother.

Sandra said something to the boy in Tagalog. The boy looked up at his sister. In English she said, "It will help Mommy. Please, Ferdy, it will be a big help." She turned to Gaston and Gilles and explained, "I've asked my brother to make some tea for our mother. Will you have some?"

"No thank you," Gaston and Gilles responded, almost in unison. "We'll ask our questions and get out of your way. I'm sure you'll want to make arrangements," Gaston added.

Sandra sat down beside her mother and Ferdy got up to make the tea.

Gaston cleared his throat and asked, "When was the last time you saw your son?"

"He was asleep when I left for work this morning," Mrs. Esperanza said.

"And what time was that?" Gilles asked.

"My mother and my little brother left at about eight. That's their usual time. She takes Ferdy to school and then continues on to her job," Sandra explained.

"How about you?" Gilles asked.

"I left very soon after my mother and brother."

"Do you work or are you in school?"

"Both, actually. I'm studying for the exams to become an accountant. I'm doing a *stage* at Gelinas, Shapiro. This week I've been working on an audit for a client whose office is on Decarie, so I leave late."

"What time did you get to your client's?"

"Eight-thirty, maybe a little before. It's not that long a walk."

"So from about eight in the morning until he was brought into the emergency room at the Gursky you had no contact with your brother. Is that correct?"

"Yes."

"Can you venture a guess as to what he did today?" Gaston asked.

Sandra didn't say anything for a moment or two. She sniffled and did her best to stop herself from crying as she thought about how her brother might have filled his last hours. "I'm sorry," she said, "this is difficult." She leaned forward and spoke softly in the hopes that her mother would not be able to follow the conversation. "My brother was a decent guy, and a talented one, but he had no direction in life. His friends were a bad influence and . . . " Sandra paused " . . . and I'm sure you've heard this story a million times. But my brother was a good guy and didn't deserve to die."

"I'm sorry," Gilles said, "but you haven't answered the question."

At this point Ferdy walked in from the kitchen with a mug of strong-looking black tea. He handed the mug to his mother who smiled gratefully at her son and used her free hand to pull him onto the sofa beside her.

Sandra sighed, "Okay, I don't *know* what he did but my guess is that he slept in until almost noon, got up, maybe had something to eat and headed out to meet his friends. Maybe they played video games; maybe they hung out in the park. My guess is that they did both."

"I saw him," Ferdy said softly, his voice partly muffled because his face was buried against his mother's body.

Sandra looked surprised by this.

"How do you mean?" Gilles asked.

"I forgot my lunch and Mik brought it to me,"

"I asked you if you had it," Mrs. Esperanza said.

"I know. But I didn't."

"What time was this?" Gilles asked.

"I don't know," Freddy replied. "Lunchtime. He was waiting for me when the bell rang."

Gilles inhaled and asked, "What time does the bell ring?"

"Noon," Sandra stated. "It rings at noon."

Gaston turned to Mrs. Esperanza and asked, "Did you understand what your daughter said? Does that sound like something your son would have done?"

"Yes," she answered. "He spent too much time with his friends and not enough working, like my daughter."

Both Gilles and Gaston smiled at Mrs. Esperanza in a way that they hoped she would find comforting.

"I forgot to ask," Gilles said, "is Mikel your older brother?"

"No," Sandra replied, "he's younger. I'm the oldest."

"Do you normally get home from work this early?" Gilles asked.

"No, of course not. My mother called me and I came home right away."

After a moment of silence Gaston got to his feet and said, "We'd like to see Mikel's room."

Sandra and Gilles got up. "Yeah, sure," she said. She walked out of the living room and down a hall past a door on the left. At the second door on the left she stopped and stood aside, allowing Gilles and Gaston to enter ahead of her. "This is the room he shares with Ferdy." She followed them into the bedroom and they were soon joined by Mrs. Esperanza and Ferdy who stood by the door.

Gilles and Gaston looked around the room and saw two single beds, one against the outside wall across from the door and the other against the shorter wall to the right. The room was a mess, with clothing strewn on the floor. A backpack was lying on the bed on the right. The backpack was unzipped and Gilles used a pen to lift the flap. He could see well-worn primary school text books and some Hilroy notebooks. Ferdy's bed was not neatly made but pulled together. The other bed, Mikel's, was a tangle of sheets and a blanket. In addition to the odours generated by two guys sharing a room Gilles also picked up the scent of stale pizza and tacos. He noticed that there were no empty dishes or other food containers in the room. This fact suggested that Mrs. Esperanza did her best to keep the room at least clean, if not tidy.

There was a dresser between the two beds on top of which were a television set and an Xbox. There was a closet to the left of the door. There was a window above the foot of Mikel's bed. The walls were covered with black-and-white drawings on letter-size paper. At first Gilles thought that they were taken from magazines or comic books or graphic novels, but on closer inspection he noticed that the drawings were originals, some drawn with charcoal but mostly done in pencil.

"Who's the artist?" Gilles asked.

"Mikel," Sandra replied. "I told you he was talented." Gilles and Gaston moved around the room looking at the art work. Most of the drawings depicted some kind of battle between mutant-looking combatants and a super-hero. It looked like Mikel had started to tell an illustrated story but there was no continuation and certainly no resolution. While Gilles and Gaston examined the artwork, Ferdy slipped into the room and stood leaning against the closet door. It had been ajar when the cops entered the room, but now it was closed.

"Your brother had talent, no question," Gaston commented. "Did he go to art school?"

"School? No," Sandra said with both sadness and resignation in her voice. "He was talented but lazy. He couldn't take the discipline of school. He took courses here and there, that's all."

Gilles and Gaston had a short conversation, following which Gilles said, "We'd like to take these drawings with us so we can examine them more closely. If Mikel knew the person who stabbed him, there may be clues in his drawings. I promise we'll take good care of them and get them back to you as soon as possible."

"Do we really have a choice?" Sandra asked.

"Well, we could station a cop here and come back with a warrant if you prefer," Gaston said.

Sandra explained what the cops wanted to her mother who sighed in resignation and nodded her agreement. Ferdy, on the other hand, had something to say. "You can't take them. They belong to me. Mik gave them to me." The boy was almost in tears but he did not move. He remained leaning against the door to the closet with his hands shoved into his pockets.

"They'll give them back, Ferdy," Sandra said. "Maybe they'll help them find out who hurt Mikel." Ferdy didn't say anything but he looked deeply unhappy as Gaston and Gilles pulled on latex gloves that they took from their jacket pockets and carefully removed the drawings from the wall.

They tapped the drawings into as neat a pile as possible and turned their attention to Ferdy. "We'd like to take a look in the closet, young man," Gilles said.

Ferdy changed his stance and folded his arms across his chest as if he was much bigger and much tougher than his twelve years.

"Please," Gaston added, sensitive to the young boy's loss and not wanting to have to physically move him.

"Ferdy!" Sandra commanded and the boy moved.

Gilles opened the door and saw what he expected to see—a closet in disarray. There were clothes on hangers but there were a number of articles on the floor as well. There was a string hanging from a light fixture and Gilles pulled it to provide some illumination. Gilles pushed the clothing aside and looked around the closet. He was certain that there was something hidden there and let out a grunt of satisfaction when he noticed a portfolio pushed against the far wall behind two heavy coats that kept the portfolio in place and almost hid it from view.

"Regarde," Gilles said as he pushed his way to the portfolio, removed it from its hiding place and carried it into the room. The portfolio was twenty-four by thirty-two inches and made of nylon with a zipper that ran around three sides. Both Sandra and Mrs. Esperanza appeared to be surprised by the discovery. But Ferdy looked defeated.

Gilles lay the portfolio on Mikel's bed and unzipped it. The top drawing was a nude of a woman's torso. Mrs. Esperanza let out a cry of surprise. Gilles and Gaston went through the drawings and discovered a number of other nudes and some portraits of a woman's face, all done in charcoal. All the drawings were signed with the word "mik," in lower-case.

"Do either of you recognize this woman?" Gaston asked, holding up one of the portraits for Sandra and her mother to examine.

"No, I've never seen these drawings," she stated. Mrs. Esperanza didn't say anything, but her shocked look told the cops that the drawings were a surprise to her. "But Ferdy has seen them, haven't you, son?" Gaston asked.

Ferdy blushed but didn't say anything. "Do you know who this woman is?" Gaston prompted. Ferdy shook his head and mumbled a "no."

"We'll take these as well," Gilles said, and took Sandra's silence as acquiescence. He placed the drawings he had removed from the walls in the portfolio and zipped it closed.

"We're done for now," Gaston explained. "If we have any more questions we'll get in touch with you. What is the best way to reach you?" Gaston pulled his notebook from his inside blazer pocket and recorded the information Sandra gave him.

"Oh, one more thing," he said, returning his notebook to his pocket. "It's about your father. Does he live with the family? Can we reach him if necessary?"

"Our father is in the Philippines at the moment. He had to return home to help his parents on their farm," Sandra explained.

"How long has he been away?" Gilles asked.

"I can't see what that has to do with anything," Sandra responded, "but he's been away for almost a year. He'll be back as soon as he can make it, believe me, if you want to talk to him."

At the door to the apartment, just before Gilles and Gaston left, Sandra asked them in a voice barely above a whisper, "We have to make arrangements. When can we get my brother's body?"

"I hope within a week. As soon as the medical examiner is finished with his investigation. We'll let you know."

Both Gaston and Gilles gave Sandra their cards and told her to call them any time she had a question, or if she remembered something that she had not told them. And with that they left the Esperanza apartment.

The drive east to the Major Crimes Division offices was a silent one. Gaston was clearly lost in thought, probably reviewing the information they had gleaned from the Esperanzas. Gilles was not the kind of person who needed to fill silences with small talk, and he too wanted to consider the evidence they had collected so far.

Over time, Place Versailles expanded to accommodate more tenants and now comprised several buildings in a variety of non-descript architectural styles. Gilles circled the parking lots looking for an empty spot. The reserved places were all occupied. Gilles had not yet become inured to the pedestrian architecture of the shopping centre. Each addition was built with different coloured and different size bricks on the outer walls. Gilles couldn't understand why the builders couldn't settle on one style and stick to it. Gaston worked in Major Crimes for a decade or so and seemed indifferent to the aesthetics of his surroundings.

Back at the office Gaston told Gilles to review all the drawings they had with them and then get them to forensics to determine if there were any helpful fingerprints on them. Gaston then went to Captain Lacroix's office to report.

Gilles took the drawings to a conference room, put on a pair of latex gloves so as not to compromise any evidence the pictures might hold, and spread them out on the table in order to examine them. Before sending them off to forensics Gilles wanted to know as much about them as possible. If the drawings held a clue, then Gilles wanted to be the one to find it. He took photographs of most of the drawings with his cellphone so he could examine them while they were being worked on by the forensics team. He called the forensics section and followed the instructions he was given to get them the drawings.

Once all that had been accomplished Gilles returned to his desk in the squad room and prepared to type up a report of what he and Gaston had accomplished that day. He had barely started on this boring but necessary task when Gaston came out of Captain Lacroix's office and walked over to where Gilles was working. He pulled a chair over from one of the other desks and sat down. "You did good work today, Gilles," Gaston said. Gilles was quiet for a moment, pleased with the praise.

Gaston Lemieux was the senior investigator in the division. Most of his colleagues thought that he should have been promoted to the rank of captain and put in charge. But Gaston had no desire to be an administrator. His skill was that of an investigator and he loved his job. All the men in the squad room looked up to him and Gilles, the newest member of the team, quickly learned that Gaston would be a perfect role model. "Merci, Gaston," Gilles said, "that means a lot to me. I won't let you down."

"I spoke to the captain and he agrees," Gaston continued, "that you can take over on this case. I have other investigations on the go and I can't take on another one. So you've inherited this one."

Gilles was thrilled. This was the first time he had been assigned a case on his own. Up to this point he had assisted other, more seasoned cops in their investigations, usually stuck with the work of writing the reports and cataloguing the evidence.

"I'm sure you'll do fine," Gaston said. "Keep me and the captain informed as you gather more information. And we want a quick resolution to the case. We can't have murderers running loose in our parks." With that Gaston stood up and went to his desk, which was situated between a pillar and one of the few windows that looked out on the large parking lot that surrounded the shopping centre.

The command to find a quick solution took a bit of the pleasure away from Gilles's feelings of pride, but he was determined not to let Gaston down.

Gilles considered his next steps and realized that it would be helpful to know as much as possible about the weapon used in the murder. If, as Gilles suspected, the weapon was a switchblade or similar kind of knife favoured by gangs in Montreal, it would mean that he should start by looking for a gang connection. He knew that the medical report would provide some needed information, but he did not want to wait for it. He decided to call Annie to see if she could provide any information that would be helpful. This was partially investigative and partially his desire to spend time with Annie whenever he could. Also, he wanted to share the good news that he had been assigned a case of his own.

CHAPTER SIX

"Did I mess up your plans?"

Gilles called Annie and asked her if she were free for dinner. He was delighted when she suggested that instead of them going out he could come to her place for a meal. She was planning to make lasagna for her and Pamela and there would be plenty for all three of them. Gilles gratefully accepted the invitation and told Annie that he would bring the wine and anything else she needed. They chatted for a while until Annie had to attend to a patient. He decided to save news of his case until he saw her.

On his way home Gilles stopped by the SAQ and picked up a couple of bottles of Château Margaux and then went to a florist for some flowers. When he got to his condo he was surprised to find Emilie camped out on the sidewalk in front of his building.

Gilles knew from experience that if his daughter showed up at his place on a weekday afternoon it was because she had had a fight with her mother. He was not pleased, but decided to play it cool.

"Que fais-tu ici, Lapin?" he asked his daughter. She got up and hugged her father. "The usual. Mom is being unbearable."

"And why are you waiting on the sidewalk? Where's your key?"

"I left in kind of a hurry, Pa. It's at mom's."

Gilles sighed and said, "Let's go inside and I'll call your mother. Tomorrow's a school day for you and a work day for me, so . . . " Gilles did not complete the sentence.

"Help me with these," Gilles said and handed Emilie the bag containing the bottles of wine and the bouquet of flowers.

"Pretty fancy," Emilie commented. "Expecting someone?"

They entered Gilles's condo and he said, "I'll tell you *after* I speak to your mother." He took the flowers and wine from his daughter and placed them on the dining room table. "Get comfortable," he told Emilie and he called his ex-wife.

Following his conversation with Yvonne he went to the living room where he found Emilie busy texting her friends. "Okay, here's the situation," he said, joining her on the sofa. "Your mother wants you to spend the night, but I'm getting you back bright and early. You are not going to miss another day of school. Understand?"

Emilie smiled and nodded. "Did I mess up your plans?" she asked without a hint of guilt.

Gilles didn't answer but went to the kitchen to have some privacy while he called Annie.

When Gilles returned to the living room he was smiling. He stood facing his daughter and said, "To answer your question, no, you've not messed up my plans. You're coming to dinner with me and Annie—at Annie's house."

"No, Dad, you go. I'll stay here," Emilie replied.

"No way. You come with me or I drive you to your mother's. The choice is yours."

Emilie was not happy with either alternative. She had no desire to see—much less spend time with—her father's girlfriend, but she was in no frame of mind to deal with her mother. She was silent for a moment or two. Her plan had been to have dinner with her father and maybe slip out to

70

check out the neighbourhood. Dinner with Annie meant an evening much less exciting than she had in mind and was very little improvement over spending the evening at home. At least at her mother's place she had her friends close by.

Before Emilie could answer her father, he said, "You know what? I don't feel like driving to the South Shore. You're coming with me."

"Christ, Pa!" Emilie exclaimed.

The drive west to Annie's house was a quiet one. Emilie had only met Annie briefly on one or two occasions and was cool towards her. She was not looking forward to spending the evening with her. She wanted her father to herself. She sulked for the thirty or so minutes of the drive. Emilie had never met Pamela but she had heard about her many accomplishments and feared being compared to her. Pamela, on the other hand, wished that she had a father like Gilles who was involved in his daughter's life.

Pamela's father, Daniel Mubende, was from Uganda. He had taken a graduate degree in the Faculty of Agricultural and Environmental Sciences at McGill University's Macdonald Campus in Sainte-Anne-de-Bellevue on the western tip of the island of Montreal. It's unlikely that Annie and Daniel's paths would have crossed had she not been cycling in Sainte-Anne with her friend Ursula. They'd stopped at a café for lunch and the only two seats available were at a table where Daniel was seated with a friend of his. The four young people struck up a conversation, and Annie had to admit that after an hour or so she was smitten. Daniel was tall, physically fit, and good-looking. But there was more to Daniel than what she saw on the surface; she sensed a caring soul within, and it didn't hurt that he had a lively sense of humour. Before Annie and Ursula left the table for the bike ride back to Montreal, Daniel had Annie's phone number and he promised to call her.

He did, a day later. He asked her to dinner, which led to more dates, and then to romance. After six months the couple decided to move in together and rented an apartment on the inexpensive side of the tracks in NDG.

Daniel put off his plans to return to Uganda when Annie became pregnant and instead got a job at Agropharm as a researcher. The pay was good and so were the hours, so he had a lot of free time to spend with his daughter.

As soon as her maternity leave was over, Annie returned to nursing. Her erratic shift schedule and the fact that she was devoted to caring for Pamela put a stress on their marriage. Daniel loved Pamela as much as Annie did but having a child made him miss his own family. He proposed that they move to Uganda so that Pamela could meet his relatives. Annie was more than happy to visit Uganda with her husband and child but made it clear that a move was out of the question. She had worked too hard to become a nurse, she wanted to remain close to her family and educational opportunities for Pamela were better in Canada than in Uganda. During a particularly heated discussion on the subject Annie made the mistake of pointing out that when Daniel decided to leave his country he must have known that he would be cutting himself off from his family. Annie tried to take back what she had said but she could tell from the hurt look in Daniel's eyes that she had crossed a line.

Finally, one day when Pamela was in the first grade, Daniel told Annie that he couldn't take another winter in Canada, and he was returning to Uganda. He didn't suggest that Annie and Pamela follow and Annie didn't propose it. A day later, on a Saturday in late September, Daniel got into a cab to the airport and then on a plane to Uganda, breaking the two hearts that loved him. For the first year or so he called Pamela on her birthday and on other holidays. But by the time she was nine even those infrequent calls stopped.

It took some time, but Annie and Pamela adjusted to their new life.

Annie's older sister Rosemary lived on Park Row East and as soon as she noticed that a flat was for rent next door she rushed over, signed a lease and paid the first month's rent even before she'd told Annie about the place. Luckily, the landlord knew Rosemary well and had no difficulty transferring the lease to Annie. Pamela was able to go to and from school with Rosemary's kids on days when Annie was working early or late shifts.

And so life went on as Pamela grew up to be the beautiful young woman now waiting to meet Gilles's daughter.

Annie greeted Gilles and Emilie with her usual warmth. She hugged Emilie in spite of the girl's resistance and said, "It's so nice to see you again. I'm thrilled that you could join us for dinner." Annie stood back from Emilie and with her hands on both of Emilie's shoulders added, "You are so beautiful. I know that your father is very proud of you." Emilie blushed. "Come and meet my daughter."

Gilles handed Annie the flowers, but carried the wine bottles as the three of them walked into the dining room where Pamela was clearing her books and notebooks off the table. "Hi, Pamela," Gilles said, and when she stood up to greet him, he placed the bottles on the table and kissed her on both cheeks. "I'd like you to meet Emilie, my daughter."

Pamela extended her hand and Emilie shook it with a weak grip. In her set no one shook hands when being introduced; a nod usually covered it. "It's so nice to finally meet you. Gilles talks about you all the time."

Emilie didn't know quite what to say so she mumbled something that she hoped would pass for a greeting and shifted on her feet.

"Dinner is ready," Annie announced. "Why don't you girls help by setting the table? And Pamela, please put your books in your room. Gilles, would you mind opening the wine? I'll put the flowers in water. They're beautiful. Did you choose them, Emilie?"

Emilie smiled in spite of herself. "Non, Papa les a choisies. My father is the one who bought them."

Pamela returned from carrying her books to her room and she and Emilie followed Annie into the kitchen to get dishes and cutlery. Gilles knew that the corkscrew was kept in the top drawer of the sideboard and he got it and opened one of the bottles of wine.

Once the table was set and all were seated Annie served portions of lasagne and Gilles added salad to each of the plates. Dinner turned out to be a pleasant affair. Annie's natural charm and sunny disposition set the mood for the table talk. She made Emilie the focus of her attention, asking the girl about school, what kind of activities she liked, and adding some amusing gossip about the people she worked with.

Gilles took charge of pouring the wine and made certain that Pamela and Emilie had only small servings, just enough so that Emilie would not feel left out. Pamela barely touched hers; Emilie was a little more adventuresome.

After the dishes were cleared from the table and placed in the dishwasher Annie offered coffee. Gilles accepted but Pamela declined and before Emilie could respond she said, "Let's let our parents talk about whatever it is that they talk about. We can listen to music in my room." Pamela got up from the table and Emilie had no choice but to follow her.

Gilles and Annie took their coffee to the living room and made themselves comfortable on the sofa. Gilles twisted so that he was facing Annie.

"How did it go with Esperanza's family?" Annie asked. "They must have been devastated."

"That they were," Gilles replied. "It turns out that our victim was an artist. I'm no judge but he seemed to have talent."

"Really?" Annie leaned forward and placed her cup on the coffee table. "What kind of art did he do?"

"Drawing. Drawings of all kinds. There were several pages of the kind of thing you see in comic books. Graphic novels, I think they call them now."

"He wrote graphic novels?"

"Well, he tried to; the writing and drawing never seemed to get very far before he ran out of steam," Gilles explained. "But there was other stuff as well. He had drawings of nudes and portraits hidden in his closet. A portfolio of the stuff."

"Did they look like drawings of real people or were they the kind of over-sexualized women you see in comic books?"

"I think they were real people, or maybe only one person. I'll show you," Gilles said. He pulled out his cellphone and scrolled to the drawings that he had photographed. "These are the nudes . . . obviously." Annie leaned closer to get a better view, her and Gilles's heads touching. "They look like a real person, like the kind of studies people do in art classes," Annie pointed out. "But they're headless. How odd."

Gilles scrolled through some more drawings and stopped at the portraits. "There were also several portraits of this woman. Maybe she was the model for the nudes."

Annie studied the portraits for a moment or two. The woman in the drawings was beautiful, with thick hair that the artist rendered as falling to just below her shoulders, a nose that was straight but also a bit on the large side. It gave her face character. The subject's lips were full and sensual.

"You know," Annie said slowly, "I think I've seen this woman."

"At the hospital? Does she work there?" Gilles asked.

"No, she's not someone I work with, that's for sure. But I have seen her. Maybe she was a patient, or maybe she does work at the hospital in some other department. The only people I know well work in the ER."

"I know I shouldn't do this," Gilles said. "But I'm going to send one of the portraits to you. Keep it on your cell-phone. Take a careful look at it and let me know if you can identify the woman. And for God's sake don't show it to anyone."

Gilles sent the clearest of the photos to Annie's phone. She smiled and shook her head, indicating that she did not need to be told about confidentiality.

"I'm betting that the nudes and the drawing of the face belong to the same person," Gilles pointed out.

"Yeah, that's probably a safe assumption for the moment," Annie agreed. "I would also guess that the reason that the drawings of the body and the head were done separately was to protect the identity of the woman for some reason."

"Good point," Gilles agreed. "I think that if the drawings were part of an art class where a model posed in the nude then he would have drawn the whole woman, so to speak. So it follows that the subject of the drawings is someone he knew personally."

"Well, that's a starting point," Annie said, "but it remains to be proven, right?"

"Right."

"What are your next steps?" Annie asked.

"Tomorrow I'm going to spend time in the park where I was shot and where the vic was murdered to see if there were any witnesses. Finding people to question is a bit of a problem in this case," Gilles explained.

"Good luck with that," Annie said.

Gilles leaned back against the cushions of Annie's very comfortable sofa. He stretched his legs out in front of him and his arm against the back of the sofa. Annie curled her feet under her and leaned her head against Gilles's shoulder. He put his arm around her. They didn't say anything for a while, relaxing and enjoying being close to one another.

Slowly but surely conversation started again. This time the topics were about Annie's day at work, her daughter, Gilles's meeting with his commander, and his daughter.

After an hour or so Gilles said, "I think I had better make this an early night. I have to get Emilie to school on the South Shore tomorrow morning and that means fighting bridge traffic in both directions."

"She can't take the metro?" Annie asked.

"She can, but I want to make certain that she gets to school."

"Oh, I see," Annie said. She was sympathetic to the difficulties Gilles faced with his daughter and, she had to admit, she was relieved that she had never had these problems with Pamela.

Gilles got up from the sofa and called for Emilie who appeared at the door to the living room rather more quickly than had she been with her school friends. "Oui, Pa," she said.

"We've got to go. It's going to be an early day for us tomorrow."

Gilles and Annie kissed goodbye and Pamela came into the room to say her goodbyes to Gilles and his daughter. Emilie thanked Annie for dinner and bade her adieu. Annie hugged Emilie and told her that she hoped she would see her again before too long. Emilie mumbled a noncommittal answer.

In the car on the way back to Gilles's condo he asked Emilie if she had a nice evening.

"Annie est très sympa," she responded, "but Pamela is a real grind. I don't think she does anything except go to school and study. It was hard to find things to talk about."

"Yeah, she's a hard worker. No question," Gilles agreed. "She's in pre-med and that is a very tough program. She'll be a helluva doctor."

"Yeah, I'm sure," Emilie said. "Did you set up this evening so that I could meet her? Is that what you want me to do? Become a grind and live the life of a hermit student? It's not happening."

"Emilie," Gilles pointed out, "you came to me. Annie and I already had plans."

"I'm just saying . . . " Emilie said, ending the conversation.

They were silent for a couple of minutes and Gilles broke the silence with a question, "Listen, Emilie, if you like I can drive you home now. But if you stay with me you'll have to get up early so I can drive you to school. And I do mean early. I have work. Which is it to be?"

"Stay," Emilie said, without a moment's hesitation.

The next morning Gilles and a very grumpy Emilie were on the road by six-thirty.

CHAPTER SEVEN

"What do you think this is? The Hells and the Rock Machine?"

Gilles made it into the office by eight-thirty, coffee in hand. He knocked on Captain Lacroix's open door. When Lacroix looked up Gilles asked, "Got time for a quick meeting, Captain?"

"Oui, bien sûr. Get Lemieux and you can talk to both of us."

Gilles called to Gaston and asked him to join him and the captain.

"OK, what's your plan?" Lacroix asked once Gilles and Gaston were seated.

"My plan is pretty straight forward. I'll hang out at the park and question as many people who are in the park as I can." Gilles went on to explain that he was aware that if Mikel Esperanza's friends spotted him they would take off. Gilles requested the assistance of a couple of squad cars, which meant four uniformed cops, to help him ensure that those young people he wanted to interview could not get away.

Gilles was not part of the team investigating his own shooting. The investigation was being handled by Québec's Bureau des enquêtes indépendantes, the BEI. The BEI had visited the scene of the shooting several times since it occurred and were unable to get much in the way of information from the people they questioned. Gilles was aware of this owing to the network of gossip in the police departments of the province.

This was not surprising; no one wanted to turn in a friend wanted by the police, especially one who had shot a cop. The captain and Lemieux had a concern that Gilles was wasting time and money trying to get information from the gang of young men who hung out in the park—if they wouldn't talk to the BEI investigators, why would they talk to Gilles? Gilles successfully argued that the young men were no different than any other group of people: when someone close to them died, the urge to get together to discuss the death of their friend would be irresistible.

This argument convinced Captain Lacroix to authorize the use of cops on patrol to assist. Once the four cops were selected, Gilles had a brief meeting with them to explain what he needed. He told them to meet him in the area of the park hidden by trees to put the finishing touches on their course of action.

Like the fathers of teenagers all over the world, Gilles knew that no one he wanted to interview would be in the park much before ten-thirty or so. He timed his arrival to get there at ten and he planned to stay out of sight until there were four or more guys at the spot he took to be the meeting place for Mikel's gang. He was not disappointed. By ten-thirty there was a group of half a dozen young men ranging in age, Gilles surmised, from late teens to early twenties.

Gilles strode to that area of the park with two uniformed cops, one on either side of him but spaced a couple of feet away. This gave the impression that running away by that route was ill-advised. Four of the guys made to rush out of the park through the trees through which Gilles had entered the park all those months ago. They turned back when the cops stationed on the other side of the trees blocked their escape. Gilles didn't recognize any of the fellows from the night of his shooting and he was not able to determine who had assumed the leadership position previously occupied by Mikel. Once the runners had returned to the area of the park bench, Gilles flashed his badge and addressed the group. "My name is Gilles Bellechasse and I'm investigating the murder of Mikel Esperanza. Did any of you know him?"

No one raised a hand but there were several mumbles that Gilles took to mean "yeah."

"There's no need to run away," he continued. "We're not here to arrest anyone. I want to know if you have any information about your friend's death. If you have any idea who might have stabbed him."

The six guys stared at Gilles and said nothing. Gilles plunged ahead "First and foremost, did Mikel Esperanza have any enemies?"

No one said anything for a moment. One of the kids said, "Denny knew him better than most of us."

Denny, a tall slim kid with long brown hair, his New York Mets baseball cap worn backwards, was sitting on the back of the park bench with his feet on the seat. "Did Mik have any enemies? Nah, everyone liked him."

"Well, not everyone," Gilles pointed out. "Someone killed him."

Another kid, a Filipino who wore his coal-black long hair in a ponytail, dressed in loose-fitting nylon workout pants and a tight-fitting t-shirt that showed off his pecs and biceps, said, "Yeah, we get that. But none of us did it."

"We save our murdering for cops," said a voice from the back of the pack. Gilles could not tell who the speaker was. One of the cops took a pace forward as if to locate the speaker and pull him out of the group, but Gilles stopped him with a restraining hand.

"Look," Gilles said, "if it will make my investigation easier I'll have no problem making arrests, and we can have this conversation at my office"—Gilles paused—"instead of yours. But I'm not here to play games or to bust anyone for dealing weed. I want to find out who killed your friend."

This reduced the level of hostility and tension considerably. Another of the young men spoke up, more politely than the previous two. "Really, Mik didn't have any enemies of the kind that would murder him. You know what kind of business he was in, and it's not without its risks, sure, but if one of his—our—competitors killed him it would mean that there was a gang war going on or that one was about to start. And neither of those is happening."

Gilles moved closer to the six young men and placed one of his feet on the bench, leaning his elbow on his knee. "Fair enough, as far as that goes. Maybe someone is trying to start a war with you. Who are your . . . competitors, let's say?"

Another of the kids said, "What do you think this is, like the Hells and the Rock Machine?"

"No, I think the drug trade is a lucrative business and competition usually leads to violence."

The kid wearing the New York Mets cap backward replied, "We're taking you at your word that you're not going to bust us, so I can tell you that it's not like that here. All of us who are in that line of work have our customers, and that doesn't change much."

"Fine," Gilles countered, "but maybe the suppliers want to increase market share."

"Not likely, we were all supplied by the same people." There were nods from the other boys in the group.

"Let me put this another way," Gilles said. "If you thought that your friend was murdered by anyone in a competing group or some other business enemy, would you tell me?"

There was silence until again Denny spoke up, "No. We would handle it. And you can check, none of us is packing and we're okay to talk about Mik. If we thought there would be trouble, do you think we would risk hanging out in a public place?"

Gilles had to admit that the kid made a good point. "What's your name?" Gilles asked.

"Denny," came the response.

"Denny what?" Gilles asked.

"Denny Marchand."

"Well, Denny Marchand," Gilles reached into the side pocket of his suit jacket and handed him one of his cards, "if you think of anything I would appreciate a call."

"Yeah," said Denny in a tone of voice that Gilles understood to mean, not bloody likely. Denny slipped Gilles's card into the pocket of his jeans.

Gilles thanked the uniformed officers for their help and told them that they could return to their regular duties. He spent an additional thirty minutes or so in the park chatting with the young men but did not gain any additional information. He hoped that by not making a big deal about the fact that they were dealing drugs he had won a measure of trust from them. The risk was that they would take Gilles's indifference to their retail activities as license to continue.

Annie's alarm went off at five-thirty in the morning. She was on the day shift for the next week and that meant that she had to be at the hospital at least fifteen minutes before her shift started at seven-thirty. She knew that she could sleep for an extra half hour but she had long since gotten out of that habit. When Pamela was a youngster, Annie learned to get up early in order to get Pamela off to school. By the time

Pamela got to high school she was able to get herself up and to class with very little nagging from Annie, but the habit of getting up early remained.

After her shower Annie was wearing a comfortable bathrobe and enjoying her simple breakfast of toast with home-ground almond butter and coffee when Pamela appeared in the kitchen.

"Good morning, Sweetie," Annie said cheerily. "You're up early."

"Ugh, yeah," Pamela said, pouring herself the second cup of coffee that Annie usually brought to work. She was wearing a pair of old scrubs that Annie had rescued from the discard pile. "I need a favour."

"What kind of favour?" Annie asked.

"The car. Can I borrow it for the day? I have to attend a special lecture at the Lachine General and I don't want to struggle with bus and metro." The Lachine General Hospital was in one of the western boroughs of Montreal, not all that far from where Annie and Pamela lived in NDG as the crow flies, but tricky to get to by public transportation.

It was too late for Annie to take public transportation to work. "Yeah, you can have it, so long as you drive me to work in fifteen minutes and pick me up at three-thirty."

Pamela sighed. "Okay, Mom." She sat down with her coffee and Annie went to her room to get ready for work. She barely needed fifteen minutes to pull on a pair of clean scrubs and apply a little makeup. She returned to the kitchen and said, "Okay. Let's go."

On the drive to the hospital Annie asked Pamela what she thought of Gilles's daughter.

"I really don't know," Pam answered. "We're pretty close in age but miles apart in everything else. I think she thinks that I'm hopelessly out of it. We talked a little about music

84

and we for sure don't like the same things. And she knows way more about the club scene than I do."

"I know," Annie said. "Gilles worries about her. She spends more time clubbing than studying."

"Well, she made me feel ancient, and that I really have to get out more," Pamela said with a smile.

"Oh, shit!" Pamela exclaimed. She'd missed the turn down the side street that would take Annie to the entrance to the ER. "I missed my turn."

"Drop me on the corner. Someone drank my second cup of coffee," Annie teased. There was a Java U coffee shop across the street from the Gursky, near the corner of Côte-des-Neiges.

Pamela pulled up to the bus stop and Annie opened the passenger-side door. "Remember, three-thirty at the ER entrance," she reminded her daughter. She jumped out of the car just as a bus pulled up behind it and honked for Pamela to get out of the way.

Annie entered the Java U and was pleased to discover that there were only two people ahead of her in line, a guy she recognized as one of the lab workers and, directly in front of him, a woman with thick black hair that fell in waves to just below her shoulders. The line moved and the woman ordered a latte and gave her name as Claire. Annie asked for a medium coffee, paid for her drink and went to the service counter to add milk. From behind her she heard the barista call "Claire!" Annie put a cover on her coffee and headed for the door. Annie had Claire in profile, and she was certain that she knew her from somewhere. As they left the Java U Annie was able to get a close look at the woman's face. Claire turned and walked south on Côte-des-Neiges. Annie headed in the opposite direction, trying to remember where she had seen her. She had just crossed the street when it hit her: Claire was the woman in the drawings.

Annie turned and rushed back across the street, hoping to catch sight of Claire and, if she was not too far away, ask her how she knew Mikel Esperanza. But Claire had disappeared.

As soon as she got to the nurses' lounge in the ER, she checked her assignment on the schedule. She was about to call Gilles with the news of the sighting when Sally, the head nurse came in and said, "Oh, Annie. Great. Sylvie had to leave and we need you in Resuscitation right away. It's crazy, we had three ambulances in the last hour."

"On it." Annie said and slipped her cellphone back into her pocket, making a mental note to call Gilles as soon as the crisis in Resus abated.

It was almost noon before Annie had a chance to call Gilles with her news. Gilles was both pleased with the information and impressed that Annie was able to recognize the mystery woman after only having seen her portrait once or twice the night before.

Who was this woman, she wondered.

CHAPTER EIGHT

"It pierced any number of blood vessels and likely the victim's liver and spleen."

The next few days passed uneventfully for Gilles and Annie. Gilles hoped to catch sight of the mystery woman from the drawings, so he showed up at the Java U across from the Gursky each morning at seven and spent an hour there nursing a coffee. But he had no luck.

There was an additional investigative advantage to the fact that Gilles was spending an hour each morning at the Java U. He got into the habit of buying coffees and croissants for the young men in the park. He showed up in the park at ten-thirty with his snacks and chatted with them. Gilles was certain that these guys knew a lot more than they had told him at their first meeting, and he hoped that he would be able to win their trust with coffee and pastry, letting conversation develop organically. It was slow work. There were long periods of silence and there were times when Gilles noticed that a hoodie-wearing youngster would approach the area where Gilles and the guys were talking, notice Gilles dressed as he was in a suit and tie, and turn away. Gilles understood that he was interfering with the gang's drug business and he anticipated that this might loosen their tongues in the hope that Gilles would leave them alone.

The mornings produced nothing in the way of leads. There was a personal benefit to Gilles in that by noon he was done trying to find the mysterious Claire and trying to elicit some information from the guys in the park, so he headed up to the Gursky and he and Annie were able to have lunch together.

◎

On Friday of that week, at about three in the afternoon, the sidewalks of the neighbourhood were clogged with university students leaving the Université de Montréal campus to get an early start on the weekend. The sidewalks were also crowded with shoppers picking up food for the weekend from the many shops that lined Côte-des-Neiges north of rue Reine-Marie. Traffic moved slowly on the street as cars and busses fought to progress up the hill.

A pedestrian wearing dark trousers, a blazer and tweed Ivy cap pulled low over his forehead moved slowly up the street, keeping to the building side of the sidewalk, away from the hustle and bustle of the street. If noticed at all he looked every inch the young academic from the Université de Montréal, not an uncommon sight in that neighbourhood. He threaded through the crowd and caught up to a young guy dressed in a hoodie and jeans.

The pedestrian got close behind the kid and stabbed him from behind on the left side. The kid screamed, twisted and reached behind him to the source of the pain. He felt the wrist of the guy that was stabbing him; as the attacker gave the weapon another thrust the victim fell to the ground. For a split second the people on the sidewalk around them froze at the sound of the scream; when they saw the victim fall to the ground they rushed to his aid. The perpetrator did not run; he let the crowd swarm around him and thus he was able to disappear.

The first person to get to the young man lying in a pool of blood was a lab technician who worked at the Gursky. He knelt down and noticed a knife protruding from the victim's back at about waist level, with blood pooling around it. He called out to the nearest bystander, "You—call 911 and get an ambulance!" Three people reached for their cellphones and made the call.

The ambulance arrived within minutes. The EMTs got the victim loaded into it and made a beeline to the Gursky, sirens blaring. In less than five minutes following the stabbing the ambulance was in the ER bay and Tom had rushed over to help the EMTs get the stabbing victim into triage. Annie was just coming off duty in the Resusitation Unit. Resus, in hospital parlance, was the unit where the most seriously ill patients, those near death, were placed. It was situated between the ambulance bay and the triage area of the ER.

Yves, the triage nurse, got to the gurney and asked, "What've you got?"

"Stabbing," the lead EMT replied.

"Christ. Get me some pressure bandages and get surgery down here," he said to the other ER nurse. "Stat!"

The commotion sounded all too familiar to Annie and she moved quickly into the triage area to see what was going on. Lying on the gurney, with both EMTs and two nurses working to stanch the bleeding, was a young man about the age of the stabbing victim that Annie had worked on a couple of weeks earlier. Two stabbings so close together could not be a coincidence. Annie called Gilles who was at that moment driving back to his office. He made a U-turn and headed to the Gursky.

"Cops called," Annie informed her colleagues.

The victim was moved to the hospital's gurney and the doctor took a close look at the wound. "We've got to get that thing out," she said, indicating the weapon, "but very carefully. I don't want to compound the damage with the extraction." In spite of Yves's efforts to apply pressure bandages to the wound it was spurting blood, indicating that the weapon had hit an artery.

Annie knew that the knife was an important piece of evidence and could not be compromised by having a lot of people touching it. Like the surgeon, she and Yves were wearing gloves, but it was also necessary to put the thing in a protective bag of some sort. Annie needed something that was a little longer than twelve inches. She turned around and rushed to the ice machine in an alcove adjacent to the triage area where bags for ice packs were kept. One of these would keep the wounding weapon safe for Gilles.

She was back at the patient's side just as Dr. Fraser slowly started to remove the weapon. Yves and Annie held the patient steady and had fresh pressure bandages ready to apply when the knife was removed. Tom stood at the head of the gurney gently holding the patient steady. The patient was unconscious, but if he suddenly awoke and jerked he could make his already life-threatening wound much worse.

"Okay, got it." Dr. Fraser dropped a dangerous looking hunting knife into the bag and Annie used the slider to seal it.

The victim was lying on his side, his arms resting on the gurney. Annie noticed that one of his hands was closed in a fist. She uncurled the fingers and found a brass button. She picked it up with her gloved hand and saw that it was convex, engraved with a lion rampant. She pulled a baggie used to send specimen tubes to the lab from a pocket of her scrubs and slipped the brass button into it, then stapled the baggie to the ice bag with the knife. She slid the bags into the side pocket of her scrubs top.

"Get him up to the OR and we'll need to get a blood match. He's lost a lot of blood," Dr. Fraser ordered.

"On it," Yves said, and showed Dr. Fraser a Vacutainer test tube with a sample of the victims' blood for the lab. No one, up to this point, had any information about the patient. Tom found a blank label, wrote Dr. Fraser's name on it along with the word "surgery—match" and put it in the pneumatic tube system to the lab. He took the precaution of calling the lab to tell them to expect the sample and to match it, stat.

"Okay," Dr. Fraser called out. "Good work, team. Let's get him upstairs." Dr. Fraser took the lead and headed to the elevators. When they got to the surgical floor, Dr. Fraser went to prepare for surgery.

"You guys, okay?" Yves asked. "I've got to get back to triage."

"Yeah," Annie replied. "I was just about to go off duty. I'll wait here for Gilles."

Yves left Tom and Annie with the patient. Less than fifteen minutes had passed since the ambulance pulled in with him.

"Do you mind taking a look to see if someone is coming to take him into the OR?" Annie asked Tom.

Tom left the room and walked around the corner to look down the long corridor to see if any of the OR orderlies were coming to get the patient.

Annie knew she had less than a minute before Tom returned but there was something she wanted to do for Gilles and she did not want to be seen doing it. She reached into the pocket of her scrubs and pulled out her cellphone. She took a photo of the victim's face. She knew that it could be a long time before Gilles had access to the patient and she wanted him to know something about him. Her cellphone was safely back in her pocket when Tom returned, followed by an OR orderly pushing an operating room gurney. With Tom and Annie's help he transferred the victim to it and said, "I've got him from here, Fraser's ready."

"Just a sec," Annie said just as the gurney was crossing the threshold, "let's see if we can find some ID."

Tom was level with the victim's waist. He held the door open with his foot, reached into the patient's back pocket, and pulled out a wallet. "Got it," he said, and the orderly took the young victim into surgery.

Annie looked over Tom's shoulder as he went through the victim's wallet. He hoped to find either a driver's license or the Quebec health card with his essential information on it. All he found was a loyalty card to a neighbourhood souvlaki joint with the victim's name written on it in blue ink. Seven of the ten numbers were punched out.

Annie pulled another plastic bag from her scrub pocket and opened it, indicating that Tom should drop the wallet and card into it. He complied and slid the baggie into his pocket.

"This'll have to do," Tom said and sat down in one of the chairs in the room. "There's something going on. Two kids in such a short time. It could be the start of a war."

"Yeah, no kidding," Annie agreed. She moved the other chair so that it was facing Tom and sat down. "I wonder if Gilles will agree with that."

Neither Tom nor Annie said anything for a couple of minutes, taking the time to get over the adrenaline rush of coping with the emergency. Tom got up and said, "I'll get the gurney back and clean it up." Annie held the door for him as he wheeled the empty gurney out of the pre-op room. "Can you send him up when he gets here?" she said. "And one more thing. Make sure that Steve wears gloves when handling the patient's wallet."

"Sure thing." Tom returned to the ER with the bloody gurney and the victim's wallet to get his information logged into the hospital's computer system.

Annie was alone in the pre-op room for another fifteen minutes before Gilles came in. They hugged and Gilles asked, "What happened?"

"Another stabbing victim. Also young. Probably the same age as the first one."

"Tabernac," Gilles exclaimed. "I've been speaking to Esperanza's friends and they're saying there's no gang war. I'm beginning to think otherwise. Do you know anything about the vic?"

"Not yet. Tom took his wallet down to the ER for registration. But I did bag the weapon." Annie held up the bag with the knife in it. She opened the bag and Gilles looked in and said, "Crisse. That's some weapon. Is the kid alive?"

"He's in surgery," Annie replied, "but this thing is deadly. It pierced any number of blood vessels and likely the victim's liver and spleen."

"Can he survive something like that?" Gilles asked.

"We'll know when he gets out of surgery. But I'd say the chances were slim," Annie explained.

Gilles did not relish having to tell another family that one of their children had been murdered.

"I have something else," she said and reached for her phone. "You can't tell anyone that this exists. I broke any number of rules to get it."

"What is it?" Gilles asked.

"A photo of the victim. I didn't know how long he'd be in surgery, I didn't know what kind of ID he might have, and I knew you would want to start your investigation."

"Amazing," Gilles said. "We should put you on the force. Let's see."

Annie pulled up the photo of the victim and she and Gilles looked at it.

"Fucking hell," Gilles exclaimed. "That's the kid who shot me!"

◉

"Shit," Annie said as she and Gilles walked out of the pre-op room. They were alone in the elevator and Annie hurriedly explained to Gilles that, officially, he did not know that the stabbing victim was also a cop-shooter. "I'm going to send you the photo and delete it from my phone." As they walked from the elevator to the registration area of the ER, Annie did just that. She also handed Gilles the ice bag and baggie with the evidence in them.

Back in the ER Annie pulled Gilles into the hallway that led to the office occupied by Steve, the person who took care of registering patients who arrived by ambulance. Steve was short and stocky with carefully styled dark hair. He tended to dress completely in shades of black in order to disguise his girth. He wore a white lab coat with his name badge pinned to the left breast pocket.

"Did you register the kid who's in surgery?" Annie asked him.

Steve looked at Annie and Gilles and said, "Hi Gilles, how's it going?" He didn't wait for Gilles to respond, continuing, "Yeah, here's his wallet back." Steve pushed the baggie containing the patient's blood-soaked wallet towards Annie and Gilles with the tip of his pen. "There wasn't much. Just a card with his name on it." He tapped the card through the plastic.

"Yeah, I noticed," Annie said.

"Luckily the kid had a file here so I got all the information I needed," Steve continued.

"His name," Gilles said. "I need his name."

"The kid's name is Ron Jardine. He's twenty," Steve reported.

Gilles was silent for a moment. The shock of discovering the guy who had shot him all those months ago had not quite worn off, and Gilles felt a surge of anger in the pit of his stomach. He breathed deeply in order to suppress the feeling.

"Christ, man, are you okay?" Steve asked.

"Yeah. I saw . . ." Gilles caught himself. "He's the second knifing in as many weeks." "Yeah, well," Steve replied.

"You said he has a file here? Do you have an emergency contact?" Annie asked.

"Yeah," Steve answered. "Let me bring up his file. Okay," Steve read from the screen, "he was here about a year ago for a broken arm. His emergency contact is his mother." Steve gave the phone number to Annie and Gilles.

Gilles reached for his cellphone, but Annie stopped him and said, "I'll call. I know the protocol." She sat down in the visitor's chair in Steve's office and pulled his phone to her and dialed the number for Mrs. Jardine. When she answered, Annie introduced herself and said, in a comforting voice, "Mrs. Jardine, I'm afraid I have some bad news for you. Your son, Ron, is in the hospital, the Gursky."

Mrs. Jardine did not say anything for a long moment and then, "Ronnie. No, no, no. What's wrong? Can he come to the phone? What happened?" The words poured out of her in a torrent and Annie waited until she had finished before she attempted an answer.

"He's at the Gursky. That's all I can tell you on the phone. But if you come to the ER, someone will explain the situation to you. Will you be able to do that? Come to the hospital?"

Annie did not hear Mrs. Jardine's answer because Gilles was whispering to her, "I can send a squad car to pick her up if necessary." Annie nodded and returned her attention to the phone call.

"Mrs. Jardine, I can have the police send a squad car to pick you up if you like."

"The police?" Mrs. Jardine cried. "Oh Christ, what's happened to Ronnie? What's he done?"

"Mrs. Jardine," Annie said firmly. "We can answer all your questions when you get here. Shall I send a squad car?" Annie read the address from the file to Mrs. Jardine and asked, "Do you still live there?"

"Yeah," Mrs. Jardine agreed. "A police car, eh? Yeah, okay."

"Okay," Annie said. "It will be there soon." She hung up the telephone.

Gilles used his cellphone to call dispatch and order a squad car to pick up Mrs. Jardine and bring her to the emergency entrance of the Gursky Memorial Hospital.

"We'll wait in the Family Room," Annie told Steve. "Let me know when Mrs. Jardine arrives." Annie led Gilles out of the triage area and down a short corridor to a room furnished with a sofa, an easy chair, and a telephone. The room was intended as a private place for the families of patients who had some sort of serious malady to wait in privacy while care was provided. It was rarely used, as family members tended to cluster around the patient, making the jobs of the medical staff harder but helping the patient—and themselves—feel better.

Annie occupied the chair and Gilles sat close to her on the adjacent sofa. "Why didn't you tell the woman that her son was in surgery?" he asked.

"Believe it or not, that's the protocol. We give as little information as possible over the phone when we call and none when someone calls us. It's not always helpful but it's done to protect the patient's privacy."

Gilles shrugged. He didn't comprehend the logic but he worked for a big city police force, which meant that he had long ago come to terms with a bureaucracy. "Yeah," Annie said, completely understanding Gilles's reaction. They sat quietly for several minutes, allowing the tension of the previous couple of hours to drain away.

It was only after she and Gilles had been sitting in the Family Room for about ten minutes that Annie realized that she had completely forgotten that Pamela was supposed to pick her up at three-thirty, over an hour ago. She pulled her cellphone out and called her daughter.

"Oh, Christ, Mum, I'm sorry," Pam said when she answered Annie's call. "We got held up. I'm leaving now."

"Just head home," Annie told her daughter. "I have to stay at the hospital, work late. Gilles will get me home. Love you."

"Love you," Pamela replied and rang off.

Annie turned to Gilles and said with a smile, "I guess you heard that. You'll be driving me home. Kids."

"No problem. But I can't be here when Jardine's family arrives."

"Why not?" Annie asked.

"Conflict of interest, a serious one. The kid is going to be charged with shooting a cop and the cop who was shot can't be seen to be talking to the kid or anyone else having to do with him or with the case," Gilles explained. "The Bureau, the BEI is handling the investigation. It was lucky that I recognized the guy from your photos. It would have been a problem if I had been in the room with him and recognized him there, or worse after I spoke to his mother."

"Yeah, I guess you dodged a bullet there," Annie said.

"No pun intended," Gilles replied.

Annie covered her mouth with her hand and exclaimed, "Oh." She hadn't intended to make a joke.

Gilles's phone beeped and he looked at it. "The patrol car has Mrs. and Mr. Jardine. They'll be here soon. I'm going to my car to call in to my boss."

Annie stood up and they hugged goodbye. "Call me when you're ready. I'll be close by and we'll go out for dinner."

Gilles walked out to his car, which was in a no-parking zone close to the entrance to the emergency room. He saw a squad car pull up to the door of the ER with the Jardines in the back seat.

Gilles called Captain Lacroix and brought him up to date. "Et vous n'aviez eu absolument aucun contact avec le gars?" Captain Lacroix asked. There was no room for error when the BEI was about to investigate. All the cops on the Montreal force knew that any seeming impropriety, no matter how innocent, would be treated as a sign of guilt, and this would be magnified a hundredfold if it got into the media. Gilles assured his commander that he had had no contact with the Jardine kid and that he had left the hospital just before the parents arrived.

"Okay. Good thinking. I'll need a full report, written and oral, tomorrow morning. And stay out of the hospital," Captain Lacroix warned.

"Yes. For sure," Gilles agreed.

After Gilles left, Annie stationed herself in the registration area with a clear view of the entrance to the ER. She wanted to be the one to escort the Jardines to the surgery floor. She only had to wait a moment or two before two uniformed cops came in with a terrified-looking couple. The two young cops towered over the Jardines.

Annie approached the quartet and introduced herself and said, "I'll show Mrs. and Mr. Jardine to the waiting room on the surgical floor."

The two cops nodded their thanks and left the hospital.

Mrs. Jardine was a short woman, no more than five feet two inches tall and very, very thin. She wore her long grey hair in a ponytail pulled back from her face. The youthful style was in contrast to her lined face. She wore no makeup and Annie guessed her age to be in the mid to late fifties. She might have been younger, but she looked old.

Mr. Jardine was a couple of inches taller than his wife. He had grey hair which he wore short. He too was very slim, but with a belly that strained the buttons of his shirt. Like his wife, he was pale and looked worried.

In the elevator on the way up to the surgical floor, Mrs. Jardine asked Annie, "What happened to Ronnie? Why is he in the hospital?"

"I'm going to let the surgeon give you the information. I can tell you that he was attacked," Annie told them.

Betty Jardine gasped and brought her hand up to her mouth. She stumbled backwards a step or two and she might have fallen if her husband, Walter, had not caught her. He held her arm as they exited the elevator.

"What do you mean, 'attacked'?" Walter asked.

Both Jardines spoke with the hoarse, raspy voices of those who smoked too much, and Annie could smell the odour of stale tobacco on their clothing.

"He was brought in by ambulance," Annie explained. "He was the victim of a stabbing. It was lucky, in a way, that he had been a patient here. We were able to find you without much difficulty." Annie changed the subject as she didn't want to give any information that might be contradicted by an investigation, and she didn't know what the results of the surgery would be.

Betty Jardine was about to ask another question but sighed and gave up. Experience had taught her and her husband that life was rarely fair and that things happened, usually bad things, for no clear reason. Annie felt for the Jardines, like any parent would,

Annie got them settled in the waiting room on the surgical floor and used the phone in the room to call the OR desk. She told the clerk to let the doctor know that the Jardines were waiting for news of their son.

Annie sat down on the sofa next to Betty Jardine, took her hand, and said, "Dr. Fraser will come and see you as soon as she can. She's the surgeon taking care of your son. If you need to call someone you can." She pointed to the phone on the small table that separated the two adjacent sofas in the waiting room. "And there are machines in the hallway just past the elevators in case you want a coffee or something." Annie gave Betty Jardine's hand an affectionate squeeze and got to her feet.

"Why would someone want to hurt Ronnie?" Betty Jardine asked, not expecting an answer from her husband. Ronnie was the youngest of their four children and the only boy. He was born late in the lives of his parents. Betty tended to spoil her son, to make excuses for his lack of a work ethic. Betty and Walter worked hard, she at a Tim Hortons and he in a warehouse. Ronnie saw that in spite of all that that his parents did they never had much in the way of money to show for it. Once expenses were covered there was nothing left over for luxuries. This was not the kind of life to which he aspired.

"Dunno," Walter shrugged

The Jardines waited silently. Walter paced and Betty fidgeted, knitting and unknitting her fingers. "I'm gonna go out for a smoke," Walter said. He paused at the door to the waiting room.

"No you're not," Betty informed her husband. "If I can make it so can you. We're gonna wait until we hear from the doctor."

Walter was about to challenge his wife, but thought better of it. He went back to pacing. He placed a cigarette between his lips but didn't light it.

After a couple of stress-filled hours of waiting, Betty fell asleep sitting on the couch in the waiting room. Her head rested on the back of the sofa and her mouth was open causing her to snore. Walter gently moved his wife so that she was more comfortably lying on her side. Her snoring stopped. Walter took the opportunity to slip out of the waiting room to go out for a smoke. Betty woke up a couple of minutes after he returned and sat up. Walter sat beside her. Rubbing sleep from her eyes she asked, "Was I asleep for long? Have you heard anything?"

"No, nothing. It's been a long time."

Fully awake, Betty stared at her husband for a moment and punched him in the kidney.

"Ow, what the fuck, Betty?"

"You shit. You went out for a smoke. I can smell it on you. For all you know someone could have come to talk to us."

Walter moved to one of the chairs and massaged the spot where his wife had hit him. Betty said nothing but continued to look daggers at her husband.

Finally, after what seemed like an eternity, Dr. Fraser came into the waiting room. She was wearing a hospital gown over her scrubs and a cap. Her surgical mask hung around her neck. There were bloodstains on her scrubs.

"Mr. and Mrs. Jardine?" she asked. Betty and Walter got to their feet. "I'm Dr. Fraser."

"How's our boy?" Betty Jardine asked.

"He's in recovery at the moment. He was stabbed and lost a lot of blood. There was damage to some internal organs.

We did our best to get everything stitched up. Now we have to wait," Dr. Fraser explained.

"Can we see him?" Betty asked.

"Yes, but only for a minute or two; he's still unconscious. Come with me. I'll take you."

The trio walked out of the waiting room and Dr. Fraser led the Jardines to the Intesive Care Unit. She stopped at the door and said, "I want to prepare you. Your son is attached to a breathing tube and a lot of other medical machinery. I know it looks awful, but it's how we do our best to make sure that our patients recover." The Jardines nodded and Dr. Fraser instructed them to put on gowns and masks. Dr. Fraser pulled her mask up to cover her mouth and nose and opened the door.

Betty began to cry upon seeing her son looking so frail and helpless. Walter too, was overcome with emotion. He put his arm around his wife's shoulders and they stood helplessly at their son's side.

After a moment or two Dr. Fraser said, "I'm sorry. We have to go. Let's keep a good thought and hope for the best."

Dr. Fraser led the Jardines back to the waiting room. "Do you want to wait here or do you want to return home? I can have someone call you when there's a change."

"We'll wait," Betty Jardine said. She was not about to desert her son in his time of need.

"That's fine," Dr. Fraser said. "I'll tell the ICU nurse you're here."

The ER was enjoying one of its rare lulls in activity. Annie, Yves, the nurse who first attended to Ron Jardine, Ursula and couple of other staff members were having a tense conversation in low tones while they waited for the next ambulance or walk-in patients to appear.

"This is the second murder in the area," Ursula said in a voice that almost vibrated with stress.

"Are the cops doing anything?" Yves asked Annie. "More patrols? Anything at all?"

"I don't know," Annie said. "I haven't heard anything, though."

Ursula folded her arms across her chest and stated, "I for one, am not going to wait for the cops or anyone else for that matter to do something. I'm going to the union and demand that they pressure the hospital to provide more security. If there is a crazy murderer around it's only a matter of time till he shows up in the ER."

There was general agreement from the rest of the people in the group. Annie knew Ursula was right about one thing: if there was an emotionally unstable person in the area sooner or later they would show up at the Gursky ER trying to get meds and, as was so often the case, threatening the staff. The week before one of the nurses had been attacked by a patient in the psych ward of the emergency department. She wasn't seriously hurt but that wasn't the point. The nurse suffered from anxiety due to the attack, and the murders in the neighbourhood added to the stress that all the front-line staff felt.

An ambulance pulled into the ambulance bay and a couple of patients walked into the ER ending the group's conversation. The respite in activity was at an end; it was back to work.

Annie was certain that Ursula would do exactly as she said and hoped she would be successful in getting extra security for the emergency department.

Annie texted Gilles to pick her up outside the entrance to the ER. Gilles pulled into the semicircular drive five minutes later, and Annie got into the car and kissed her boyfriend. "I hope you like Indian food, I've made a reservation at Rasoï," he said, naming one of the newer eateries on Notre-Dame West. "After the day you've had I thought we deserved a special treat."

"That is a special treat. Wonderful."

They were enjoying their main courses, when Gilles's cellphone vibrated. He was about to hit the red icon to send the call to voice mail when he noticed the call was coming from his commander. He said, "Sorry, chérie, I have to take this. Oui, âllo?" He listened in silence and then said, "That's another kid lost for no reason. I'll want to question his parents as soon as possible and see if there is any physical evidence that helps us learn who did this."

"Écoute-moi, Gilles," Captain Lacroix said. "For the moment you're still not to go near the Jardines. You said he was the kid who shot you, and that investigation is in the hands of the BEI. I've called them and there'll be a couple of their investigators at the office first thing tomorrow. You're to meet them here."

"D'accord," Gilles replied. He was about to argue with his boss but thought better of it.

"The BEI will have a warrant to search the Jardine home. You can drive over with them but stay out of the house until the BEI is finished. Once they're done you can talk to the parents. But remember, you can't be in the Jardines' house or apartment building while the BEI is investigating. We have to be absolutely certain that there is nothing to cast doubt on any evidence they might find regarding your shooting."

Captain Lacroix did not state it explicitly, but it was clear to Gilles that he hoped the BEI would find the gun that Ronnie Jardine had used.

After Gilles completed his call with Captain Lacroix he gave Annie the news and told her what he couldn't tell his boss, "I would have liked to be with the BEI when they went to question the Jardines but Lacroix won't allow it. There are times when I . . ." Gilles let the sentence trail off.

"The poor parents. It's such a waste and so sad," she said.

"Crisse, two stabbings and both victims not much older than our kids," Gilles agreed.

Annie and Gilles talked about the next steps in the investigation while they finished their meal, but the news of the murder put a damper on their evening. They forewent dessert and coffee and decided to call it a night.

Gilles drove Annie home and then continued on to his place. He promised to let her know how the investigation proceeded the next day.

CHAPTER NINE

"I'm not saying Ronnie was an angel."

Gilles had a restless night and was up before his alarm clock went off. He was in the office by seven-thirty. Captain Lacroix was not yet there and Gilles made certain that his reports concerning the stabbing of Ronald Jardine were completed and filed. He managed to get all this done before his boss arrived at eight-thirty. The investigators from the BEI arrived a couple of minutes later. It was clear to Gilles, as both officers were carrying cardboard cups of coffee that they had been waiting for Lacroix in one of the cafés in the shopping centre downstairs.

Captain Lacroix convened a meeting with Gilles and the BEI investigators in one of the conference rooms. Following introductions, they got down to business. Camille Vinet was in charge of the investigation. A slim blonde whose hair was held away from her face with a large black clip at the back of her head, giving her a severe look. She opened the meeting by telling Gilles and his boss how her team intended to proceed. Her partner, Simon Charpentier, tall and burly, carrying more than a few extra pounds, did not say much other than to indicate his agreement as Camille spoke.

The plan was straightforward. They would arrive at the Jardines's apartment on Barclay, a block of apartment buildings similar to the Esperanza home. Vinet and Charpentier would ask the Jardines for permission to search their son's room. Putting it as a request was a formality that they were prepared to accord the family because of their loss. The BEI had obtained a warrant for the search and if the Jardines put up any resistance then Camille and Simon would present it.

The BEI investigators told Gilles that he could be in his car close to the apartment building if he wished, or he could wait at some other spot and they would let him know when their search was over so that he could begin his investigation. Finally, Lacroix, Gilles and the two BEI cops agreed that if the BEI found anything that was not connected to Gilles's shooting they would leave it for his investigation.

Before they left for the Jardines's apartment, the BEI cops reviewed the events that led to Gilles being shot.

Gilles gave the BEI team a fifteen-minute head start and then made his way for a café in the neighbourhood.

Camille and Simon pulled up in front of the Jardines's building and made their way to their apartment on the third floor. Suzanne knocked on the door and announced, "Police. Ouvrez la porte, s'il vous plaît." She and Simon waited for a minute or so and then she knocked again and repeated her order more loudly. She made enough noise that a neighbour a couple of doors away opened his door to see what the commotion was about. "Jesus. Shut the fuck up," the neighbour, a young guy wearing a bathrobe, shouted. "People are trying to sleep."

Simon turned to the neighbour with a withering look which caused him to close his door.

Walter Jardine opened the door to the family's apartment. "What, what?" he asked. His eyes were bloodshot from lack of sleep. His facial muscles were slack, giving him a sunken cheek look.

Camille, in a less aggressive tone of voice, asked if they could come in. Walter stood back to let the two cops enter. "This is about Ronnie, isn't it," he asked. "You couldn't wait and give us a bit of peace?"

He, Camille, and Simon were standing in the small foyer of the home. Camille could see the living room straight ahead. It was furnished with a sofa and easy chair that were old, tattered and mismatched. There was a coffee table close enough to both pieces of furniture so that it could be used by people seated on either of them. There were two ashtrays overflowing with cigarette butts on the coffee table. There was a large-screen television on the wall opposite the sofa and there were a couple of end tables with lamps along with a standing lamp as well. The apartment was redolent of stale cigarette smoke.

Camille looked at a haggard-looking, unshaven Walter Jardine and said, "We're sorry for your loss, but we have to search your house for evidence of a crime."

By this time Betty Jardine, looking sleep-deprived and stressed, joined the conversation. She cleared her throat, phlegm gurgling its way down her throat, and said in an aggressive tone of voice, "Our son was the victim of a crime. He was murdered. Why are you harassing us? Go and find our son's killer." Betty folded her arms across her small, sagging breasts and spread her legs slightly as if to block entry into the rest of her home.

"Oui, we understand," Simon said. "But we have reason to believe that before he died your son was implicated in a shooting, and we want to see if there is any evidence of it."

"Our son didn't shoot anybody," Betty said. "How many times do I have to say it? He was murdered!" She started to cry. "Say something," she said to her husband. She sniffled, trying to stop her tears.

"You have to leave now," Walter said. "There's no reason for you to be here." He moved to get around the two cops to open the door. Camille and Simon held their ground.

"Look," Camille explained, "we have a warrant. We can do this the easy way or the hard way. Up to you."

"Let's see it," Walter said. He was standing very close to Camille, glaring at her. She had to take a step backward to avoid hitting Walter with her elbow when she reached into an inner pocket of her nylon jacket with the word "Police" emblazoned on the back. She pulled out the warrant and extended her arm to hand it to Walter, forcing him to back up a couple of steps.

"Christ. Do you expect me to read this?" he shouted.

"Frankly, we don't care. Now show me to your son's room. You can watch what we do but stay out of our way."

Betty sighed loudly, careful not to say what was on her mind, turned and led the two cops down a corridor to their son's room. Walter followed, his fingers drumming against his legs. Betty opened the door and was about to enter when Camille stuck out her arm. "Stay here," she commanded. She and Simon crossed the threshold to Ronnie Jardine's messy, sparsely furnished bedroom. A single bed was placed a couple of feet away from the window, its head against the narrow interior wall. There was a dresser against the wall opposite. A small table with a lamp next to the bed and a wooden chair completed the furnishings. There were clothes and comic books strewn all over the floor. The room smelled of body odor and unwashed clothing.

The two cops exchanged a look. Simon wrinkled his nose and each of them pulled on a pair of blue latex gloves. Simon was carrying a briefcase with evidence bags and a Sharpie.

He pulled the chair over to where he stood and placed his briefcase on it. Camille searched the bed and, finding nothing in the way of evidence save the residue of lonely nights, began methodically going through the clothing and comics on the floor. Simon joined her. After they inspected an article of clothing they tossed it on the bed. They did the same with the comic books. They then searched the dresser and still found nothing. Camille and Simon were experienced investigators and they knew to search the unlikely hiding places first so as to eliminate them. They were well aware that the majority of people who wanted to hide something from the police hid it in a closet. Once they were satisfied that the search of the bedroom had provided nothing of interest they turned their attention to the closet.

There were hangers on a bar that ran the length of the closet but there was very little hanging from them. Most of the clothing was on the floor. They searched the clothing and then turned their attention to the closet itself, looking for a hidden compartment. There was none. There was one shelf that ran the length of the closet and there were a dozen shoeboxes on the shelf. Simon took one of the boxes and opened it. He expected to find it empty or holding something other than shoes. He was wrong; the shoebox held a pair of new Nike running shoes. Camille found that all the shoeboxes they searched contained pairs of pristine name-brand athletic shoes. In the sixth box they found a pistol in a pair of Kyrie 3 basketball shoes. The pistol was placed upside down, with the muzzle pointed into the toe of the shoe and the grip protruding upward from the opening.

Camille tilted the box so that Simon could see into it. "Trouvé," she exclaimed.

Simon went to the briefcase and pulled out an evidence bag. He wrote the date and place of the found piece of evidence and noted that it was a pistol. Camille used her cell-phone to take a photograph of the contents of the shoebox, then removed the pistol by hooking her little finger in the trigger guard and dropping it into the evidence bag. Simon placed it in the briefcase and returned with a much larger bag to accommodate the box and the shoes it contained.

Walter and Betty watched the procedure, a mixture of awe and horror on their faces. They were well aware that Ronnie had had brushes with the police but they were surprised that he had a gun hidden in his closet. "That's not Ronnie's," Walter said weakly. "We've never seen it before."

"It's a plant," Betty said.

Camille looked dismissively at the Jardines but did not say anything.

"We'll search the rest of the house now," Simon explained.

Walter and Betty followed the cops from room to room as they went through their possessions. The search took a couple of hours and did not turn up anything else of interest, which is what Camille and Simon expected.

As the two cops prepared to leave, Camille told the Jardines, "We're done. Very soon, probably within fifteen minutes, you'll be hearing from the detective from the Major Crimes Division who is investigating the murder of your son. His name is Sergeant Gilles Bellechasse. He'll want to ask you some questions. Don't leave your house until you've spoken to him."

"You're saying our son was both a criminal and a victim?" Betty asked. "That makes no sense."

"Well, that's the situation," Simon responded. "You can ask Sergeant Bellechasse for details."

Simon and Camille turned and left the apartment, closing the door on the stunned Jardines.

Gilles knew that the BEI search could take some time, so he brought the most recent Louise Penny novel with him to read while he waited. He had consumed two coffees and a chocolatine and was well into the novel by the time he received a text from Camille informing him that they had completed their search, that they had found a gun, and he was free to question the Jardines.

Gilles gathered his things, left the café and drove to the Jardine apartment building. His knock on their door resulted in an almost immediate response, as if Betty Jardine was waiting by the door for Gilles to arrive. She opened the door and stood in the doorway, her small frame blocking entry to her home.

"I was told that a cop would be coming to see us. I can't say that I like the idea," she said.

Gilles knew that he had nothing to gain by being aggressive with the Jardines. Losing their son and undergoing a police search probably brought them to the limit of their tolerance for stress. "I don't expect that you would like to have the police in your lives. But we want to catch the person who," Gilles searched for the right euphemism—"harmed your son. It's important that we get as much information as possible as soon as possible."

Walter called from the living room, "Christ, Betty, let's get this over with." Betty stood aside and Gilles walked into the apartment. He headed directly to the living room and Betty followed. "Do you mind if I sit down?" he asked politely.

"As if we could stop you!" Betty exclaimed. Gilles sat down in the chair adjacent to the sofa and Betty joined her husband on the sofa.

Gilles pulled a pad and pen from the inner pocket of his blazer, flipped open to a fresh page and asked, "Can you think of anyone who would want to hurt your son?"

Betty ignored the question, looked straight at Gilles, and said, "The other cops said that Ronnie shot someone. That can't be. Ronnie was a sweet boy."

"Wouldn't harm a fly," Walter put in.

"Yeah, well anyway," Betty continued, "Ronnie was not a thug. So why not find the person who claimed Ronnie shot them and start there? That would be a kind of person who would hold a grudge. A person who believed, even wrongly, that Ronnie had done something to them."

Gilles understood that the BEI investigators had apparently not told the Jardines that their son was accused of shooting a cop. Gilles decided that withholding the information would not help his investigation. Sooner or later the Jardines would learn the truth, and better sooner and from Gilles.

"Under normal circumstances you would be right. But not this time. I'm the person that Ronnie shot."

"Oh, fuck! Ronnie shot a cop?" Walter asked incredulously.

"Shit," was all that Betty said.

"Right. So, can you tell me who might have wanted to harm your son?" Gilles repeated.

The news that their son had shot a cop took the edge off the Jardines' belligerent attitude. They thought for a couple of moments before answering, speaking more conversationally now. "No. Really. I can't think of a soul who would want to hurt Ronnie," Betty said. She turned to her husband and asked, "Can you, Walt?"

"No, Betty is right. He hung out with friends that he's had since high school."

"His friends were Mikel Esperanza and a kid named Denny?" Gilles asked.

"Yeah, Denny Marchand," Walter answered. "Poor Mik was killed a week or so ago. Do you think the crimes are related?"

"Well, I don't believe in coincidence," Gilles said. "So yeah. Until I have evidence to the contrary, that's my working hypothesis."

"Jesus," Walter said.

Before anyone could say anything else the front door opened and Cathy Jardine and her two sisters walked into the apartment. Betty had called her daughter after the BEI investigators left and told them what had transpired, and that another cop was on his way. Betty got to her feet and met her daughters in the small foyer to the apartment. Walter and Gilles also stood but didn't leave the living room. The three women formed a circle around their mother and they all spoke at once. Gilles could only pick up snippets of the conversation. "Fuckin' cops. They got no fuckin' respect."

"Is that one of them?" Cathy, the oldest of the three asked, indicating Gilles with a nod of her head.

Cathy strode into the living room, mumbled a greeting to her father and turned her attention to Gilles. She was tall and blonde and looked nothing like her short parents. "How much longer you going to harass my parents?" Gilles got to his feet, extended his hand, and introduced himself. Cathy looked at his outstretched hand, but did not shake it. "I'm Cathy and I'm going to make sure you leave my parents alone."

Gilles used his extended hand to motion in the direction of the other two women who came in with Cathy. "And these, I presume, are your sisters?"

"Yeah. Norma and Liz. Now how about you leave my parents alone." It was not a request.

The two younger women bore more of a family resemblance to their parents. Norma had short brown hair and was wiry, like her mother. Liz, the youngest of the three sisters, was also the largest. She had enormous breasts and carried an extra fifty pounds. Her black hair was shoulder length, her eyes were similar to her father's and of the three she had the kindest face.

"You get any sleep?" Cathy asked her parents. Betty and her other two daughters had crowded into the living room. "How're you feeling?"

"Like I've been hit by a truck and then run over," Betty replied. Walter nodded.

Betty and Walter brought their daughters up to date. Cathy and Norma sat on the sofa with their parents and Liz pulled a hassock over and sat on it. Gilles returned to the easy chair.

Gilles had so far received no useful information from Walter and Betty Jardine, so he turned his attention to Ronnie's older sisters. He asked his question of all three of the women, but he looked straight at Liz when he posed it. "Do any of you know anyone who would want to harm your brother?"

"No." Liz held Gilles's eyes and answered before Cathy could speak. "I'm not saying Ronnie was an angel. He wasn't. He was the baby of the family and spoiled by his three older sisters. He was impulsive and often acted without thinking. And I'm sure that he and his buddies had sources of income that we don't want to know about. He and his friends barely finished high school and they really didn't do much of anything for work." She reached forward and touched Gilles on the knee. "I can't explain what he was doing with a gun, much less shooting someone with it."

"He's the one Ronnie shot," Betty interjected. "Or so they say."

"Fuck," Liz said. Her two sisters stared, open-mouthed.

"I think he was showing off with the gun and it went off," Gilles said. "It was not a smart thing to do and if we had found him—and believe me, we were looking, but his friends protected him—well, he would have been in serious trouble.

"Look. When he shot me, I was confronting him and his friends because I believed they were selling drugs in the park. Is it possible that someone with whom they did business, if that's the right word, stabbed Ronnie and Mikel for some reason?"

"It's possible," Cathy answered. "But if they were doing what you said they were doing, these guys were small time. It's not like they were in trouble with a cartel or something."

Gilles had to accept that he was not, at the moment, going to get any additional information from the Jardine family. He handed a card to each of the Jardines and said, "Please call me if you remember anything. Before I leave, I would like to take a look at your son's room."

Gilles's cellphone buzzed and he took it out to see that it was Annie calling. He thought it best not to take the call while he was with the Jardine family.

Betty felt comforted by the presence of her daughters and some of the fire returned to her. She got up and said, "Jesus, don't you guys talk to each other? The other two cops tore his room apart and searched the rest of the house. Follow me."

Betty marched out of the living room and Gilles and the Jardine daughters followed. When she got to Ronnie's room she stood aside and motioned Gilles in. "See," she said, "his stuff is piled on his bed. They went through everything."

Gilles entered the bedroom and poked at the piles of his stuff with his pen. He went to the closet and tapped the walls looking for a hidden compartment.

"Tell me," Gilles said after he had examined the closet. "Did the other cops find any drawings?"

"Drawings? No, just the gun."

"Okay, thank you," Gilles said.

He knew that the BEI cops had searched the entire apartment and if they had found anything else even remotely useful they would have taken it with them or let Gilles know where and what it was.

"I won't disturb you any more today," Gilles told the family. "But call me if you think of anything."

Annie was assigned to the Resuscitation, Resus, Unit that morning. True, all patients were equal and equally deserving of the best care, but she found the stress of Resus to be unrewarding. Even though there were fewer patients than in the other units of the ER the rooms were larger because they had to accommodate a lot of medical equipment and it was not uncommon for there to be two nurses and a doctor treating the patients. They were usually in serious distress and connected to a collection of machines that helped them breathe and kept fluids flowing in and out in proper proportion, monitored bodily functions and supplied them with meds. The stress came not from caring for the patients, but from the relatives who hovered around, getting in the way, asking questions that could not be answered and making demands that could not be fulfilled. All of this interfered with the care the person needed.

Annie usually skipped her breaks, but when working in Resus she found she needed a break after a couple of hours. She asked one of the other nurses to cover her patients and she headed off to the café in the hospital's food court. Modern hospitals were designed like shopping malls; the cafeteria was now replaced with a food court with a variety of choices and a common seating area. Annie arrived when the restaurants were at their busiest so she had to give up hope of having a table to herself where she could relax. Coffee in hand, she looked for an empty chair at any of the tables in the food court. She almost dropped her coffee when she noticed an empty chair at a table occupied by the mysterious Claire.

"Excuse me," Annie said, "would you mind if I sat here?"

Claire smiled and pointed at the chair. "Please."

Claire was more beautiful in person than in the drawings. She had black hair the shine and colour of a raven's eye. It was thick and wavy and cascaded to just below her shoulders. Her eyes were also black. From what Annie could see, Claire had a slim, athletic body with small firm breasts. Annie noticed that Claire was wearing neither a uniform nor a hospital ID.

"Is it as hectic in your department as it is in Emerg?" Annie asked.

Claire smiled and replied, "Oh, I don't work here."

"I'm sorry," Annie said and then added sympathetically, "I just assumed. I guess you're here to visit a patient. I hope it's nothing too serious."

"No, nothing like that," Claire answered. "My husband's a doctor here. I'm meeting him. But he's in a meeting, so . . . " Claire didn't finish the sentence as it was self-evident that she was having a coffee. "Where do you work?"

"I'm a nurse in the ER," Annie told her, hoping to keep the conversation going so she could determine which of the doctors Claire's husband was.

"Right, Emerg, I should have known," Claire replied but did not say anything to encourage further conversation. She looked at her watch, picked up her coffee container, and got up from the table. "I've got to run. It's been nice meeting you . . ." Claire looked at Annie's ID and said, "Annie."

Annie also got up and said, "Nice meeting you too . . ."

"Claire."

"Claire," Annie echoed. The two women shook hands and Claire walked off in the direction of the corridor that could take her to any of the interconnected buildings that comprised the Gursky Memorial Hospital.

Annie sat back down and pulled her cellphone from one her scrubs pockets and called Gilles. When he didn't answer, she left a message.

◉

As soon as Gilles was outside the Jardines's apartment building he returned Annie's call. Luckily, she was not with a patient but in the supply closet looking for an infusion pump.

"I only have a minute," she said when he answered, "but I have some news."

"What is it?" Gilles asked. He knew that Annie would not call him to gossip. If she had news about something it had to be important.

"I met Claire, the mysterious woman from the drawings."

"What? Fantastic! Where did you meet her?"

Annie recounted her coffee-break meeting with The Mysterious Claire and ended by saying, "I know it's not much but I hope it's helpful."

"Very helpful, darling," Gilles said. "It's more than we knew before and now we just have to find out which of the hundreds of doctors at the hospital has a wife named Claire."

"A daunting task," Annie said drily.

"Daunting, but not impossible. Good work, chérie."

CHAPTER TEN

"Thank you. You make me cry."

Before she headed to the main building to meet her husband, Claire stepped outside to make a phone call. She moved away from the smokers who congregated, even at a hospital, in the area close to the entrance. She was nervous about her lunch date with her husband and wanted to talk to her best friend.

"Marji, hi," Claire said when her friend answered. "Do you have a minute?"

"For you, absolutely."

"I'm on my way to meet Eric for lunch and I'm really stressed that he's going to say that he wants a divorce. Can I come over afterward? I think I'm going to want to talk."

"Sure, come over whenever you want. But what makes you think that Eric wants to divorce you?"

"I think he knows . . ."

"How could he?"

"I don't know," Claire said. "But he's been acting strange for the last little while."

"What do you mean?" Marjorie asked. "Cool, or suspicious?"

"No, not really. More the opposite, really. He's been super nice, very calm and solicitous. Very unlike himself. As if he's made a tough decision and now has to carry it out."

"Shit," Marjorie exclaimed. "Are you sure? You've been pretty stressed lately because of Mik's death. Maybe you're misreading the signs."

Marjorie could hear Claire breathing before she answered. "I don't want to talk about that on the phone. I hope you're right about Eric, but I don't think so. That's why I want to talk to you afterwards. I've got to run now. I'll call you when I'm on my way to your place."

Claire walked back into the hospital and snaked her way through two pavilions to the main building where she was to meet her husband.

Normally Claire would have met Eric at his office, but he was in a meeting with the executive committee of the board of directors in the hospital boardroom so he and Claire agreed to meet in the main lobby. Claire paced back and forth while she waited.

Only a few minutes late, unusual for the chronically overbooked Chief of Medicine, Eric strode into the lobby and greeted Claire with a kiss and a hug. He was wearing a dark blue suit with an orange and blue silk Hermès tie. At five feet nine he was an inch shorter than his wife, but she had to admit that he looked good in his suit. It was cut to emphasize his athletic build. Only his grey hair indicated that he was almost twenty years older than she was.

"Hi darling," he said. "I hope I haven't kept you waiting too long."

"No. You're right on time," Claire said, and returned his kiss. "Where do you want to go?"

"I've made a reservation at the Duc d'Orléans," Eric said. It was one of the better restaurants in Montreal and the best one in the neighbourhood of the Gursky. On the odd occasion that Claire met her husband for lunch at the hospital they usually went to one of the many sandwich shops on the streets near the hospital. The Duc d'Orléans was the kind of place reserved for special occasions, and this added to Claire's concern about what was on Eric's mind.

As Claire and Eric walked up Côte-des-Neiges toward the restaurant Claire was struck, as she usually was, by the beauty of the tower of the library at the Université de Montréal a little to the east. Ahead of her the dome of the St. Joseph Oratory dominated the skyline. She made a mental note to return to the neighbourhood to do some urban sketches some with the tower in the background, others featuring the Oratory.

Eric kept the conversation light and impersonal. He told Claire about his meeting and the personalities involved in hospital politics. Claire only half listened. This kind of chatter, too, was unusual for Eric. When he talked about hospital politics it was usually with vitriol, not with the kind of humour he was now showing.

The maître d' at the restaurant greeted Eric formally as Docteur Kavanaugh and fussed over Claire. The Duc d'Orléans was Eric's restaurant of choice when entertaining dignitaries and donors on behalf of the hospital.

They were seated in a quiet corner. Over the meal, Eric continued to keep the conversation light, talking and gossiping about friends. When the table was cleared and coffee served he covered Claire's hand with his and said, "There's something I'd like to do. It's sort of a surprise." Claire braced herself. "I've been working a lot of hours recently and I can see it's been hard on you. I want to take some time off and take a cruise."

It was only when she exhaled that Claire realized that she had been holding her breath, expecting the worst.

"Wow, what a wonderful idea," Claire replied. "Where do you want to go? It's a little early for the Caribbean, I would think."

"Yeah. You're right. I was thinking European. Mediterranean or Baltic or something like that." Eric reached into his jacket pocket and pulled out some colourful pamphlets describing different cruise lines and their offerings. "We don't have to decide now. I just wanted to propose the idea."

"I'll look these over," Claire said, gathering up the leaflets. "I have to admit I've always wanted to see Turkey."

"I'm sure that one of these goes there," Eric agreed. He was about to say something more when his cellphone sounded. He pulled it out of his pocket and said, "I'm sorry. I didn't realize the time. I have another meeting."

Eric settled their bill and they left the restaurant. Just before he turned to head back to work he said, "Do you want me to flag a cab for you? Are you heading home?"

"I'm going to walk for a while," Claire said. "And then I'm meeting Marjorie."

Eric kissed Claire goodbye and said, "Great. Have a nice afternoon." Claire returned his kiss and her husband strolled back to the hospital. Claire watched him for a second or two and then walked north on Côte-des-Neiges on her way to Marjorie's. As she walked she called her friend and told her that she was on her way to her studio.

Claire had met Marjorie Reynolds about ten years previously, six months after she married Eric. She met her husband when she worked at the Gursky, and following their marriage, his second, he convinced her that it looked bad for the wife of the chief of medicine to be holding a job as a lab technician. It would, he explained, be more appropriate for her to work on one of the volunteer committees. Claire had a few meetings with various members of various committees and found she had nothing in common with the women she met. They tended to be settled into a lifestyle that involved children, vacations, and good works. Claire respected the good works part of their lives, but had almost nothing else in common with these women. Claire had an artistic streak and decided to indulge it.

One day while waiting for a friend to meet her for a coffee Claire was leafing through a copy of *Reflection* magazine, one of Montreal's free weeklies, in which Marjorie advertised. She flipped the page and then went back to the ad. Claire had enjoyed drawing when she was a student but had given it up for some reason. Now that she had the time she decided to take a course and develop her talent. If it turned out she was not a talented artist at least she would have something to do that had meaning for her.

Claire enrolled in a beginner's class and loved it, signing up for as many other courses as Marjorie offered. In the process they became good friends. Marjorie was in her late forties, fifteen years older than Claire, and so occupied the role of older sister and sometimes that of a mother surrogate.

During her second year taking courses with Marjorie Mik turned up at the studio. He was the last to arrive and Marjorie welcomed him and introduced him to the rest of the class. Mik smiled shyly and bobbed his head in response to the introduction. He was clearly unsure of himself. Marjorie put a hand on his back and said, "Why don't you take the easel next to Claire?" She walked Mik to where Claire was standing and made another introduction. Over the weeks that followed Claire, and the rest of the class, could see that the shy Filipino guy had a lot of talent.

He and Claire had little conversations about perspective or the best charcoal or something equally innocent. After a while Claire suggested that they have a coffee after class and, in the nature of these things, one thing led to another. Mik had the habit of walking Claire to her car after their coffees together. They usually parted with a Montreal two-cheek kiss. On one occasion Mik turned it into a full kiss. Claire responded by kissing Mik with the same passion. Their affair escalated from that point.

Marjorie's combined studio and townhouse, was located a block east of Côte-des-Neiges in a disused primary school that an enterprising developer had turned into four combination town house/lofts. The school was a three-storey red-brick building built after the First World War. Because the construction was done with interior supporting walls, the developer could not gut the place and turn it into eight condos. So he did the next best thing—he divided the building vertically and created four townhouses with studio space on the top floor of each. The first two floors housed the living space the third floor was almost completely open. Marjorie turned this space into a studio. There were large windows on three sides which gave the studio a lot of natural light.

The living space was nicely furnished with comfortable colourful furniture, some of it expensive, some of it from second-hand shops and friends and neighbours.

After walking a block or so, Claire hailed a cab. Marjorie greeted her with a hug and offered her the choice of tea or wine. Claire opted for the wine and Marjorie poured two glasses. They sat in comfortable chairs in the corner of the living room.

Marjorie Reynolds was able to afford her somewhat bohemian lifestyle because she was the youngest daughter of a wealthy businessman who had left her well provided-for. She inherited her father's business acumen and so made some very wise investments with the money she had inherited. That, plus the fact that her paintings and drawings sold reasonably well for a living artist, meant that she was able to do what she wanted when she wanted.

Marjorie was a couple of inches shorter than her friend. She had steel-blue eyes and sharp features. When her face was in repose she looked aristocratic, but her face was rarely in repose. When she was painting, her lips were usually pursed and her gaze fixed. With friends, her smile was warm, the kind that invited people to share their thoughts and feelings.

Marjorie's grey hair swung along her jaw line as she led Claire to the living room. She didn't say anything to her friend for a couple of minutes, allowing her time to relax and take a couple of long sips of her wine.

"So, lunch. How did it go?" She resisted the temptation to ask, "Still married?"

"I can tell you one thing," Claire replied, "It was not what I expected. Eric wants to go on a cruise."

Marjorie almost choked on a mouthful of wine. "A what? A cruise?"

Claire smiled. "Yeah. It took me completely by surprise."

"So he doesn't . . ."

". . . suspect anything. Apparently not."

Claire had known that her fling with Mikel wouldn't last. She was lonely in her marriage and he was a sweet young man who paid her attention; he complimented her art and enjoyed her company. The fact that he was very handsome was just icing on the cake. She didn't expect the affair to end with the death of her lover.

"How are you feeling?" Marjorie asked. "You've had quite a shock."

Claire sighed and didn't say anything for a moment. "Yeah. But I have to . . . well . . . you know."

Marjorie leaned closer to her friend and took her hand.

"So what are you going to do?" Marjorie asked.

"Go on a cruise, what choice do I have?"

"Well, you can always say no," Marjorie said. "Let me ask you something: do you love Eric? I mean, are you in love with him?"

Claire refilled her wine glass and looked at its contents as if it would provide her with an answer. After a long moment she said, "Actually, no. I'm not in love with him. But I don't feel ready to leave him. Not now. I feel too vulnerable."

"And you feel that putting off what appears to me to be inevitable will make it easier? The next time you meet a person like Mikel, a person for whom you have real feelings, he may not want something casual."

"I know," Claire said. "But I can't change the fact that I'm not ready. I'm not over Mik and the great thing about Eric is that he works so hard that I have time on my own to deal with it. To grieve."

"I guess," Marjorie said, very uncertain that her friend had made a good choice. "But you know you can always move in with me if you need to. I have extra room here. Whatever else you feel, you have options. And a friend who cares about you and is here for you."

"Thank you. You make me cry," Claire said and sniffled. She used her fingers to wipe away tears. "You're the best. I don't deserve you."

"Oh, Claire, you deserve so much more. You deserve to be happy."

CHAPTER ELEVEN

"I want to talk to you privately. Off the record."

Gilles was very pleased with Annie's news that she had not only found the mysterious Claire but also had managed to chat with her. But at the moment he wanted to talk to Denny Marchand. He had formed the conclusion that the deaths of two guys who were part of a gang that dealt drugs out of the park were connected to a territorial war or, worse, a battle for control of the illicit drug trade in Montreal which the legalization of cannabis had done nothing to stop. He knew that if this proved to be the case then he would have to pass the investigation off to the division that dealt with the gangs. Gilles wanted to be sure before he gave up his first murder investigation. He decided that it would be a good idea to try to find Denny Marchand to see if he could get any information from him.

How to get Denny to talk openly was a problem Gilles intended to solve when he found the young man. The logical place to look for Denny Marchand was the park where one of the murders and most of the drug deals in that part of the neighbourhood took place. He drove to the park and left his car in the hidden area that he had used on the day he was shot.

He saw through the bushes that Denny was where he expected him to be. He was sitting on the back of a bench with his feet on the seat, hanging out with his friends. Gilles surveilled the scene for long enough to see that, as usual, these guys were dealing drugs. He did not want to push his way through the bushes to where the group was hanging out; it would make too much noise, and the guys would probably run off. So he took the long way around and came up behind Denny and his friends. Gilles placed his hand on Denny's shoulder, startling the young man. "What the fuck?" Denny exclaimed. He would have slid off his perch had Gilles's grip not held him in place. He turned his head.

"Cop," Denny said loudly, and his friends ran off in different directions, one of them taking the brown bag that had been sitting on the bench six inches or so from Denny's left foot. He turned back to Gilles and said, "Happy?"

"Actually, yes," Gilles said. "I want to talk to you privately. Off the record."

"I'm going to leave go of you if you promise not to run, to stay and listen to me. Then you can run if you like," Gilles explained. "Deal?"

"Like I have a choice. Deal."

Gilles released his grip and quickly, before Denny could get off the bench, circled around so that he was standing in front of Denny "Just stay where you are and listen," he said.

Denny slid down so that he was sitting on the bench seat, manspreading his legs and stretching his arms out on the back of the bench. Gilles moved slightly to one side to avoid being kicked as Denny spread out.

"OK, cop, I'm all yours."

"My name is Detective Sergeant Gilles Bellechasse. This is an unofficial conversation, so save the attitude."

This was the first time in Denny's life that he was having a conversation with a cop that did not have the risk of a sanction of some sort, and he didn't quite know how to handle it. Gilles could see that Denny was confused and certainly not ready to trust him. "Look," Gilles said in a conversational voice, "I'm investigating a murder, two murders actually, and I don't care about your petty drug deals. I'm not on the narcotics squad; I'm in the Major Crimes Division. And anyway, I don't even think the narc cops care about marijuana dealers anymore."

Gilles removed his foot from where he'd placed it on the bench and sat down beside Denny. "If you care about the murder of your friends then you'll help me find out who killed them. It's that simple."

"Yeah, so you say," Denny retorted. "Are you taping this conversation?"

Gilles pulled out his cellphone and showed it to Denny. "As you can see, I'm not. But if it will make you happy I'll turn it off." His phone went dark. "And," Gilles added, "we can have this conversation somewhere where there is a lot of ambient noise which makes recording impossible."

Denny smiled and said, "It's okay, dude. I'll take your word for it."

"So were your friends up to anything that could get them murdered?"

"No. Really. We're not in that deep."

"Tell me about them. Maybe I'll see something that will help. Start with Mikel Esperanza."

Denny took a deep breath and said, "Mik was my best friend. We met in primary school and we've been buddies ever since. We went to the same high school. I'm not particularly good at anything but Mik is—was—different. He had talent. Have you seen his drawings?"

Gilles nodded and Denny continued, "He could do anything. He made up graphic novels and he could draw a street scene that looked like the street. He was incredible. I asked him to make a portrait of my mother for a present for her and he did it. It's beautiful and it's hanging in her apartment. There was no reason why anyone would want to hurt him."

"What about Ron Jardine?" Gilles asked.

"Same thing. He went to school with us and liked it about as much as we did. Ron was more like me. Not terribly good at anything but reliable. In our biz trust means everything and we trusted each other."

"I get that," Gilles agreed, "but in the drug business competitive problems tend to get settled with violence, no?"

"Look, man, we're not the Rock Machine or the Hells Angels," Denny said. "We're just not that important."

"Why don't you explain how your business worked, then?" Gilles asked.

Denny thought about this question for a couple of minutes. To answer it was to admit to a felony no matter what the possibilities of legalization were. He decided to take Gilles's commitment at face value. Denny wanted to see the person or people who'd murdered his friends caught.

"It's pretty simple," he explained. "We have a supplier and we have a territory. We look after Barclay, Plamondon and one or two side streets."

"And that's it?" Gilles asked. "There are no other gangs?"

"I wouldn't exactly use the term gangs, but yeah, there are others. There's a group of guys like us who have a couple of other streets. Our supplier set all of us up like McDonald's franchises. We each have a small territory, and like the owners of McDonald's, we don't encroach. And there's enough money so we all do okay."

"What happens when another gang wants to take over from your supplier?"

"I told you, we're all supplied by the same people. If there's a conflict they take care of it. No one is stupid enough to get into a fight with these guys. Anyway, everyone has been on their best behaviour since the arrests and trials. It's like any other business, when there's a crisis everyone just keeps their head down and waits for the bullshit to end." Denny was referring to Operation SharQc, which saw the arrest, trial, and conviction of the major biker gangs in Quebec several years previously. In theory this brought an end to the control of the drug trade by the two main motorcycle gangs, the Rock Machine and the Hells Angels. In fact, the drug trade continued with the remnants of the two gangs and other major players in the Montreal underworld. They all agreed that it was better to work together quietly than be pulled apart by the cops.

"To be clear," Gilles concluded, "there's been no hostile action of any kind in your world?"

"None," Denny agreed. "I don't know who killed my friends or why, but it has nothing to do with our business. Believe me."

Gilles got to his feet and said, "I do believe you. You've been very helpful. Thank you." Gilles extended his hand. Denny shook it and said, "Good luck then, dude. I hope you find the fucker who did this to my friends."

"I intend to," Gilles said. He again gave Denny one of his cards this time with his cell phone number written on the back and said, "Call me if you think of anything else."

Denny nodded and slipped the card into his jeans pocket. As Gilles walked away Denny pulled out his phone and called his friends, telling them the coast was clear and they were again open for business.

When Gilles got back to his car he called Annie and suggested that she come to his place for dinner. "I'm cooking,"

he said. He had a bœuf bourguignon in the freezer which he had made for the next time Annie came over for dinner.

"Then I'm in," Annie agreed. "I'll let Pam know and I'll come over as soon as I'm off."

Gilles went shopping and then home to start preparing dinner. Annie arrived just as he took the boeuf bourguignon out of the oven. He placed it on the stovetop to let the flavours blend, and let it cool a bit to a temperature where it could be eaten. He poured Annie a glass of red wine from the bottle that had been opened and breathing on the table. They chatted while he cut a warm baguette into chunks large enough for dipping in the sauce. When Gilles was satisfied that the boeuf bourguignon was at the point of perfection, he dished out two generous portions and carried them to the dining room table. Annie came through the open-plan kitchen to the dining area with the bread basket and the salad.

Over dinner they talked about their daughters. Annie was aware that Gilles's daughter, Emilie, was a rebellious handful who missed her father and took advantage of her mother. Annie listened sympathetically to Gilles's description of his daughter's latest, mischievous exploits. Both of them understood that Emilie's behaviour was intended to ensure that she was the most important person in Gilles's life. She was very clever about getting into just enough trouble to keep Gilles on his toes, but not so much that she was at serious risk of doing irreparable damage to her life. For example, she skipped school but did well enough on her exams to ensure that she graduated with her friends. From time to time she was delivered home by the local police from a house party that had gotten out of hand. But the cops in that suburb knew Gilles was a brother in blue and ensured that there was no official report of Emilie's transgressions.

"Sooner or later she'll understand that you love her and your problems with her mother will never stop you from being her father, being there for her," Annie said.

"Oui," Gilles agreed. "But I hoped it would be sooner, not later. How is Pamela doing? I wanted Emilie to see her as a sort of role model."

Annie did her best not to brag about her daughter. The fact that she was an exceptional young woman didn't mean that she should be trotted out as an example for other parents to cite as a model of behaviour. "She's great. I think she works too hard and I wish she had some of Emilie's joie de vivre. It would be nice if she went out with her friends more." Annie smiled and added, "I guess we're never satisfied, are we?"

"Parenting," Gilles said, the one word expressing it all. They moved to the comfort of the sofa. "Not to change the subject," Gilles said, changing the subject. "What are the odds of finding The Mysterious Claire? It's important that I talk to her. If the stabbings had nothing to do with gang competition in the drug trade, then Claire may know something important."

"Yeah, if for no other reason than to give some sort of insight into what Mikel was up to. How he ended up making drawings of her. Nude and all," Annie said. "Now that I know she's married to one of the doctors at the Gursky, it shouldn't be too difficult to find her."

"What's your plan?" Gilles asked.

"Simple," Annie said. "I'll ask people I know if they know of a doctor who's married to a woman named Claire?"

"That won't cause people to ask a lot of questions about why you want to know?"

"Not really. As a group we're pretty gossipy. They'll think I just want some hospital scuttlebutt."

Annie moved close to Gilles and curled against him, her legs tucked under her. "Enough about kids and crime," she said softly. "Now it's Annie time."

Gilles leaned into Annie's body and kissed her. Annie felt the strong affection and passion Gilles felt for her and returned the feeling and the kiss.

The dishes would wait until the next morning.

CHAPTER TWELVE

"A guy's been stabbed . . . we need an ambulance!"

Gilles got up very early to do the dishes from the previous evening. He closed the bedroom door so Annie could sleep. The smell of coffee brought her into the kitchen. Gilles held his arms open and Annie moved into them for a good-morning hug. Gilles could feel the warmth of Annie's body under the t-shirt she had donned when she got out of bed and made a move to lead her back to the bedroom. Annie smiled and said, "I'd love to." She felt his hardness against her. "You're obviously ready for some action. But you know I'm not a quickie kind of woman. I've got to get to work . . . and so do you."

Gilles kissed her and then said with a sigh, "Yeah, I suppose you're right. Coffee's ready. Toast? Or would you like me to whip up some eggs?"

"Toast and coffee will be fine."

Gilles put bread into the toaster and brought the coffee pot to the table along with two cups. Annie brought the butter and jam.

"What kind of day do you have?" Gilles asked.

"I told Ursula that I would work her shift so she could take care of some personal business or something. I think one of her kids is having trouble at school."

"You're working a double?" Gilles sipped his coffee. It was not uncommon for nurses to work two shifts in a row, either to help a friend or because the hospital was short staffed.

"What about you?" Annie asked while buttering her toast.

Gilles added some jam to a piece of toast and took a bite. He swallowed and said, "A lot of paperwork. Not to mention that the BEI investigators will want to talk to me and the boss. And I want to talk to someone on the gang squad about drug dealers in the neighbourhood around Kennedy Park."

Annie finished her coffee and said, "Then we'd better get moving."

On sunny autumn days, Hari Deshpande treated himself to a walk through the park on his way to work. On this day, he was more than an hour later than usual, owing to the fact that he had been at the office until well after midnight the night before. Winter would make walking unpleasant soon enough and Hari did some of his best thinking while in motion and away from his desk. He lived with his parents in the family home on Lacombe Avenue, a tree-lined street with prosperous-looking duplexes on both sides of it. The detour through the park also involved a walk along the tree-shaded streets of his neighbourhood. He took childish pleasure kicking at the leaves as he made his way along the sidewalk.

Hari had graduated from McGill University the year before with a degree in computer science. He was six or so months into his first job with a firm that specialized in writing security software for computer networks. Hari had developed a program that added an additional level of protection to two-step verification. He worked out a way of embedding the code in the second of the two steps so that once installed the user didn't have to do anything further to utilize the program, there was a device-to-machine communication. This made computer networks impenetrable. The beta test of Hari's software proved it to be invulnerable to attack from viruses such as the Wannacry, for example.

On many of his walks through the park, both on his way to work and on his way home, Hari saw some of the guys with whom he'd gone to high school hanging out in a corner of the park, doing nothing much other than selling weed. Hari knew it was wrong to feel superior to these guys, but, really, it was hard not to.

As he strolled he noticed the bench they usually hung out at was empty. Probably too early for them, Hari thought, even though it was late in the morning. Then he noticed Denny, one of his former classmates, walking toward him on the path.

The two barely knew one another. Hari was part of the nerd crew in high school and Denny was a Spicoli wannabe. When their paths crossed in the park or in the neighbourhood they usually exchanged a nod and a greeting comprised solely of "'Sup." Out of the corner of his eye Hari spotted a guy in reflective wraparound sun glasses and a black hoodie approaching at a forty-five-degree angle. Hari spotted the glint of something in the guy's hand. It was a knife. As black hoodie guy got close to Denny he swung his right arm up intending to stab Denny. Hari reacted quickly and pushed Denny out of the way.

"What the fuck, man!" Denny yelled as he grabbed at Hari. Denny fell to one knee, but by grabbing Hari as he fell he pulled him into the arc of the knife. Hari felt the blade pierce his right side and yelled in pain.

Hari landed in front of Denny, who saw the blood seeping from the wound. Both of them were frozen for a moment. "Help me," Hari moaned. Denny crawled a little closer to Hari and said, "Don't move, man. I'm calling 911."

"A guy's been stabbed," he yelled. "We need an ambulance!"

The operator was about to hang up when Denny screamed, "What do I do, man, what do I do? This guy is bleeding."

The operator gave him instructions to best to stop the blood flow and told him that she would remain on the line until the ambulance arrived.

Denny dropped his phone and covered Hari's hands with his, putting pressure at the point where the knife had entered. He could hear the ambulance's siren in the distance. Denny had regained some of his composure and said, "The ambulance is almost here. Hang in there, dude."

The ambulance drove right up to them. One of the EMTs moved Denny out of the way and ripped Hari's shirt to expose the wound. The second EMT handed his colleague a pressure bandage which he applied to the injury. They hoisted Hari onto a gurney and got him into the back of the ambulance. One of the EMTs got into the ambulance with Hari and Denny jumped in after him. The other EMT drove, siren blaring.

"Vous ne pouvez pas être ici," the EMT said pointlessly to Denny. The ambulance was speeding to the hospital, siren blaring.

"Yeah, right," Denny replied. He dug around in his pockets until he found the card with Gilles's phone number on it and called the cell number.

"Listen, man," Denny shouted. "Another guy just got stabbed. I'm in the ambulance with him."

"Another of your friends?" Gilles asked.

"No man, just a random guy. I think I was the one that was supposed to be stabbed," Denny explained, the adrenaline beginning to wear off.

"Tabernac," Gilles exclaimed. "Where are you being taken?"

Denny asked the EMT where they were going and reported to Gilles, "The Gursky. We're there!"

"Wait for me. I'm on my way," Gilles commanded.

Gilles told Captain Lacroix what had happened and that he was on his way to the hospital. He moved swiftly out of the office and to one of the unmarked cars in the lot. He used the siren to clear traffic out of his way and called Annie as he drove. He quickly explained what was happening and asked her, if she was not already there, to get to triage to see what was going on. "Do your best to keep the other kid, the one who is not wounded, there until I arrive," he said.

Under normal circumstances the drive from the Major Crimes Division office in the east end of the city to the Gursky would take forty-five minutes or more. With siren blaring, Gilles made it in fifteen.

He arrived and strode into the waiting room where he found Denny looking pale and worried. He was sitting in one of the chairs staring at his blood-covered hands. Gilles sat down beside him and said, "Where are they?"

Denny indicated the general direction of triage with his chin. "Okay," Gilles said. "Wait here for me. I'll need to know what happened."

Denny nodded his agreement and went back to staring at his hands. He went in search of a bathroom to wash off the blood.

Gilles found Annie and the doctor he recognized as Christine Fraser standing around the gurney that bore Hari. Annie was not on triage duty at that time but got one of the other nurses to cover for her when she heard about another stabbing victim in triage. She wanted to be sure to observe any details that would be helpful to Gilles.

Gilles approached them and asked, "How is he? Can he talk?"

"He's lucky," Dr. Fraser said, "no organs were hit. He'll need some stitches but the wound is not serious."

"That's great," Gilles said. "When can I talk to him about what happened?"

"It would be best if you waited until we had him stitched up. He might not feel like talking until the meds wear off."

Annie spoke directly to Hari. "Is there someone we can call?"

Hari answered groggily, "God, no. Please. If you call my parents they'll freak."

"I understand," Annie said, "but you're going to need someone to come and take you home."

"Okay," Hari agreed. "But let me call them . . . and my office," he added as an afterthought. He pulled his cellphone out of his trouser pocket.

"I'm going to take him up to surgery," Dr. Fraser explained. "I want to get some X-rays and make absolutely certain that no internal organs were damaged before I patch him up." She signaled for Tom Andreadis, who suddenly appeared in the triage area, to help her wheel the patient to the surgery floor.

As they moved Hari out of the ER, Gilles could hear him on his cellphone trying to explain to his parents where he was and that he was okay. Gilles could not hear Hari's parents' side of the conversation, but he was certain that they would soon be at the hospital.

Obviously it would be some time before Gilles could question Hari, but he had the next best thing—a witness to the attack. Denny was in the ER waiting room looking very worried. Gilles sat down beside him. "Can I get you something? A glass of water, a coffee?"

"Thanks, man. I think I'll be fine."

"Listen," Gilles went on, "there's a Second Cup in the next building. Let's go over there and talk. I could sure use a coffee, but I think a tea might be better for you." Gilles smiled and rose from where he was seated. Denny got up and followed. There weren't many tables, but once they had their drinks they were able to find a free one with two chairs.

Gilles took out his pen, flipped his notepad open to a fresh page, and laid it on the table. Denny sipped at his tea and looked a little more relaxed.

"Can you tell me what happened?" Gilles asked.

"Yeah. It's fuckin' sick, man," Denny exclaimed. "I was walking through the park and I saw this guy I recognized from high school and from seeing him from time to time in the park. It's one of those things, you know. You see a guy you recognize but don't really know, so you say hi or something and keep moving. No biggie."

"But that's not what happened, is it?"

"No way. We were gonna . . . I could tell because he kind of slowed down. But then I saw panic in his eyes. So I turned to see what it was and I saw this guy rushing at us and he was heading right for me. At first I didn't get what was happening—if Hari hadn't given me a shove I would have been knifed." Denny leaned forward in his chair, twisted and pointed to a spot just below his rib cage on his right side to emphasize his point. "Probably would have killed me," Denny concluded.

"And you're sure he was aiming at you and not Hari?"

"Absolutely. What the fuck is going on, man? Is someone trying to kill all of us who hang in the park?"

Gilles didn't say anything for a moment or two as he thought about what Denny had just said. He'd been focused on the stabbings being part of a fight amongst drug dealers over territory. But it now occurred to him that Denny might be onto something. Perhaps the stabbings were part of some vigilante action to get the drug dealers out of the park.

"Well, if it's not a territorial thing . . ."

Denny interrupted Gilles before he could finish his sentence, "It's not, man. I told you. I even checked with some of the other guys, our competitors, I guess you would say. They have their customers and we have ours. It wasn't them. There's no reason."

". . . then vigilante action is something we have to consider," Gilles said.

"Yeah. No fuckin' kidding," Denny agreed.

Gilles made a few notes in his pad and thought about the possibility of what Denny thought was obvious: that one or more people had taken it on themselves to get the drug dealers out of the park. Gilles thought about how he would go about investigating such a notion. He concluded that he would have to check the internet to see if there were any postings or blogs or whatever having to do with getting drug dealers out of the park. Denny's idea was not completely ridiculous; far from it.

As Gilles thought about the possibility of some kind of vigilante murders he remembered something Tom, the ER orderly, had said to him when Mikel Esperanza was brought in. Tom had commented that the neighbourhood and the park used to be safe places and now they were overrun with drug dealers.

Gilles determined to talk to Tom if he was still around when he went back to the ER.

Gilles turned his attention back to Denny. "Are you feeling any better? You were pretty shaken up."

"Yeah, man, thanks," Denny answered. "It's fuckin' scary."

Gilles took the last sip of his coffee and got up from the table. "I may want to talk to you again," he said to Denny. "Please write your information here." He handed Denny his pad and pen. Denny wrote his name and phone number and looked up at Gilles. "Do you need my address too?"

"Yes, it would be helpful."

Denny added his address to the information and hoped he could trust the cop not to harass him or use the information to bust him for dealing weed. He knew he was taking a chance, but Gilles seemed like a decent sort. More interested in catching a murderer than messing with grass sellers.

Gilles left Denny in the café and walked back to the ER. It was quiet and, just as he hoped, Tom was lounging in one of the patients' chairs in the enclosed triage area chatting with one of the nurses.

Turning to Tom, he asked, "Do you have a minute? Is there somewhere we can talk?"

Tom was more than a little surprised that Gilles had questions for him. Like the rest of Annie's friends in the ER, he knew Gilles as a casual acquaintance. Still, he was nervous that he was about to be questioned by Gilles the cop, not Gilles the friend.

"It's not busy, we can talk in the waiting room," Tom said. "Unless it's something confidential, that is."

"No, the waiting room will be fine." They found a couple of chairs next to the window and sat down.

"How can I help you?" Tom asked.

"On one of my trips into the ER, you mentioned that the park where the stabbings took place used to be a peaceful place, and that things have changed. What did you mean by that?"

"The obvious," Tom answered. He felt relieved that he was being asked about something he cared about and not a crime. "The park used to be a family kind of place. Parents brought their kids there to play on the swings and in the sandbox, that kind of thing. It's a really large park and years ago we started a neighbourhood group and organized sports for the youngsters. So we had baseball teams and soccer teams, that kind of stuff. Our teams played teams from other parts of the city."

"I see," Gilles said. "So what changed?"

"Four or five years ago a different element moved in." Tom spoke with passion. It was clear that he had a very low opinion of the people he referred to as "a different element." "Mostly young guys," Tom continued, "with nothing but time on their hands. They turned the park into a drug market."

"Were they violent?" Gilles asked.

"I have no idea," Tom replied. "My kids are grown and they moved out of the neighbourhood. I used to bring my grandkids there when they visited but I stopped when the dealers moved in."

"Do you know if there are people in the neighbourhood who are angry at what occurred, occurs, in the park and want to do something about it?"

"Angry," Tom said pensively, "yeah, I would say that most of the people who've lived here for a long time are pretty angry. But what can you do? Nothing, that's what! We've asked the police to do something but that never happened. We asked our city councillor to do something but he said it was a police matter. So we went in circles for a while then just gave up on the park. No more sports for the kids. The only people who use the soccer pitch or the baseball diamond are adults who play pickup games after work."

"So no one was proposing some kind of citizen action?" Gilles asked. He noticed a middle-aged Indian couple with worried looks on their faces approach the information window and he assumed they were the parents of the stabbing victim. Gilles wanted to talk to them.

Gilles was on his feet when Tom answered the question after a brief pause. For some reason the question seemed to upset him. "No, nothing like that." Tom, too, got to his feet and said, "I've got to get back to work now," and walked away.

Gilles caught up with the Indian couple as they were waiting for the elevator that would take them to the ward where their son was being treated.

"Mr. and Mrs. Deshpande?" Gilles asked.

Mrs. Deshpande, a short woman dressed in a sari, her greying hair in a neat bun, nodded and her taller husband said, "Yes we are. Are you a doctor? We're here to see our son." He pushed his glasses up to the bridge of his nose.

Gilles showed the Deshpandes his ID and explained, "I'm with the police. I'm investigating the stabbing of your son."

"It's awful," Mrs. Deshpande said. "Our son leaves for work and is attacked. Who would do such a thing to a nice boy?"

Mr. Deshpande took his wife's right hand in both of his and patted it. "Do you know what happened?" he asked Gilles.

By this time the elevator arrived and the threesome stepped onto it. Gilles pressed the button for the surgical floor. "At the moment I don't have much information. I want to talk to your son. But it appears that he was stabbed helping another guy who was likely the intended victim. Can you think of anyone who would want to harm your son?"

Mrs. Deshpande was quick to answer. There was a flash of anger in her tone of voice. "Absolutely not. Hari is a wonderful person. A help. You just said that he was trying to prevent an attack."

"I had to ask," Gilles said, somewhat embarrassed. But he knew that he would have to ask Hari the same question for the record. Gilles wanted to hear Hari's story, but he was pretty certain that events had occurred as Denny described them.

They got off the elevator and Gilles asked the Deshpandes if they knew where their son was. Mr. Deshpande showed

Gilles a slip of paper with the number of one of the ICU wards on it.

"It's this way," Gilles said, ushering the Deshpandes down the hall. Hari smiled at his parents and they rushed to him, his mother in tears.

"Oh, dear, oh, dear," she exclaimed. "Are you hurt?"

"No, Maan. I'm fine. Just a surface wound."

Mrs. Deshpande hugged her son and he returned the hug. Mr. Deshpande took Hari's hand and squeezed it with fatherly affection.

Gilles felt like an intruder and was touched by the strong feelings the three Deshpandes had for one another. He wanted to ask the few questions he had for Hari and then leave the family in peace. "Do you feel up to answering a few questions?" Gilles asked.

"Why should he have to answer any questions?" Mrs. Deshpande said. "He's done nothing wrong."

"Of course not," Gilles said. "I just want to hear from your son what happened."

"Now, Mira," Mr. Deshpande said softly. Like his wife, he spoke with an accent of the subcontinent. "I'm sure the officer is just doing his job. We should be thankful that he wants to help." He put a comforting hand on his wife's arm.

"No problem," Hari put in. "I'll have no trouble answering your questions." His parents took this comment as their cue to step a couple of paces away from his bed to allow him to make eye contact with Gilles.

"Please tell me what happened."

Hari told Gilles essentially the same story that Denny had earlier told him. Hari remembered Denny from high school and from the various times he had seen him in the park and was about to greet him, but had no intention of stopping for a chat. He and Denny were not friends; they were barely acquaintances. "I caught some movement from behind Denny from the corner of my eye and I turned to get a better look at what it was. At first I just thought it was some guy running up to talk to Denny. Then I saw the knife and I pushed Denny out of the way of the attack."

"Quick thinking on your part."

"I don't know if you would call it thinking. I just reacted," Hari explained.

"How was the assailant holding the knife?" Gilles asked.

Hari closed his eyes to replay the scene in his mind. Speaking slowly, he said, "Underhanded, in his fist, and he was swinging the knife up when I shoved Denny."

"Thank you. I just have one more question and I'll leave you and your parents alone. Did you recognize the guy with the knife? Another high school friend, for example?"

"No," Hari replied, "I didn't recognize him. I couldn't. He was wearing a hoodie and wraparound sunglasses, the kind that reflect. And everything happened so fast. Sorry."

"You've been very helpful," Gilles said. "I doubt that I'll be bothering you again. Although you may be called as a witness when we catch the guy."

"And you think you'll catch him?" Mr. Deshpande asked, apparently unconvinced that such an event would come to pass. "Is my son in danger?"

"I don't think so," Gilles said. "I can't promise anything, of course, but I am determined. We can't have people being stabbed in parks in broad daylight, can we?" Gilles smiled in what he hoped was a reassuring fashion. He handed Hari one of his cards and said, "If you think of anything else please call me."

CHAPTER THIRTEEN

"I'm following Dr. Kavanaugh."

Annie returned to her assignment in the Resuscitation Unit. The patients there were usually elderly and suffering from a large number of ailments, any one of which could end their lives. But medical science had found a way of keeping these poor souls alive with the use of medications and machinery and a great deal of attention from the nursing staff at the Gursky Memorial Hospital. It was Annie's least favourite service.

She was pleased that Resus was quieter than usual. It gave her a chance to talk to the doctors who were with her at the nurse's station. There were two doctors working in the unit with her and she asked both of them if they knew if there was a doctor at the hospital with a wife by the name of Claire.

Dr. Goodfriend, the first person she asked, couldn't think of anyone offhand. He was young and new to the hospital and it didn't surprise Annie that he didn't know all of the other doctors that worked there.

Dr. Sternberg, the second person she asked, was much more helpful. He was one of the senior staff members, likely to be the next person to be named head of the emergency department.

"The only Claire I can think of is married to the chief of medicine, Eric Kavanaugh. Why do you want to know?"

"I met her in the café. We chatted for a couple of minutes and she said she was married to a doctor. I was curious, that's all."

"She used to work here," Dr. Sternberg went on. "In one of the labs. She was beautiful then and still is. Fragile, though. Anyway, just about every single guy, including a number of married ones, hit on her. Somehow, Eric ended up with her. Never understood it. It broke up his first marriage—he's older than she is. Still, she must have seen something that we didn't . . . don't."

"Maybe she was attracted to a successful doctor," Annie said. "It wouldn't be the first time." Annie was not unaware of the various affairs and relationships that started, and sometimes ended, at the Gursky.

"Yeah, you're probably right," Dr. Sternberg agreed. "But Eric is kind of full of himself and more than a little arrogant, even by the generous standards of our profession." Dr. Sternberg chuckled.

A heart monitor beeped and Dr. Sternberg and Annie rushed to the patient's bedside. The last time Annie had seen Dr. Kavanaugh was at the official hospital holiday party. The event was held every year in the food court and Dr. Kavanaugh always made a short, insincere speech about the high esteem in which he held all those in attendance. Each of the departments in the hospital also held their own holiday party, which was a lot more fun owing to the large amount of drinking and dancing.

At the end of her shift Annie changed out of her scrubs into regular clothes. She and some of the other staff were having a girls' night out. She walked through the hospital to the main building and down the hall where Dr. Kavanaugh had his office in the hope that Claire might be meeting him again.

The door to the outer office was open and she slowed her pace so she could look in. The secretary's desk was unoccupied and clear of any files, holding only a couple of framed family photos, a computer keyboard, mouse and monitor, and a cupful of pens and pencils. She heard the door to an inner office open and close just as she passed. She half-turned and saw Dr. Kavanaugh, dressed in a blue suit and the red tie that alpha types thought denoted power, walking through the secretary's office, closing the outer door behind him. He walked toward the main entrance, away from Annie. Without thinking, she took a couple of additional paces which brought her to an alcove that held a bank of elevators. A large number of people were getting off one of the elevators just as Annie got there, and she joined the crowd heading towards the main entrance.

She got to the lobby just in time to see Dr. Kavanaugh walking along the sidewalk that bordered the crescent drive of the front doors. He turned west on Côte-Sainte-Catherine Road. Annie quickened her pace, left the building and followed him. When he got to the corner he crossed to the south side of the street and continued walking west. Annie remained on the north side of the street and followed the doctor. Annie had never tailed anyone before and was a little surprised by her own behaviour. But she felt compelled by curiosity to see where the doctor was headed. Home, she assumed.

Annie pulled out her cellphone and called Gilles. "Hi," she said when he answered, "listen, I'm following Dr. Kavanaugh and I need some pointers on how to tail someone without being seen."

"Are you serious?" Gilles asked. "Why? And who is Dr. Kavanaugh?"

"He's the chief of medicine and he's Claire's husband," Annie explained. "I don't really know why I'm following him.

I thought it would be a good idea to walk by his office in case I had the chance to run into Claire again. She wasn't there but he left the hospital just as I spotted him so I decided to follow him. A foolish notion, but I'm doing it anyway. What should I be doing to avoid being spotted?"

"Well, you can stop playing detective and go home, for one thing," Gilles said.

"Not happening."

"Okay, then. Where are you in relation to the doctor?"

"We're walking west along Côte-Sainte-Catherine. He's across the street on the south side," Annie explained.

Gilles let out a brief laugh and said, "You've figured out the best way to tail someone. Stay out of sight. If there are a lot of people on your side of the street, try and stay in the crowd. That will provide you with cover. If you get to a deserted street the only thing you can do is stay as far back as possible. If he makes you, then turn away, give up. Got it?"

"Yeah, thanks. I'm guessing that he's heading home but we'll see."

"Call me when you're done. And for god's sake be careful," Gilles told her.

"Will do."

She followed Dr. Kavanaugh as he made his way along the street until it ended at Decarie Boulevard. He crossed Decarie and headed south for a while before turning west again. So far he was walking along busy streets and thus it was easy for Annie to follow him without being spotted. When he got to Dufferin Street in Hampstead, things became a little more risky. Dr. Kavanaugh didn't know Annie, but he might have noticed that a woman was following him. The street was deserted except for Dr. Kavanaugh. Annie hung back and peered around the corner to see where her prey was headed. Just before he got to the corner of Ellerdale he turned onto the walkway to a two-story red-brick house. Annie waited until he entered and then strode down the street to check out Dr. Kavanaugh's home. She wanted to pause in front of it and snap a photograph with her cellphone but feared that she would be noticed, so she walked past the house and turned east on Ellerdale.

She was able to get a good look at it. The black door was in the centre of the building, with windows on either side. In the few minutes that Annie had to observe the house she formed the opinion that its design was pleasingly symmetrical. Now she knew where Claire lived.

Annie returned to the Gursky to meet her friends for their night out.

Following his interview with the Deshpandes, Gilles left the hospital and headed back to the office of the Major Crimes Squad. He was driving east when Annie called to tell him that she was tailing Dr. Kavanaugh.

As Gilles walked through the shopping centre to the elevators that would take him up to the squad he realized that he was hungry. He stopped at one of the fast food outlets and bought a pad thai, which he ate in the food court while he thought about the case. Two murders by stabbing and one attempt. He realized he had, so far, collected a lot of information, but very little real evidence that pointed in the direction of any possible suspects. He had spent most of his investigative effort looking for a motive connected to the drug business in the neighbourhood and had so far come up empty; now, following his conversation with Tom Andreadis, he decided to look on the web to see if there were any posts from so-called "concerned citizens." He hoped that a search for irate residents of the neighbourhood would be more fruitful.

Gilles also realized that his boss would more than likely expect a full report. He decided that it would do no harm to curry favour with his colleagues, and to that end he stopped at the Second Cup in the shopping centre and purchased a cardboard urn of coffee to replace the sludge that the coffee maker in the squad room produced and a dozen muffins to bring up to the squad room.

Gilles placed the box of muffins on the counter, poured himself a coffee, and went to his desk as the others in the office made a beeline for the coffee and muffins.

Gilles logged onto his computer and was about to begin searching the web for posts regarding the events in Kennedy Park when his intercom buzzed.

"Quoi de neuf, Bellechasse? Je veux un rapport."

Gilles looked up and saw that Captain Lacroix was motioning him over to the commander's office. As he strode across the squad room he got his notebook out of his pocket.

Captain Lacroix's office was little more than functional. There were photographs of his wife and children on his desk and a couple of photos on the wall of the captain shaking the hand of one or another of the mayors of Montreal. There was enough room for Gilles to sit in the visitors' chairs in front of the file cabinets, but not much more than that.

"Tell me you've made some progress, Bellechasse."

"I've interviewed the families of the victims and one of their friends and have so far determined that we are not looking at a gang war, a fight over territory."

"Thank heaven for small miracles."

"Yeah. There are two more avenues I plan to follow up on," Gilles continued. "The first is the possibility that there is some kind of vigilante action taking place in the neighbourhood. I've interviewed someone who lives in the area and there was something in the way he responded to my questions that made me suspicious." Gilles was exaggerating, but he was not being untruthful. He could not take the risk of appearing to be at a dead end.

"What's the second avenue?" The captain did not seem all that convinced by the possibility that some sort of neighbourhood group was murdering drug dealers.

"We found drawings of a woman in Mikel Esperanza's bedroom. He was the first victim. I was able to determine that the woman's name is Claire and that she has an association with the hospital." Gilles felt a pang of guilt at not giving Annie credit for finding The Mysterious Claire but he did not want to have to explain to the Captain that his girlfriend was helping him. "I want to question her as soon as I can. She's married to one of the bigwigs at the hospital."

Gilles paused for a minute and added, "I'll also try to find out something about the murder weapon and also the button that the second vic managed to pull off the perp's blazer."

Captain Lacroix leaned forward and placed his elbows on his desk. He continued to stare at Gilles. "Forty-eight hours, Bellechasse. That's the amount of time you have to produce something concrete before I assign the case to someone else—someone more senior. Get it?"

Gilles got to his feet. "Yes sir," he said, with more conviction than he felt.

"Now get back to work," the captain said. "Oh yeah, one more thing, Bellechasse." Gilles turned to face his boss. "Thanks for the coffee and muffins."

"You're welcome, sir." Gilles said. He returned to his desk. Captain Lacroix headed to the table that held the food.

Gilles got to work searching for evidence that someone in the neighbourhood of Kennedy Park had threatened action against the drug dealers in the park.

Gilles typed Kennedy Park into the Google search engine and got thousands of hits before he could add the word Montreal. This narrowed down his choices considerably but as he scrolled through the list he did not come on any web addresses that looked helpful to his investigation. After about twenty minutes Gilles got to his feet, stretched and massaged his neck. He finally found a site, Patrol Our Parks, or POP, that looked like it that might produce results. The splash page had an animation of the letters P, O, and P in bright yellow exploding out of a jagged red circle on a field of blue, very much like the POW drawings that appeared in old comics when the superhero punched a villain.

Gilles scrolled through the site and discovered that there was a bulletin board that was open to the public and a messaging section that was open only to members of POP. The postings on the bulletin board tended toward the angry; what they lacked in correct grammar and spelling they made up in vitriol. The main theme of the messages was that the drug dealers had taken over Kennedy Park and that someone or a group of someones had to do something about it. Gilles rocked back in his chair with a satisfied smile. This was exactly the thing he had hoped he would find. The posts on the bulletin board were all signed with pseudonyms such as Cote Des Noways, a clumsy pun on the name of the neighbourhood, and the word ACTION, all in caps, the T in the form of a knife dripping blood. Gilles made a note of the URL in his notebook and determined to ask the computer crimes division to see if they could pull information from the site.

He decided to try to join the group using a made-up name and address. He read through the criteria for membership. It was restricted to those who lived in the neighbourhood of the park, and a map was provided to indicate exactly what the system administrator believed the neighbourhood to be.

Using Google Maps, Gilles had no trouble coming up with an address in the area, and he started to fill in the questionnaire using the phony street address and a new Gmail address he created for the purpose. When he got to the bottom of the form he had to indicate which active member was sponsoring his application. This presented an obvious problem. He could not make up the name of a sponsor. Gilles took a chance and typed in Tom Andreadis's name. Gilles was prompted for Tom's email address, which he did not have. After a couple of minutes another message popped onto the screen informing Gilles that he could not be granted membership until his sponsor confirmed his sponsorship. Gilles could not be certain that Tom was an actual member of the group and he could progress no further.

He left the membership page and returned to the splash page to consider his next steps. He decided that the logical next step was to call the Computer Crimes Division and ask them to look at the website to see if they could find a way of hacking into it to get information on the membership of the group.

Gilles called the Computer Crimes Division and was put on hold while the person who answered the phone went in search of an investigator. After a short wait a woman came on the line and identified herself as Constable Chantal Rigaud. She asked Gilles a few questions to ensure that he was who he said he was and asked how she could help.

Gilles explained his investigative problem with the POP website and gave Constable Rigaud the site's URL. She agreed to try to find a way to hack into the site and get back to him in a day or so.

He next called his contact at Identité judicaire to see if they'd been able to get any prints from the knife used to stab Ron Jardine. "Rien d'utilisable," he was told. "There were some blood smears on the blade where the vic grabbed it but nothing on the handle. Your perp was wearing gloves or had it wrapped in a cloth of some sort. Nothing on the button either."

"Was there anything distinctive about the weapon? Some kind of marking that can identify where it came from?" Gilles asked, knowing it was a faint hope at best.

"Rien," came the response. "The thing is available from any number of stores including Amazon for eighteen bucks. Unless you find the store or have access to Amazon's invoices it's impossible to trace."

Gilles sighed, thanked his contact, slammed down the telephone and muttered, "Fuck, fuck, fuck."

A couple of minutes after he got off the phone, Annie called him back with the news she had identified Dr. Kavanaugh's address, which meant that he would be able to pay Claire a visit and, he hoped, learn more about the first murder victim. Gilles held the phone against his ear with his shoulder and confirmed the doctor's address at Canada411 while he talked to Annie.

Annie made the point that it would be best to find a way to get to Claire without tipping off her husband as it was possible that he did not know about the nude drawings, and she would probably be more forthcoming owing to the nature of the drawings if her husband was not involved.

"Have a nice evening, chérie."

"Always fun to get out with the girls and blow off some steam." Annie sent Gilles a kiss and hung up.

Gilles strode into Captain Lacroix's office and reported on his progress.

"Bon travail," Captain Lacroix said. "What's your next step?"

"I'm going to think of a way to get to Claire Kavanaugh without her husband finding out. I suspect that whatever the reason for the drawings, she would not want to talk about them or Esperanza with him present."

"You're probably right," Lacroix agreed. "But be careful not to give the impression that you're harassing the woman."

"No, for the moment, my approach will be that I want to protect her privacy. I have no reason to embarrass her in front of the husband."

On his way home, Gilles took a forty-five minute detour. He drove west to Hampstead to check out the Kavanaugh house.

CHAPTER FOURTEEN

"Talk to me? About What? I hardly know you."

Gilles's last thought before falling asleep, and his first thought upon waking the next morning, were how to best approach The Mysterious Claire. The obvious way was to show up at her house, identify himself, and interview her. He was concerned, though, that the direct approach might not yield the results he wanted. It was tough enough getting a straight story out of witnesses and suspects; at this point in the investigation Claire was neither. Moreover, Gilles was certain that whatever Claire's relationship with Mikel was, it was clandestine, thus making it even less likely that she would want to talk about it. Gilles hoped that she would give him some background information about Mikel that he had not been able to get from anyone else, and so he believed a softer approach would be better. Ideally, Gilles thought, he would like to be eavesdropping on a conversation between Claire and a close female friend of hers.

The solution to his problem was to get Annie to make the first approach to Claire and convince her that talking to Gilles would not be a cause for worry. There were obvious ethical problems with this approach and it put Annie in a difficult position. It wouldn't hurt for them to get together and see if there was a way for Annie to approach The Mysterious

Claire. And so after a quick shower, at about eight-thirty, he called Annie.

"I didn't wake you, did I, chérie?" he asked when Annie answered after the fifth ring.

"No, not really," she answered sleepily. "I'm off today so I was kind of lazing about. Not sleeping though."

"I need your help, chérie," he explained. "Can I buy you breakfast?"

"Charmer," Annie replied. Gilles could sense the smile that went with her answer. "You know the best way to get me to do something is to bribe me with food. Especially breakfast."

"How about if I pick you up in half an hour, forty-five minutes?"

"Works for me," Annie answered.

An hour later Gilles and Annie were seated in a window table at L'Avenue on Notre-Dame Street West. Over omelets and coffee, Gilles explained his dilemma to Annie.

"I get it," Annie said. "But I'm a little unclear as to exactly how I'm to get her to have a coffee with me. It's one thing to run into her in a café, quite another to get her to have one with me."

"I thought of that," Gilles said. He fell silent while the waitress refilled their coffee cups and continued, "Here's my plan. You drive over to Claire's house and ask her to join you for coffee. In all likelihood she won't agree, she hardly knows you. But if you tell her that you want to talk to her about Mikel Esperanza, she'll agree."

"Yeah, I can see that. I'm more than happy to try to talk to her and even to see if she'll agree to talk to you but," Annie covered Gilles's hand with hers and lowered her voice and continued, "I can't be in the position of pushing her to meet with you. Acting as bait, I guess you could say. If she doesn't want to talk to me or to you, for that matter, you'll have to try the direct approach."

"Absolument," Gilles agreed. I'll find a café where I can wait. If she doesn't want to meet me, tant pis pour moi."

"And you'll be waiting for us at a café?" Annie asked.

"Yeah, right," Gilles agreed, proving the wisdom of getting Annie involved in his scheme.

"Of course, the whole plan falls apart if she's not at home or if she flatly refuses to have anything to do with me," Annie pointed out.

"Let's hope it doesn't come to that," Gilles said.

"Just so you know, even though I don't know her, I'm going to approach her as a friend. If she doesn't want to talk to me then that's it."

The couple talked about other things as they finished their breakfasts. Gilles paid the bill, and on the drive back to Annie's flat to pick up her car, they agreed that Gilles would wait for Annie and Claire at the Starbucks on Queen Mary as it was close to where Claire lived. If Annie could not convince Claire to accompany her, she would call Gilles and he would drive to Claire's house and approach her directly—the Plan B Gilles hoped he would not have to put into action.

Thirty or so minutes later, Gilles was ensconced in a booth at the Starbucks on Queen Mary near the corner of Earnscliffe. At about the same time, Annie parked a couple of doors away from Claire's house. She rang the doorbell. "Yes?" Claire asked when she answered the door. She gave Annie a blank stare. Obviously she didn't recognize Annie from when they met at the café in the hospital.

"Claire, hi," Annie improvised. "Do you remember me? We met at the hospital. I hope I'm not disturbing you."

Claire stared at Annie trying to place her.

"I shared your table at the Second Cup," Annie said and added, "At the hospital," when Claire showed no sign of recalling the meeting.

"Oh, right," Claire said but made no move to invite Annie in or to continue the conversation.

"If you don't mind, I'd like to talk to you for a minute," Annie said.

"Talk to me? What about? I hardly know you."

"Mikel Esperanza," Annie said. This had the desired effect. Claire froze and her mouth fell slightly open. In the moment it took Claire to regain her composure, Annie saw a look of sadness cross her face.

"I see," Claire said coldly. "What about him?"

"Is there some where we can talk? Would you like to go out for a coffee?"

Claire was silent. Annie could see that she was enduring an internal conflict of sorts. Part of her wanted to shut the door and another part of her wanted to know why this virtual stranger wanted to talk to her about Mik?

"I know this comes as a shock to you," Annie said. "A stranger comes to your door and wants to talk to you about . . . well . . . about your private life. You can shut the door and I'll leave. But if you talk to me for a couple of minutes you can still ask me to leave and I'll do so. Promise. May I come in?"

"I suppose," Claire said and stood aside to let Annie into her house. Claire led the way to the kitchen and indicated that Annie should sit at the small round table where she was having a coffee and reading the newspaper. "Would you like a coffee? She offered.

Annie held the cup of coffee with both hands and said, "Again, I'm sorry for intruding. I know that you knew Mik Esperanza."

"How? How on earth would you know such a thing?"

"I'll explain. My boyfriend's the cop investigating the murder in Kennedy Park. He thought it would be best to talk to you off the record. More discreet. Better than showing up on your doorstep and flashing his badge."

"I'm a suspect?" Claire asked, fear in her voice. "That's nuts."

"No, of course not. That's why Gilles, my boyfriend, wants to talk to you off the record. He doesn't want to embarrass you. That's why he asked me to approach you."

"How did you know I knew Mik? And, while we're on the subject, how did you know where I lived?"

"The cops found some drawings Mik had done of you and Gilles showed them to me and then I spotted you in the café," Annie said.

Claire had her elbows on the table and she put her head in her hands. "Oh, dear God, the drawings. How many . . . are there . . .?" Claire couldn't continue and was on the verge of tears.

Annie reached across the table and placed a comforting hand on Claire's wrist. "I understand," she said. "We don't want to embarrass you. A couple of cops have seen them, that's all."

Claire dropped her hands and looked straight at Annie, hurt and vulnerability showing in her eyes. "That's all? Isn't that bad enough?"

Annie hadn't removed her hand from Claire's wrist when she lowered her arms so the two women were holding hands. Annie gave Claire's hand a comforting squeeze. "It must be awful for you. I understand. Really, I do. We've all done things that maybe weren't such a good idea. Don't you think it would be a good idea to meet Gilles now, informally, instead of . . . well you know . . ." Annie let the alternative hang. She was sure that Claire had no desire to have a cop appear on her doorstep and have to explain to her husband.

Claire sighed. She looked Annie straight in the eyes trying to decide whether or not to trust this stranger who appeared at her door. Claire saw sympathy in Annie's blue eyes. "I suppose you're right." She got to her feet. "Let me get my jacket."

"I'll call Gilles and tell him we're on our way," Annie said.

CHAPTER FIFTEEN

"Bringing witnesses to my boyfriend works up an appetite."

Annie and Claire walked into the Starbucks and Gilles rose to greet them with a welcoming smile. The two women sat down and Gilles went to the counter to get the drinks they wanted, a cappuccino for Annie and a tea for Claire.

There was a long moment of awkward silence as Gilles and his two companions sipped at their beverages. Gilles cleared his throat, looked at Claire, and said, "I'm sorry for the unconventional way in which I arranged to meet you. I didn't want to surprise or embarrass you by showing up on your doorstep and flashing my badge."

"Well, I can't say that I wasn't surprised, but I suppose I appreciate the effort," Claire responded. "How did you find me, anyway?"

Gilles looked briefly at Annie and smiled. "I have to say that it was Annie who figured out who you were. We found the drawings of you that Mikel made and Annie recognized you, first in the Java U near the hospital and then in the hospital coffee shop."

Claire blushed, thinking about the nude drawings that the police had found, and said, "Annie explained all that but how were you able to work out where I lived?"

"Well, no," Annie place a comforting hand on Claire's forearm, "I have to admit to following your husband home the other day, when I saw him leave the hospital."

Claire stared unhappily at Annie and Gilles but said nothing. Gilles brought the conversation back to the subject at hand—his investigation into the murder of Mikel Esperanza and Ron Jardine. "How did you know Mikel?" he asked.

Claire took a deep breath. "I suppose I should have known that it was only a matter of time until the police found me." She sighed. "Mikel and I met at an art class." Claire paused and looked at Gilles and then Annie.

"At art class," Gilles repeated. "Where was it?"

"My friend Marjorie, Marjorie Reynolds, gives art classes at her studio and Mik happened to enroll in the same class I was taking." Neither Gilles nor Annie said anything and after a moment of silence, Claire continued, smiling at her recollection of her first meeting with Mik. "He was shy and unsure of himself, not his talent, but being in a room full of strangers. Marjorie put him next to me. I don't know if it was by chance or intention." Claire sipped at her tea. "Anyway we got to talking and, I'm not sure exactly how it happened, I think I offered him a lift somewhere and, well, one thing led to another. A lift turned into coffee which turned into spending time together. You know how these things are."

Annie put a hand on Claire's forearm indicating that she understood. Gilles nodded, a neutral expression on his face. "He was so sweet. If I mentioned that a certain brand of charcoal was better than some other kind he would appear with it at our next class. That kind of thing." Claire fingered the small silver covered onyx cone on a delicate silver necklace she was wearing. "We would visit museums together and if he saw something he thought I would like he bought it for me. He was both considerate and impulsive. A lovely soul." Claire paused for a moment to let the emotion of the memory pass. "I know it was wrong of me. Married and all. But . . . well . . ."

"I understand, of course I do," Annie said.

Speaking softly Gilles asked, "Did anyone know of your . . . your," he searched for a neutral word, ". . . time together?"

"No, just Marjorie. And she didn't say anything to anyone, if that's what you're asking."

"Yes, exactly. No one else knew, not your husband, nobody?"

"No," Claire said. "He would have had a cow, he would have lost it."

"And he didn't, as you said, lose it?"

"No. You have to understand, my husband is a doctor and as such likes to be in control."

"No question. That's the way they are," Annie agreed.

Gilles took a sip of his coffee, which was now cold. "In the time that you and he . . . was there ever an event, no matter how minor it seemed at the time that would indicate that there was anyone who meant Mikel harm?"

"No, nothing," Claire said. "That's what's so upsetting about this whole thing. I told you, Mikel was a really nice person. I can't imagine why anyone would want to hurt him."

"Were you aware of the way in which he earned money?" Gilles asked.

"Not in any detail. I knew that he had no, how would you say it . . . visible source of money. So I knew he was up to something. But I purposely didn't talk about that side of his life."

"I'm sorry, but I have to ask again, to be clear," Gilles said, "what about your husband? Was he aware that you were"—Gilles paused again—"seeing someone?"

Claire thought for a couple of minutes before she replied. "First of all, my husband is a doctor, not a murderer. But in any event, as I said, he didn't give any indication that he knew a thing about Mikel. He was busy with the hospital, attending conferences, running to Quebec City to deal with the health minister, and so on. During the time I was with Mik, my husband barely knew I was alive."

Annie, who had been very quiet during Gilles's questions, nodded.

Gilles offered to get refills for Annie and Claire and both women declined. "Are we done here?" Claire asked.

"Yes, we are," Gilles told her. "I appreciate your talking to me and I hope you understand that I did my best to conduct this interview as a conversation, not an interrogation."

"Yes, I appreciate that."

"But," Gilles continued, "There will likely come a time in my investigation when I'll need more information from you. How would you like me to get in touch with you?"

"Call my cell." She gave Gilles her cellphone number, which he wrote into his notebook. Annie noted it in her cellphone.

"One more thing," Gilles said to Claire. "Take my phone number in case you think of something." He handed Claire his card and added, "My cellphone number is probably the best way to reach me."

Claire fiddled with the card for a moment; instead of putting it in her pocket she tapped Gilles's number into her phone and left the business card on the table.

Claire got up and Annie asked her, "Would you like a drive home?"

"No thanks, I'd rather walk."

Gilles went to the counter to get fresh coffees for Annie and himself. When he returned to the table, he asked Annie what she thought of Claire's story.

"I believe her, if that's what you mean," Annie replied. "She never was a suspect, was she?"

"Not a suspect, no," Gilles said. "More a person of interest, because all aspects of a victim's life have to be investigated."

"I also thought you were very nice to her," Annie said with a smile. "I can't believe that you're usually that circumspect when questioning a witness."

Gilles returned the smile. "You're right. As I told her, I considered this a conversation, not an interrogation. It was more or less off the record, given that it took place in a coffee shop and you were present. Not to mention the unconventional way in which we made the whole thing happen."

"That's sort of what I figured," Annie said. "Now it's getting on to time for lunch and I expect a nice one. Bringing witnesses to my boyfriend works up an appetite." Annie's smile could have easily illuminated the darkest cave.

CHAPTER SIXTEEN

"Should I bring a lawyer?"

After lunch, Gilles drove Annie back to where she had left her car and had to refuse her invitation to spend the rest of her day off together. He wanted to get back to the office and report to his boss that he had another lead to follow up: the possibility that Mikel's murder had something to do with his affair with Claire. Gilles knew that this left the question of the second murder and the attempted murder unexplained, but it had to be considered.

He also hoped that the tech division would have some news from the Patrol Our Parks website.

He found a spot in the parking lot of the shopping centre and, again, stopped to buy coffee and muffins for his colleagues.

He barely had time to put them on the lunchroom table before Captain Lacroix appeared at his office door, called Gilles's name, and waved him into his office.

"Qu'est-ce que tu as, Bellechasse?" The captain sat down behind his messy desk and motioned for Gilles to take one of the visitors' chairs.

"The woman in the drawings. I found her," Gilles reported. He thought it best to leave out Annie's role in the investigation. "I was able to arrange to meet her for an off-the-record interview."

"Off the record?" Captain Lacroix asked incredulously. "Since when do we conduct murder investigations 'off the record'?"

"Je sais. But she's a married woman and she wouldn't talk to me at all unless it was unofficial. If anything comes from her information I'll be able to have another go at her—this time on the record."

"I hope you have more than that. An affair won't explain the other two crimes, will it?"

"Yes, sir," Gilles replied. "I haven't ruled out some sort of vigilante action. There is a great deal of hostility in the neighbourhood against the police for not having a strong enough presence, for allowing drug dealers to make the park their shopping centre, so to speak."

"Maybe it would be better if their kids didn't buy the drugs." Captain Lacroix shuffled through some papers and picked up his phone, indicating that the meeting was at an end.

Gilles went to the lunchroom to get a cup of coffee and then to his desk. He said a silent prayer and called Constable Rigaud at the tech centre.

"J'ai des nouvelles pour toi, Gilles," she said. "Check your email."

"Merci, Chantal. I was busy this morning. I should have checked. Stay on the line in case I have any questions." He found Chantal Rigaud's email and was pleased with what she had unearthed. She had figured out the commands to get into the Patrol Our Parks website so he could see who was posting. "This will give you admin status," she wrote, "so be careful not to change anything. Look but don't touch."

"Got it," Gilles said. "But what happens if another administrator is logged in?"

"Nothing, so long as you don't do anything but navigate around the site and read whatever it is that you find."

"Okay, that's great. Thanks."

Gilles pulled his keyboard closer to him, opened Google and copied the character string that Constable Rigaud had provided him. A lot of code rolled down and then disappeared, leaving his screen blank. Gilles wasn't sure what to do so he shrugged and hit the Enter key. To his delight he was at the Patrol Our Parks landing page. Using his mouse he navigated to the comments section and read the postings, careful to keep his hands off the keyboard. The comments were uniformly angry, poorly written, and full of bravado, including threats to commit bodily harm against the drug dealers. Gilles discovered that by placing the cursor on the alias of the person who wrote the post, he could bring up their real name and email address. He guessed that this was the way the administrators of the site could ensure that only those who were part of the group could post.

Gilles scrolled down, reading posts and taking down the names of the people who made them. After scrolling through three pages of angry screeds he hit pay dirt. He found a post written by Tom Andreadis, who hadn't mentioned the Patrol Our Parks group when Gilles questioned him.

Gilles was concerned that if he tried to print them he would give himself away so he took screen shots of the more vitriolic comments. He found several additional postings that carried Andreadis's alias, Mr. T. Gilles guessed he took it from the old TV show, *The A Team*, which was hardly appropriate. He found taking successive screen shots to be a cumbersome process so he called Constable Rigaud and asked her if there was a way to print them without giving himself away. She congratulated him on having the good sense to call her before he did anything and promised to copy all the postings made by Mr. T. along with some examples of other threatening posts and send them to Gilles as PDF documents.

Anticipating his next question, she asked Gilles, "Do you need access to information on the members? Names and addresses and so on?"

"Yes, my next step is to track down as many members as I can so we can interview them," he told Constable Rigaud.

"I thought so," she agreed. "I'm going to send you a link to the membership page. You can copy the information but don't do anything else in the file."

Gilles exited the POP website and mentally reviewed the information he had gleaned. In addition to Tom Andreadis, Gilles had half a dozen names in his notebook and the emails Constable Rigaud was about to send him would add another ten or so, names of frequent authors of posts on the website. If, as Gilles suspected, the deaths were the result of vigilante action to clean the drug dealers out of the park, it would be necessary to locate and interview every person on the list, and possibly many more. This meant that Gilles would have to find a way to get Captain Lacroix to authorize more officers for the investigation.

He relaxed in his chair, closed his eyes, and pushed his lips in and out as he thought of the best way to approach the problem in order to get the result he wanted.

After a couple of minutes he sat up straight and rolled his chair closer to his desk. The link to the membership page had arrived and Gilles printed out the information and left the site. He looked over the printout and decided to check it against the Canada411 website. He had two reasons for doing this: to see if the information was current, and so he could say he got it from Canada411.

He opened Canada411 and started to search the names on the list. Three of the names were Greek and easily identified. English and French names presented more of a problem. Two of the names, Lefebvre and McKenzie, resulted in a large number of hits. Gilles narrowed his search to the streets around the Kennedy Park, and his perseverance paid off. He was able to identify most of the names on the list. Gilles assumed those that he could not confirm were false. He wondered why so many of those who had opened accounts on the POP website had provided truthful information about themselves. Didn't they understand how easy it was to access?

While he was in the process of searching the names on his list he received an email from Constable Rigaud with a batch of posts along with the names of those who had written them. Gilles again researched the names on Canada411 and got as many addresses and phone numbers as he could. He knew that there were errors on his list which had grown to twenty names. It would be up to the team interviewing the twenty people to determine which of them to eliminate from the investigation. By the same token, the interviews would likely add names to the list.

Gilles entered the information on a spreadsheet and organized it by street and postal code. He printed a couple of copies and walked over to Captain Lacroix's office. Gilles knocked on the glass of the door and entered without waiting for an invitation.

Captain Lacroix looked up and asked, "Qu'est-ce que tu as?"

Gilles placed a copy of the printout on the captain's desk. "I did some research and found a list of people who might have taken some action to clean the drug dealers out of the park."

"Really? How can you know this?"

"That's the point," Gilles responded. He explained that his list of names was compiled from those who had written posts to the POP website that could be construed as threats of bodily harm against the drug dealers. In order to determine which of them were possible suspects in the two murders it would be necessary to interview all of them to see who had an alibi for the times of the murders, who was in contact with whom and so on. "One of my prime suspects is a guy by the name of Tom Andreadis. He works at the hospital and I want to check his alibi. And even if he has one that doesn't mean that he wasn't an organizer of the criminal behaviour. The investigation will help to determine that."

Captain Lacroix was impressed.

"I need some help to interview all these people and any others we come up with. I think three or four uniformed cops can handle it. That would be four or five names for each of us, not counting Tom Andreadis. I want to leave him for last."

Captain Lacroix smiled. He had to admire Bellechasse's balls, appearing in his office and asking for four cops to be assigned to his case. "You don't ask for much, do you?" he said.

Gilles didn't respond, not wanting to say anything that would damage his request. "I'll give you two uniforms for a couple of days. I can't do more than that. But if you develop some promising leads . . . well, we'll see," said Captain Lacroix.

"Can we start tomorrow morning at the beginning of shift?" Gilles asked.

"Absolutely."

"See you at seven-thirty," Gilles said.

He looked at his watch and saw that it was five-thirty. He called Annie and asked, "Are you still on your day off?"

She laughed and said, "Subtle, aren't you? Yeah, I'm still not at work. Would you like to come over and have dinner with me and Pam?"

"I thought you'd never ask," Gilles said.

"Fair warning," Annie replied, "I'm on early tomorrow."

"So am I," Gilles informed her. "I have to be at the office by seven-thirty, latest."

"So, an early night."

"See you soon," Gilles said. "I'll pick up some wine on my way over."

◉

Gilles was the first person in the office the next morning, even beating Captain Lacroix. He took the time to prepare before his meeting with his boss and the cops who would be helping him with the canvass. He worked out what kind of open-ended questions would yield the maximum amount of information in the least amount of time. He knew that the risk to asking general questions as opposed to those that required a simple factual answer was that people tended to either ramble on or say nothing. His plan was to instruct the officers to let people talk to the point where they started to repeat themselves or to dissemble, and then to ask them about their whereabouts at the times of the stabbings.

He printed three more copies of the addresses of the members of POP, indicated which ones he would visit, and finally highlighted Tom Andreadis's name. He wanted to make special mention of him.

The uniformed cops showed up about ten minutes after Captain Lacroix, and Gilles was thrilled that his former partner, Constable Nicole Bélanger, was one of them. They kissed on both cheeks in greeting and Nicole introduced Gilles to her new partner, Constable Marc Parent.

The three of them went into Captain Lacroix's office and Gilles briefed the two. He ended by calling their attention to Tom Andreadis's name. "It's highlighted because I don't want you to go anywhere near him or his house." He explained how he knew Tom and that Tom had already lied to him about the nature of the group he had organized and its activities and he wasn't about to give him a second opportunity. Tom had claimed that the group was created to organize sports and other social activities. Once he had had the opportunity to review the information from the canvass, Gilles planned to have a formal conversation with Tom.

Marc Parent asked, "What do we do if one of the people we interview mentions his name?"

"Good point," Gilles replied. "Get as much information as you can as to the person's relationship with Tom, but don't introduce his name into the conversation. We want to see what people say about him without being prompted. And there's a strong possibility, a certainty really, that Tom will know about our interest in the group before I talk to him. For me, that's a good thing. Let him worry a bit.

"There's one more thing," Gilles said. He took his phone from his jacket pocket and brought up the photo of the brass button Ron Jardine had clutched in his hand. "This is a picture of a brass button that one of the victims, Ron Jardine, was holding. So far it and the knife are the only solid clues we have. It may have come from the murderer's blazer or sports jacket. At the end of your interviews, do it as kind of an afterthought, ask the person you are interviewing if they have a blazer or sports jacket and ask to see it. Don't mention the brass button you are looking for. No reason to tip them off."

"Oui, je comprends," Marc replied. "But what happens if the person says they have more than one?"

"Ask to see them all," Gilles instructed.

"And if they say that their jacket is at the cleaners?" Nicole put in.

"That would make me suspicious," Gilles said. "Get the information about the dry cleaner and get over there to look at the jacket before its owner has a chance to pick it up."

"Got it," Nicole and Marc said, almost in unison.

There were no additional questions so Gilles and the two uniformed cops set off on their mission. Gilles wished them luck and told them that he expected to see them back at the office at the end of their shift for a report, even if they hadn't questioned everyone on their list. They would decide at that point whether or not to continue with that aspect of the investigation.

◎

Gilles's first call at about nine-thirty was at a duplex on one of the more prosperous streets in the neighbourhood. He rang the doorbell of the ground-floor unit belonging to the McKenzie family. A woman about sixty years old opened the door. She was short and trim. Her salt-and-pepper hair, in need of a shampoo, hung to her shoulders. She looked at Gilles quizzically and said, "Yes, can I help you?" She kept the door ajar with her foot and her hand on the door handle. If Gilles turned out to be a salesman or a Jehovah's Witness the door would be unceremoniously shut.

Gilles identified himself and showed the woman his ID, consulted his list and said, "I'm looking for Albert McKenzie. Is he at home?"

"I'm his wife," the woman said. "What on earth do you want with my husband?"

"I'd like to tell him that myself," Gilles explained, placing his foot just inside the doorjamb. "Is he at home?"

"Yeah, I'll get him," Mrs. McKenzie said. She did not move from her sentry position at the door. She turned her head and called out, "Al, there's someone here to see you. He's a cop."

"Bullshit," came a male voice from within the house. "Probably a salesman. Tell him to go away."

Mrs. McKenzie sighed and gave Gilles a look that said, what could you possibly want from him? Aloud she said, "Al, for Christ's sake, he's a cop. Don't you think I know enough to check his ID?"

Neither Gilles nor Mrs. McKenzie said anything for a couple of minutes. Finally, Albert McKenzie appeared at the door. He was a little more than a head taller than his wife and bald, with a semicircle of wispy white hair. He hadn't shaved that morning and he was not fully dressed, wearing a sleeveless undershirt and a pair of grey slacks. His feet were stuffed into a pair of well-worn slippers. His wife stood aside when he came to the door. She did not relinquish her hold on the inside door handle, but she had to move her foot to allow her husband to open the door wider.

Gilles showed his ID to Albert McKenzie. "We're investigating some stabbings in the neighbourhood, two of which took place in Kennedy Park. I was wondering if you were aware of them?"

"Yeah, so what?" Albert McKenzie asked.

Gilles made a note on his sheet that contained the names of the POP members and asked, "Are you a member of the group Patrol Our Parks?"

"Yeah, so what?" Albert repeated. "That's not illegal, so what business is it of yours?"

Gilles placed a tick mark beside Albert's name and asked, "Can we talk inside?"

"No," Albert said.

"Yes, of course," Mrs. McKenzie said and pulled the door open. She turned and walked to the kitchen at the end of a long hallway. Gilles and Albert followed.

She invited Gilles to sit at the kitchen table. "Would you like a cup of coffee?"

"No thank you," Gilles replied, "but I'd appreciate a glass of water."

Mrs. McKenzie went to the fridge and poured Gilles a glass of water from a Brita pitcher. Albert sat down at the table and pulled a coffee mug to him. It was half-full.

Gilles took a sip of water and asked Albert, "What can you tell me about the Patrol Our Park group?"

Albert took a long sip of his coffee, practically draining the cup. He held it out in his wife's direction and she refilled it from a pot on the stove. Albert added his own milk and sugar and as he stirred his coffee he answered Gilles's question. "My . . . our kids grew up playing in that park. Now it's become a drug-dealing supermarket. Nobody does nothing to get rid of them. So Tom Andreadis got us together to form a group. Our plan is simple: patrol the park ourselves and make it safe for all those who want to use it, young or old. It used to be a place where I could meet my friends, old guys like myself. We could have a coffee and shoot the breeze."

"And how many of you patrol the park?" Gilles asked.

"We haven't started yet. Our group is new; we've only had a couple of meetings. We're still signing up members. But the group is growing and pretty soon we'll have enough members to send people into the park to clean it up."

"Two of the stabbings took place in the park, and in the other case the victim was one of the guys who hung out there?"

"Yeah." Albert stopped talking for a moment to shift his chair to make room for his wife, who joined him and Gilles at the table. "Tough luck, eh?"

"Albert," Mrs. McKenzie said, "we can't have people going around killing each other. Murder doesn't make the park a safe place."

"You don't know what you're talking about, Hildy," Albert pronounced. "These guys are in a dirty business and that's the way it goes for them."

"Hari could have been killed," Mrs. McKenzie said, turning to Gilles for support.

Gilles nodded and said, "Did you know Hari Deshpande?"

Albert was about to answer but his wife beat him to it. "We knew his parents, not Hari. He's younger than our children. His parents are very nice. Hard-working people."

"Exactly," Albert put in, "and he should be able to walk through the park without being accosted."

Hildy McKenzie shook her head slowly. "Albert," she said, and was about to add something else, but thought better of it. Instead she turned to Gilles and said, "My husband is very upset about some of the changes to the neighbourhood." She patted her husband's hand affectionately.

"I have one more question," Gilles said. "Would you consider that Tom Andreadis was the leader of your group?"

"Yeah, but, as I said, we weren't really organized yet. He was the one who started it and got us together and figured out how to use the interweb and things like that."

"I see," Gilles commented. "Where did you meet?"

"We only had about six meetings. And we rotated houses. The first meeting was at Tom's and then someone else's and so on," Albert explained.

"We even had a meeting here," Hildy McKenzie added.

"And all you discussed was patrolling the park?"

"Yeah, that and things we want to do to identify ourselves, arm bands or jackets or something. We also want to have walkie-talkies or something so we could communicate with each other if we saw anything," Albert explained.

"Did you have any meetings with the police from the local station?" Gilles asked.

"We wanted to, but they wouldn't send anyone."

Gilles took his notebook out of his inner jacket pocket and made a note to talk to the commander of the local station to get his perspective on the POP group.

Gilles got up from the table and said, "I think I have enough information for the moment, thank you. If I need

anything else, I or someone from the force will drop by again."
Gilles extended his had to Albert, who shook it without getting up from where he sat.

Before either of the McKenzies could say anything, Gilles
said, "I have one more question I'd like to ask." He looked at
Albert McKenzie. "Do you have a blazer or sports jacket in
your wardrobe?"

Albert looked up at Gilles and replied, "That's an odd
question, and none of your business really."

Hildy was on her feet and said, "Now, Albert, it's not a
secret. He has a blue blazer."

"Thank you," Gilles told her. "I'd like to see it, if you don't
mind."

Hildy turned and walked out of the kitchen to retrieve
her husband's jacket. While they waited, Gilles and Albert
did not exchange a word, sharing instead an uncomfortable
silence.

After a couple of minutes Hildy returned carrying a
double-breasted blue blazer that looked well-worn and had
black plastic buttons, not brass.

"Thank you," Gilles said. "Does your husband happen to
have any clothing with brass buttons?"

Albert snorted in response and Hildy said, "No, nothing
like that."

"Then I'm finished. I won't take up any more of your time.
I'll get back to you if I need more information."

"I'll show you out," Hildy McKenzie said, and walked
Gilles to the front door. Gilles thanked her for her hospitality
and left the McKenzie home.

Gilles made half a dozen additional visits that day and
met with a cross-section of the population of the area. He
met with elderly couples like the McKenzies, families with
grown children still living at home, like the Deshpandes, and

families with young children. Some of the people he interviewed were French speakers and others, like the McKenzies
spoke English. In some homes he was offered chai tea and
one couple suggested a Red Stripe beer, which Gilles would
have accepted had he not been on duty. All in all, the stories
they told were more or less the same: Tom Andreadis was
the organizer and driving force of the group. He called the
meetings and encouraged those who attended to bring their
friends and neighbours in order to have the largest number of
people possible from which to create patrols. All the people
Gilles spoke to, with the exception of the McKenzies, commented on how angry Tom was at the presence not only of
drug dealers but also anyone who looked like a dealer. He
held the view that able-bodied young men should be doing
honest work like him and his children.

All the men he questioned had a sports jacket or a blue
blazer and often both. None of them were missing brass
buttons.

Gilles planned his canvassing so that his last interview
would be close to the hospital. He wanted to arrange to have
Tom come by the police station the next day, and he wanted
to speak to him in person if at all possible.

Gilles walked into the ER and, as luck would have it, Tom
was the first person he saw. Before Gilles could say anything,
Tom spoke. "So, I hear you've been asking about me."

"You're right," Gilles replied. "That's why I'm here. I want
to talk to you about the POP group you've organized."

Tom did not look happy. "Well, I'm at work now, but
I have a break in an hour or so, if you want to wait."

"No, Tom, I don't want to wait. It would be better if you
came to my office tomorrow morning." Gilles took out one
of his cards, wrote the address on the back, and handed it to
Tom. "Can you be there by ten?"

Tom looked pensively at both sides of the card, as if there was some information inscribed there that would be helpful, before he answered. "Do I have a choice?"

"Not really," Gilles informed him. "I need to talk to you as part of a murder investigation."

"I see," Tom said playing with Gilles's card. He paused and asked, "Should I bring a lawyer?"

"Your choice, Tom. But you should know that you're neither a suspect nor a witness. Just someone with information that we would like to have," Gilles explained, "at this point." As an afterthought Gilles added, "If you have a blue blazer I would appreciate it very much if you would bring it when you come to my office."

Tom gave Gilles a half-smile and said, "Are you kidding? There's a dress code for being questioned?"

"Humour me," Gilles said.

"Okay, I'll see you tomorrow." Tom turned and walked away without another word.

Under normal circumstances Gilles would have looked for Annie, but in this case he thought it best to leave the ER.

Gilles got back to the office fifteen minutes ahead of the two constables, Bélanger and Parent. Over coffee they compared notes and agreed that they had no strong suspicions about any of these people, but there were those amongst them who could have committed the crimes.

Bélanger and Parent had checked the wardrobes of all the people they questioned but did not turn up any clothing with missing brass buttons.

CHAPTER SEVENTEEN

"I'd like to say it's been a pleasure. . ."

Even though Tom was unfamiliar with the area of Montreal east of Papineau, he had no problem finding Place Versailles, which occupied a large swath of land on the corner of rue du Trianon and Sherbrooke Est, the shopping centre where the Major Crimes Division of the Montreal police was located, but he had to wander around the centre for a while before he found the elevators that would take him up to the division. The receptionist, a chatty woman in her fifties, asked Tom who he wanted to see. She paged Gilles and directed Tom to some chairs in the waiting area. While he waited, the receptionist asked Tom about the weather and commiserated with him when he complained about the traffic situation in the city.

After about ten minutes Gilles appeared in the reception area and brought Tom into a room with a long table and a dozen chairs around it. The room was painted institutional green and had no furnishings other than the table, chairs and a credenza with some pads, pens, and a telephone on it. To Tom the room looked more like a boardroom or an office meeting room than an interrogation room. He was comforted by this.

As requested, Tom arrived wearing a blue blazer and Gilles could see at a glance that it did not have brass buttons. He chose not to comment on this fact.

"I see you decided to come alone," Gilles said when both men were seated, Gilles at the head of the table, Tom a few seats away facing the windows that looked out over the parking lot.

"Yeah, I haven't done anything wrong—so no lawyer," Tom replied.

"What's in the folder?" Gilles asked, indicating the thick maroon Pendaflex file with an elastic around its flap that Tom had with him.

"Information about our group. Just in case," he answered.

"Okay, that seems like a good place to start," Gilles said. "I gather that you're the driving force behind Patrol Our Parks. Tell me about it."

"Think about it," Tom said. "If there had been proper policing in the park, you probably wouldn't have been shot."

Gilles did not want to admit it but the thought had occurred to him. He nodded, indicating that Tom should continue.

"I didn't want to wait for some kid to be shot or killed. So I decided to do something. If the cops weren't going to do anything, even after one of their own was shot, then it was up to us who lived in the neighbourhood. I called some people I knew and arranged a meeting. And then these people called friends of theirs, and so on, and the group grew."

"Yeah, I get that," Gilles said. "What I want to know is what your plans were, beyond holding meetings."

"Patrols, citizen patrols," Tom said, a little exasperated. "It's in our name. The plan was—is—to wear something that identifies us and to tell the undesirables that if they do not move on we will be on the phone to the police." Tom opened his folder and pulled out some photographs of blue nylon windbreakers. He slid them over to Gilles and explained, "These are samples of the kind of jackets we wanted to buy.

We'd have the name of the group on the back and a design of some kind on the front, on the left side."

"And how did the police react to your plans?"

"Badly," Tom stated. "I had one conversation with the commander of the local police station and he told me to drop the idea of patrolling the park. He told me to leave police work to the police."

"And you did what?" Gilles prompted.

"Nothing. The police might not like the idea but they can't stop people wearing jackets and walking in the park. If they did anything to stop us they'd look pretty stupid, no?"

"No," Gilles said. "I'm concerned with murder and attempted murder. So let me ask you bluntly: Is it possible that one of your members, frustrated by the lack of support from the police, decided to take matters into their own hands?"

"C'mon, Gilles," Tom answered. "You met our members. Do they look like murderers to you?"

"I don't know what murderers look like. But you haven't answered my question."

"Well then, the answer is no."

"You have to remember, Tom, that you lied to me when I asked you about the group you organized." Gilles flipped through his notes and continued, "You told me that the group was devoted to sports and now that your kids were grown the organization disbanded. This turns out not to be the case as I discovered and you just confirmed. I found no shortage of evidence that the members of Patrol Our Parks are very concerned about drug dealing in the park so I'll need more than your say-so not to be concerned that someone in your group didn't stab three people, killing two of them." Gilles paused to let his words sink in and then asked, "Do you have a list of all your members and all the people you've contacted in your folder?"

Tom sat silently, his fingers drumming on the file folder. He didn't want to subject the people whose names he had to the type of police harassment some of the members had recently experienced, but he did not want to face the consequences of interfering in a police investigation. And he didn't know everyone who had showed some interest in his group. It was possible that there was a murderer amongst them.

Tom sighed and slid the file to Gilles, "See for yourself."

Gilles went through the folder and pulled out several sheets of paper with names and contact information on them before he handed it back to Tom.

Before reviewing the names, Gilles asked, "How do people join your group? Can anyone sign up?"

"Not exactly. Your membership has to be approved by someone already in the group."

"So you know all the members?"

"No," Tom answered. "I know all the original members, but now any other member can approve one of their friends. So I don't know all those who have expressed an interest in our work."

Gilles read over the list of names and recognized several of the people he or the two uniformed cops had spoken to. "I want to ask you some questions about these people." He motioned for Tom to take the chair adjacent to where he sat so they could go over the list together. Gilles was more interested in people Tom didn't know than those he did. Tom had an alibi for the times of the stabbings, he was at work. It was remotely possible that Tom had somehow convinced someone to take direct and violent action, but Gilles doubted it. Tom didn't have that kind of charisma.

Gilles and Tom spent an hour going over the names, and in the end Gilles had a list of a dozen people who merited a closer look.

All the listings included email and street addresses. Gilles decided that he would do a fast check of the information against the police database and Canada411 to see if any of the people had police records or if there were any other anomalies.

Gilles got to his feet and said, "I won't keep you much longer, Tom. There is one more thing I want to check." Gilles walked to the door that led to the room where the detectives worked. "This will only take me a couple of minutes. Can I get you a coffee while you wait?"

"No thanks," Tom said.

Fifteen minutes later Gilles returned to the conference room and sat down, again beside Tom. "I just checked these names against our data base and also against Canada411. None of these people has a police record, but there is one name that does not check out." Gilles pointed to the list. "Do you know this guy, Jack Earnest? There's nothing in Canada411 or anywhere else on the web."

"Not one of mine," Tom explained. He flipped through the documents in his folder looking for additional information. "As far as I can tell, his request for membership was approved by one of the original members, Allan Wexler."

"How well do you know Allan Wexler?" Gilles asked.

"I've known him since we were kids. We went to the same primary school. We grew up in that neighbourhood," Tom told Gilles. "His father owned the dry cleaners and Allan went into the business."

"Do you have a phone number for him?" Gilles asked.

Tom checked the contacts on his cellphone and said, "Yeah, I have it. You can call him if you like, but I should tell you that none of us really scrutinize people who want in. The approval is pretty automatic in most cases."

"Actually," Gilles replied, "I'd like you to call him and see what he can tell you about Jack Earnest."

Tom stared at Gilles before he said anything. "Let me get this straight: you haul me down here as a suspect in a murder and now you want my help? Unbelievable."

"First off," Gilles explained in a calm voice, "I didn't haul you down here as a suspect. I thought I made that clear. If you hadn't lied to me about your involvement in the Patrol Our Park group we might have had this conversation at the hospital. We take lying seriously around here." Gilles paused to let his words sink in. He didn't know Tom all that well but he knew him well enough to know that he was on the stubborn side. "So, yes, I'm asking for your help in solving two murders and one attempted murder. I would have thought that, given your commitment to having a safe park, you'd want to help."

Tom didn't say anything. He stared at Gilles, sighed and reached for his phone. He scrolled through his contacts and tapped on Allan Wexler's phone number.

"Put it on speaker," Gilles commanded.

"Hey Allan," Tom said. "Tom Andreadis calling. I hope I'm not disturbing you."

"Never too busy for you, Tom. What's up?"

"I'm with the police and they have a question about one of the guys in our group."

"The park group?" Allan asked.

"Yeah. He wants to know about one of the guys in the group. Jack Earnest he's been on the website. You authorized him. How well do you know him?"

Tom mumbled a few "yeahs" and "I sees" while his friend answered his question. Finally Tom said, "Yeah, well we may work at tightening that up in the future. Thanks, Allan."

Tom turned to Gilles and reported, "Okay, as you heard my friend doesn't actually know this guy, Jack Earnest. Allan happened to be on the site when his request to join popped up and he okayed it."

"Are you telling me there's no filter or waiting period in the approval process?" Gilles asked.

"Yeah, we see ourselves as a group of friends and friends of friends and couldn't imagine anyone else being interested," Tom explained. "I guess we didn't really think it through very carefully. We're just a neighbourhood organization."

"Anyway," Gilles concluded, "no one seems to know this Jack Earnest fellow."

Tom didn't say anything, choosing not to comment on the obvious. Gilles thought for a couple of minutes and then said, "The address he gave is a fake. The street exists but not the house number. I'd like you to test his email. Send him a message asking if you can get together for a coffee or something. Say that you like to meet the new members of your group. I'm going to do a little more research as well. One of us should be able to find him." It occurred to Gilles that Jack Earnest might not exist, that he was a decoy who could have been planted by anyone including Tom Andreadis.

"And what do I do if he agrees?" Tom asked.

"You let me know and you meet him somewhere for coffee. What did you think?"

"Okay, I'll take care of it later, when I get home," Tom said, and half-rose from his chair.

Gilles put up a hand. "We'll do it from here," he said. "It would be best if you sent him the email from the website."

They went to Gilles's desk and he pulled an extra chair over for Tom. Gilles brought the website up and scrolled through some of the recent postings. There were dozens of them, and they all concerned the visits certain of the members had from the police. The postings were overwhelmingly hostile to the cops and in many cases were incoherent with vitriol.

"Crisse," Gilles exclaimed, "don't you exercise any editorial control over what appears on your website?"

Tom smiled and responded, "Freedom of speech, Gilles. We don't allow threats or slander or that kind of thing but no, we don't censor the free exchange of ideas—in this case the idea that we should not be harassed by the cops!"

Gilles chose to drop the subject. He had no desire for Tom to take any additional pleasure from the postings.

He shifted the keyboard to Tom so that he could log in and send an email with a blind copy to Gilles. Tom did what he was asked and said, "Okay? Are we done here?"

"Almost," Gilles told him. "I want you to authorize my membership in your group so I have full access to your website." Gilles did not wait for Tom to answer. He pulled the keyboard back and typed his information, all of which, except for his first name, was false. "I'm a cop, I don't want to leave a trail on a website that I'm surveilling," he said and shifted the keyboard in Tom's direction again so that his membership in the group could be authorized. Tom didn't do anything. He slid both hands on his thighs while he considered Gilles's request. He didn't like the idea of the cops spying on him and his friends but to refuse was to call more suspicion to himself. Tom stared at Gilles and accepted him into the POP group.

Gilles stood and so did Tom. "Thanks for your help." Gilles offered his hand to shake. Tom hesitated for a moment and then shook hands with the detective.

"I'd like to say it's been a pleasure . . . but . . . well, I suppose you're just doing your job," Tom said as Gilles walked him to the elevator.

"Exactly," Gilles replied as the elevator doors were closing. "Call me if this Earnest fellow gets in touch with you."

Gilles's strong suspicion was that Jack Earnest was not a real person but an avatar for someone who wanted to know what the POP people were up to. The question was: why?

Was the person behind the Jack Earnest persona someone who wanted to use the anger expressed on the POP website as a cover for their own actions?

Tom was scheduled to work the three-to-eleven shift and so had time to stop for a sandwich before heading to the Gursky. He was upset by having been treated as, what—not a suspect, but a person of interest in a murder investigation—and he wanted some time alone to cool down before getting to work. He knew that he would be working with Annie and he didn't want his recent interaction with Gilles to damage his relationship with her. Everyone who worked with Annie thought highly of her. She was one of the most popular members of the ER staff, loved by her patients and colleagues alike.

Tom chose not to eat in the food court at the shopping centre. He had no desire to run into Gilles. He drove to the hospital, parked in the employee parking lot, and headed to one of the restaurants that lined Côte-des-Neiges. Tom made it to the hospital with time to spare. He changed into scrubs in the employee locker room and, uncharacteristically, strolled into the ER ten minutes prior to the start of his shift. The first person he saw was Annie, who was talking to Ursula, the nurse she was replacing in the triage unit, getting information on the patients being handed off to her. She waved at Tom and gave him a big smile. Tom waved and smiled back.

Dr. Eric Kavanaugh left the meeting he was attending at one of the Gursky's off-site clinics late, a full half-hour late. This meant that he would be very late for his next meeting at the main building of the Gursky Memorial Hospital. Eric was, by nature, punctual, and found it physically painful to be late. The clinic was located in a building on Côte-des-Neiges, a few blocks north of the hospital. Most of the office buildings on that part of the street housed doctors, dentists, and clinics. The shortest route back to the hospital was to cut through Kennedy Park.

Eric, dressed as usual in an expensive bespoke suit, dark blue today, with a starched white shirt and a Pancaldi Fantasy pattern silk tie, turned into the park, striding toward his office. He slowed his pace as he felt sweat beginning to dampen his underarms. In order to save some time he took a path through a thicket of bushes, careful not to get any of nature's detritus on his clothing. He stopped for a moment to get his bearings and felt a prick on the fleshy part of his lower back. He reached behind him and his hand came away sticky with blood. Eric's first thought was that his expensive suit had been ruined. That thought did not last. He rushed out of the bushes. "Help me. Call an ambulance. I'm hurt," he screamed and collapsed on the bench of a picnic table. Two young women pushing their children in carriages stopped and turned when they heard him yelling.

They froze for a couple of seconds. "Oh God," one of them said, panic in her voice. Her friend reached for her cellphone and called 911.

"I'm a doctor at the Gursky," Eric yelled. "Tell them that."

The woman who was not on the phone rushed to Eric with a baby wipe. He took it with his right hand, his left hand covering his wound. He transferred the baby wipe to his other hand and rose slightly so as to be able to reach behind him and apply pressure to the wound. He tried to support himself by placing his right hand on the picnic table but found it too high so had to resort to using the rim of a garbage receptacle next to it. After a moment or two he again collapsed onto the bench to await the ambulance.

The second woman joined her friend and asked, "What happened? Who did this?"

Eric looked up at them. "I've been stabbed," he repeated, his voice trembling

The two women, themselves looked around nervously. "Did you see who did it?" one of them asked.

They heard the yelp of the siren of the approaching ambulance. A minute later two EMTs wheeled a gurney over. One of the technicians got a pressure bandage on Eric's wound. Eric dropped the baby wipe into the garbage can as the EMTs helped him onto the gurney.

On Eric's instructions, the ambulance driver called ahead to the hospital and informed Annie, the triage nurse on duty that they would soon be arriving with Dr. Kavanaugh, who had been stabbed. Annie and Tom along with Dr. Klein, the doctor working triage, met the ambulance.

In the examining room one of the EMTs tossed Eric's suit jacket onto a chair. The rest of the team transferred him to the hospital so that he was lying face down. Annie pulled his shirt up, removed the pressure bandage and cleaned the wound. Dr. Klein examined it and said, "It's a clean wound, not too deep. Were you moving when you got stabbed?" he asked. "It looks like you were moving away from the attack."

"I must have been," Eric replied. "I was late and rushing."

"A few stitches and a tetanus shot and you should be fine," Dr. Klein explained. "You were lucky,"

"Yeah," Eric agreed.

"Is there someone I can call?" Annie asked. "Your wife? Anyone?"

Eric didn't want to worry Claire. Better to tell her what had happened once he had been released from the ER. "Yeah," he replied. "Please call my secretary and tell her that I won't be back at the office for a while. I'll call her when I can."

Annie thought the request was strange but called Dr. Kavanaugh's secretary and told her what had happened. Dr. Kavanaugh's secretary was obviously upset at the news that her boss had been stabbed. "I'll be right there," she exclaimed in near hysteria. Annie told the woman to remain at her desk; that the doctors and nurses had the situation under control. The secretary gave no indication that she was listening to Annie as she asked where in the ER her boss was being treated, and after repeating her question several times asked if he was okay. Annie raised her voice to get the secretary's attention and told her in no uncertain terms to stay away from the emergency department.

Dr. Kavanaugh's secretary was about to ask if he wanted her to call his wife when the line went dead. As she hadn't been told not to call Claire, she made the call and told her what had transpired.

Annie and Dr. Klein took care of the chief of medicine and when they were done, Tom wheeled him to a room in the emergency department. Eric wanted to go home but Dr. Klein overruled him; he wanted to keep an eye on him for the next few hours to ensure that there was no sepsis or other complication.

Annie called Gilles and told him that Dr. Kavanaugh had been stabbed. Thirty minutes later he was at the hospital with a couple of uniformed cops. Gilles took Eric's statement and sent the cops to the park to check out the scene of the attack. He called the Identité judicaire and asked them to meet the uniformed cops at the scene. Gilles would meet them there when he finished at the hospital.

The cops had no trouble finding the picnic table where Eric had been sitting; they only had to follow the ambulance tire tracks into the park. They saw the bloodstains on the bench; they took a couple of scrapings and slid them into evidence bags.

A city garbage truck had been in the area to empty the bins in the park about ten minutes before the cops arrived at the scene, so when they checked the garbage pail closest to the place where the stabbing occurred they found it empty, its contents on the way to the city dump.

The cops searched the area around the bench and the bushes where Eric had actually been stabbed looking for a weapon, but did not find one. It was easy enough to follow the blood trail from the bushes to the picnic table but there were only partial footprints, none of them clear. The cops checked the shrubbery hoping to find some material from the perpetrator's clothing but found nothing.

Claire got to the hospital while Gilles was talking to Dr. Klein. Annie directed her to her husband's room. She was somewhat relieved to see him looking so well. She perched on a corner of the bed and stroked his hair. Eric moved in order to give her a bit more room.

"God, Eric, what happened?" Concern had drained the blood from Claire's face and her voice held a tremor of worry.

"I was attacked in the park," he said. "How did you know I was here? I asked them not to call you."

"Eric," she said. Her tone of voice implied the foolishness of his not wanting her to be informed. "Well they did, of course they did. But what were you doing there in the first place?"

"I was late," he responded. "A meeting I was at ran long and I had to get back to the hospital for another meeting. So I took a shortcut through the park." Then he added, "There were no cabs."

Claire was about to say something about being careful in the future but she knew it was pointless. If an action as benign as walking in a park could turn out to be dangerous then her counsel was meaningless.

Encouraged by her husband's healthy-sounding voice and demeanor, Claire was able to stop worrying. "Can I get you anything?" she asked, the colour returning to her face.

Eric stroked her arm and said, "No. I'm sure I won't be here long."

After determining from his conversation with Dr. Klein that Kavanaugh was not in any medical danger, Gilles returned to his room, opened the door a crack, and asked if Eric felt well enough to talk to him.

Eric sighed and Claire said, "Perhaps later, my husband is not well."

"No," Eric said. "Let's get this over with."

Gilles came into the room and stood near the foot of Eric's bed, close enough to have a clear view of him but not so close as to be intimidating. "Please tell me what happened," Gilles said. Claire got up from where she was sitting on Eric's bed. She caught Gilles's eye and gave her head a quick, almost imperceptible shake.

Eric repeated the story of his attack.

"And you didn't get a look at the person?"

"No," Eric replied. "I was stabbed in the back, the lower back."

"I won't trouble you any further," Gilles said. "But I'll probably want to talk to you again."

"No problem."

Gilles returned to the triage area and sought out Dr. Klein again. "I have a couple more questions," Gilles explained. "Is there somewhere we can talk privately?"

Dr. Klein led Gilles to an empty examining room and leaned against the examining table, his arms folded across his chest. There was a visitor's chair in the room which Gilles turned so that its seat was against the wall opposite where Dr. Klein was standing. Gilles leaned against the chair back so that his and Dr. Klein's eyes were at the same level.

"I just spoke to Dr. Kavanaugh," Gilles said, "and he did not seem any the worse for wear. What can you tell me about his wound?"

"I can tell you that it was not serious, not life-threatening in any way. Maybe he pulled away from his assailant, or maybe he was moving or maybe he felt something and arched his back away from the stab. He was lucky. It could have been a lot worse."

"Can you tell me anything about the kind of weapon that was used?"

Dr. Klein thought for a minute and said, "I know about the other stabbings, about the kind of weapon that may have been used. I have no way of knowing what the weapon was other than to say it could have been similar to the others."

"But the wound was not deep?" Gilles asked again.

"No, it was only a little more serious than a surface wound."

Annie was busy with a patient so Gilles waited until she was free so that they could say their goodbyes and arrange for the next time they could be together.

He then went to the park to join the uniformed cops and the forensics team.

CHAPTER EIGHTEEN

"I'm going to do the only thing I can."

Criminals are no different than anyone else; they followed patterns of behaviour. Gilles believed this and so was troubled by the fact that he could discern no pattern to the activities of the Kennedy Park stabber. Gilles thought that he under-stood his quarry; he could make allowances for the fact that one of the stabbings took place on the street instead of the park. He could make allowances for the fact that one of the people who was stabbed while walking through the park, Hari Deshpande may not have been the intended victim, and luckily had survived. Gilles was certain that the intended vic-tim was Denny Marchand. But once he factored in the stab-bing of Dr. Kavanaugh, which seemed unrelated to the drug dealers, these conditions together were not consistent with the hypothesis that Gilles had formulated—that the attacks were part of a misguided vigilante action to clean the drug dealers out of the park. If all the stabbings were perpetrated by the same person, and because Gilles was certain that this was the case, then he either had to consider different *actus causas,* reasons for the actions or different perpetrators for some of the crimes.

As Gilles drove back to the office he replayed events in his mind and considered other explanations. The only conclusion he had reached as he approached the parking lot of Place Versailles was that Tom and his friends and allies, with the possible exception of the mysterious Jack Earnest, were guilty of some of the stabbings but not others. You would have to be blind to consider Dr. Kavanaugh a drug dealer. Therefore, Gilles concluded as he pulled into a parking spot, there was something else about Dr. Kavanaugh that made him a target. This begged the question: what did the other two victims and the one intended victim have in common with one another and/or with the doctor?

It was possible, Gilles considered as he walked from his car to the entrance to the shopping centre, that the hospital was the connection. Maybe there was something connecting Esperanza, Jardine, Denny Marchand, maybe even Hari Deshpande, and the Gursky. Did any or all of them work there at one time or another? Were they all patients of Dr. Kavanaugh? Who was Jack Earnest, and was he somehow connected to the hospital?

When he got to his desk he put in another call to Chantal Rigaud in the Tech Crimes Division and asked her to check the POP website to see if she could track down Jack Earnest.

"That's pretty easy," Rigaud told Gilles, "I can do that while you're on the phone."

"Great," Gilles said, encouraged that he would have some hard evidence to follow up on. He could hear Constable Rigaud typing and muttering to herself. Finally she cleared her throat and reported, "Well, this guy is pretty smart. He didn't make that many posts, none of them were that long, and this is what makes it difficult if not impossible to figure out who he is: he didn't use the same IP address twice."

"What does that mean?" Gilles asked.

"He made the posts from internet cafés. I know the location and I know the day and date, but that's about it. To get any more information you'll have to visit each of the three or four cafés and hope that someone there remembers him. I wouldn't count on it, the posts are pretty old."

"One more question," Gilles put in, doing his best to hide his disappointment, "Were any of the IP addresses from the area around the Gursky Memorial Hospital, or better yet from the hospital itself?"

Constable Rigaud said nothing while she typed away on her computer. After about five minutes she informed Gilles, "I have one address on the corner of Queen Mary and Côte-des-Neiges. That's pretty close according to Google Maps. I can give you the dates and times of all the posts. But he just as easily could have been in his car in front of the café using their internet."

Gilles wanted to check the internet café closest to the hospital at the same time of day that the post was made to the POP website. He knew that this was the best way of finding an employee who might remember Jack Earnest. He checked his watch and saw that he was three hours too late for today, so he tidied his desk and headed home. Checking up on the elusive Jack Earnest would have to wait until the next day.

Once home, he changed into sweats, cooked a steak for dinner, and settled in to watching Netflix.

The next few days passed uneventfully. Gilles re-examined the information he had collected regarding the stabbings. He had the unmistakable feeling that things were not adding up as they should; the evidence was pointing in a direction that Gilles could not quite follow. He reviewed his analysis and conclusions with Captain Lacroix and the senior detective on the squad, Detective Sergeant Gaston Lemieux. Both men agreed that the four stabbings were related and that something was not making sense. Captain Lacroix pushed Gilles to find other investigative paths to follow but Gaston urged Gilles to reflect on the evidence so far uncovered and try to determine if it allowed for another conclusion. Gilles thought that Gaston's advice was the better course to follow but he could not disobey a direct order from his boss, so he gave every impression of following it while he sought another conclusion that accommodated all the known facts. He came up empty. The visit to the café where Jack Earnest had used the internet proved fruitless.

During this time Annie was on the night shift and she and Gilles spoke on the phone on a daily basis. Finally, her scheduled night shifts came to an end and she had a few days off before she switched to the day shift.

She spent a day catching up on chores and napping in order to reset her circadian rhythm. On her second day off she spent time with Pamela and that evening she and Gilles had a planned dinner together at his condo.

Before having been stabbed, Dr. Eric Kavanaugh had made plans to attend a medical conference in Toronto several days hence. Claire was worried about her husband. She felt that due to his injury he should not be travelling. Eric had a contrary opinion. On the day that he was to leave, he showed Claire that his wound had almost completely healed and explained the medical reasons, which Claire did not fully understand, why flying would not be a problem.

"And anyway," Eric concluded, "if something does go wrong I'll have a large choice of doctors to patch me up." He laughed at his own joke.

"What are your plans?" Eric asked his wife just before he left.

"A quiet evening with Marjorie," she told him. She kissed him goodbye and told him to be careful of his wound.

Eric took an Uber to the airport, arriving in plenty of time to catch the two-thirty Air Canada flight to the Toronto Island, Billy Bishop Airport. This meant that Claire had the house to herself for a good part of the afternoon. She loved the quiet of the house when her husband was absent. Eric always had the TV on, usually tuned to the Fox News channel. And if the TV was silent then he was listening to some crap on satellite talk radio. Even during meals there was a constant barrage of dumb noise filling the house. Eric felt compelled to comment on what he was hearing. Claire rarely said anything, which her husband took to mean that she agreed with him. Nothing could be further from the truth. Claire's silence meant that she was trying to think about other things.

She watched from the bay window of the living room as Eric's Uber drove off. She had several hours before she had to leave to have dinner with Marjorie. It had been a long time, too long a time, since the two of them had spent an evening together, and Claire had a lot she wanted to talk about with her best friend and confidante.

Earlier in the day, while her husband was packing, she had placed her sketch pad and charcoals in the sun room that looked out on the garden at the back of the house. She intended to spend the afternoon sketching and her favourite place to do that was in the sunroom. It was comfortably furnished and Claire could work standing up at an easel or, as she did on this day, sitting in an easy chair, her sketch pad on her lap and her charcoals arrayed beside her on a small table upon which there was room for a glass of wine or cup of tea. This afternoon it held a cup of tea; there would be time enough for wine when she got to Marjorie's.

Claire made several sketches of the big old walnut tree, popular with the squirrels, which was in the far left corner of the backyard garden. The tree, Claire was certain, was a hundred years old or more, and had been there before the house was constructed. Claire slipped into a nap with her sketch pad on her lap and charcoals in her hand. It was just coming on five-thirty when she snapped awake.

She put her drawing materials aside and went upstairs for a quick shower before leaving for her friend's house. Thirty minutes later she was in the vestibule looking for her car keys. Halfway to the car she realized that she had forgotten her cellphone, so she returned to the house to retrieve it. She found it on the kitchen counter; it would soon need a charge. She would charge it at Marjorie's. It took her another couple of minutes to find the charger, which she threw into her purse.

It was an unseasonably warm evening and Claire decided to walk to Marjorie's studio. The walk would take her about forty-five minutes, but it would have the effect of returning her to the relaxed state she had been in before having to hunt for her phone and charger. She pulled her phone out of her bag and called Marjorie to tell her that she was walking to her place. Marjorie said, "Call me when you're a couple of blocks away and I'll meet you on Côte-des-Neiges. We'll go for a drink at the Fleur des Vins." This was a new wine bar that had opened close to where Marjorie lived and was becoming a favoured place for a glass or two of wine in the late afternoon.

"Sounds like a plan," Claire agreed, and slipped her phone back into her handbag.

The walk was every bit as enjoyable as Claire thought it would be. Under normal circumstances Claire would have cut through the Kennedy Park. Even though she did not consider herself a fearful person she decided not to take any chances and stuck to city streets. The sun was setting as she headed north and she enjoyed the Rorschach patterns made by the dusky light filtered through the trees and buildings along Côte-des-Neiges.

She had just passed the point where one of the pathways in the park joined Côte-des-Neiges, about a block and a half from Marjorie's when Claire heard the sound of someone running up behind her. She thought it was probably a jogger. She tensed and moved to the relative safety of edge of the sidewalk to let him pass. The jogger stopped behind Claire and she nervously looked back over her left shoulder to see what was happening. Joggers normally ran past pedestrians. The fact that this one stopped for some reason made her anxious. She saw a man in a hoodie, the hood pulled over his eyes, making it impossible to see his face. Claire was about to say something when she caught the glint of something in the man's hand. Fear overtook her and just as she ran into the street the man thrust his hand forward and Claire felt herself being stabbed. At that moment the 165 bus heading south was pulling away from the curb about half a block away. Its headlights illuminated Claire and the angry honk of the bus's horn caused her to jump out of its path to the double line that divided the lanes of traffic. Her assailant, who had attempted to follow her, jumped back onto the sidewalk.

Claire made it to the far side of the street. She slid her hand under her sweater and felt blood, wet and sticky. She kept moving and reached into her purse for her cellphone. She had it in her bloodstained hand "Call Marjorie!" she yelled. She said and fell. She heard the bus behind her but could not hear her assailant. She did not know if he was coming for her. Worse, she was not certain she had the energy to run if he was.

Marjorie's phone rang and when she answered she heard nothing but street noises. She knew the call was from Claire and she said, "Claire, Claire, did you ass-dial me?" There was no response and she was about to hang up when she heard what sounded like Claire screaming. "Claire, Claire!" she repeated. "What's wrong?" There was no answer. Marjorie ran outside to see if Claire was nearby and in trouble.

Claire had fallen to her knees. She could see that the man in black had spotted her, and she reached out for something for support so she could pull herself to her feet. She had to get to safety. Her hand grasped the bar of a bicycle stand. She pulled herself up as her assailant dashed across the street. She looked north and south and saw a trio of pedestrians, young people, laughing and joking as they walked in her direction. She stumbled a few steps toward them, screaming for help. The scream that Marjorie heard on her phone. They, stopped for a moment trying to get a sense of what was going on, and saw Claire fall. They rushed towards her just as the man in black reached the sidewalk where Claire had fallen.

The young woman in the trio rushed toward Claire and shouted at the man in black, "Tabernac, espèce de merde!" The attacker was close to Claire, but not close enough to stab her again, and the young woman was closing in on him. He took off running across Côte-des-Neiges and disappeared into the park.

Just as the three young people got to Claire, Marjorie got to the corner of Côte-des-Neiges and Van Horne and saw the commotion on the opposite side of the street. Claire was on the ground.

"Hey," she screamed as loudly as she could as she ran toward her friend.

Claire looked up from where she was on the sidewalk and gasped, "Marjorie," and then passed out.

Marjorie ran to her friend thinking that the three people close to her were the attackers. The young woman who scared the attacker away was on her phone. "What happened," she said loudly. One of the three people said, "Une attaque." Marjorie was on her knees next to Claire. The woman who had been on her cell phone said, "J'ai telephoné 911." Claire awoke and said, "Marji, thank god you're here. A guy attacked me."

Claire tried to get up. "An ambulance is on its way," Marjorie told her, "Don't try to move."

"Call the cop," Claire said just before she collapsed again. It took Marjorie a minute to realize that Claire meant Gilles Bellechasse. She found Claire's phone on the sidewalk and scrolled through her contacts and found Gilles's number. She called it.

Gilles and Annie were in Gilles's living room chatting. Gilles had his legs stretched out in front of him, his feet resting on an ottoman. Annie was curled up beside him, her head on his shoulder. He held her close. A perfect moment. The autumnal darkness enfolded them. The marimba ringtone of Gilles's cellphone interrupted their perfect moment. Gilles reached for his phone. It was a number that he did not recognize in the call display; he worried that someone was calling to tell him that Emilie was in some kind of trouble.

"Oui," he said, sitting up, alert.

"Detective Bellechasse, it's Marjorie, Marjorie Reynolds."

It took Gilles a couple of seconds to place the name. "Yes, Marjorie, how can I help you?" He looked quizzically at Annie who was now sitting up and paying attention to the conversation.

"Claire's been attacked," Marjorie said. "Stabbed."

"Where are you?"

"What happened?" Annie whispered.

"Where are you?" Gilles asked again.

Marjorie told him where they were and added, "An ambulance is on its way."

"I'm on my way. I'll meet you at the Gursky."

Gilles got to his feet. "Claire's been stabbed," he told Annie. They rushed out to his car.

There wasn't that much traffic, but navigating through Montreal's maze of construction detours made the drive maddingly slow. Gilles didn't have a siren in his personal car but he was not averse to speeding, weaving in and out of traffic, when he had the chance. If a cop stopped him, he would get the officer to provide an escort, sirens blaring.

Gilles and Annie arrived at the Gursky just after the EMTs had wheeled Claire into the triage area. The nurse on duty was looking at the wound, Marjorie was nearby making small nervous movements. Gilles identified himself. "Thank God you're here," she said.

Annie consulted with the nurse on duty.

"It's not life-threatening, that's for sure," said the nurse to Claire and Annie, "but it does require some attention. It'll need stitches and she'll certainly require a tetanus shot." She looked up at Claire. "You'll have to go up to surgery. We want to get you patched up as soon as possible."

The EMTs handed the nurse their report and left.

"Can I ask a couple of questions," Gilles asked, "before you take her?"

"You'll have to make it fast," said the nurse.

"I won't be long," Gilles said. He turned to Claire. "What can you tell me about the attack?"

"Not much," Claire told the detective. "I was walking along Côte-des-Neiges and heard someone running up behind me.

I moved to let them pass and when he didn't I turned to see why and he tried to stab me."

"How do you mean 'tried'?" Gilles asked.

"I saw something shiny in his hand and somehow sensed danger so I tried to run into traffic. Not quite fast enough." She gestured with the hand holding the corner of her shirt.

"Was there anything familiar about the man? Anything you recognized?"

"No, nothing. He was wearing a hoodie that covered his face."

"Can you tell me something about his build? Was he tall? Short? That kind of thing."

"He was shorter than you. It was hard to tell as I was concentrating on getting away," Claire said.

The ER nurse returned from calling the surgical floor and returned with an orderly to wheel Claire's gurney away.

"I'll only be another couple of seconds," Gilles said and turned to Claire. "What were you doing, exactly, on that part of Côte-des-Neiges?"

"Oh," Claire said. "I was walking to Marjorie's. We have—had—plans to spend the evening together."

"And your husband?" Gilles asked. "Where was he?"

Claire brought a hand to her mouth and exclaimed, "Oh Christ, Eric. I forgot all about him. He's in Toronto at a convention. I'd better call him."

"That will have to wait," the nurse said. "We have to get you upstairs."

The orderly wheeled Claire away.

Gilles turned his attention to Marjorie who gave him as much information as she had about what happened. "There were three other people there, where it happened," she said.

"Do you know who they were?" Gilles asked.

"No but one of them called 911."

"Lucky they were there. Nine-one-one will have the number of the person who called. I'll track them down."

Marjorie asked the detective, "Do you think there's a mad stabber type of predator roaming the park or do you think something else is going on?" The question surprised Gilles because it reflected his thinking almost exactly.

"I can't answer that question," Gilles said. "I can't discuss an ongoing investigation." He had formed the conclusion that the stabbings were neither random events, nor some kind of vigilante action. Up to the attempt on Claire's life, Gilles supposed that there was the possibility that some person or group of people were fighting an imaginary war in some sort of modern demented fashion. But then why would both Claire Kavanaugh and her husband be victims of vigilante action. The question remained: who was the perpetrator? If Mikel had had a jealous girlfriend she might be a suspect. But so far no girlfriend had been found. A jealous husband was always a good bet, but the jealous husband in this case was 540 kilometres away in Toronto.

Gilles and Annie along with Marjorie waited for Claire to be cared for by the surgeon. They only had to wait about ninety minutes before Annie learned that Claire was in recovery. They prepared to head up to the recovery room to see if Gilles could continue to interview her. Marjorie insisted on accompanying them to satisfy herself that her friend was recovering from her wounds.

They found Claire sitting up on a gurney while the doctor attended to her wound. Claire had her cellphone in her hand. She motioned with it to Annie, Gilles and Marjorie and said, "It's dead. Can someone lend me a phone? I have to call my husband." It was a little after 8:30 by this time.

Gilles handed Claire his cellphone and she tapped in her husband's phone number.

"Eric, it's me . . . Because mine is dead, that's why. Listen to me. Someone stabbed me and I'm in the hospital." No one could make out what Eric Kavanaugh was saying but they could hear that he was talking quickly and excitedly. "No, I don't think that's necessary. Stay where you are. I'll stay with Marjorie when they let me leave."

Gilles gestured to Claire that he wanted to speak to her husband and Claire handed him his phone.

"This is Detective Gilles Bellechasse. I'd like to ask you some questions but I want to get to a more private place. Can I call your hotel?"

Gilles went back down to the ER floor. He could see Steve in his office behind the triage station. "I need to make an important call," he explained. "Is there a private room I can use?"

"You can use my office. I can work at another terminal," Steve said.

Gilles locked the door and called the number Eric Kavanaugh had given him. After a wait of no more than a minute or two Dr. Eric Kavanaugh came on the line. "Hello," he said.

"Dr. Kavanaugh, Gilles Bellechasse speaking. I need to ask you some questions about your whereabouts this evening and earlier today."

"First," said Dr. Kavanaugh, "tell me how my wife is. Is she okay? Is she receiving medical attention? I can make a phone call and she'll have the best people in the hospital looking after her."

Gilles didn't know for a fact that the so-called "best people in the hospital" were looking after her but he was confident that with Annie on the case, and probably in charge of it, Claire was being well looked after. "Your wife is being well cared for. She appears to be recovering nicely."

"Let me speak to the doctor in charge," Eric Kavanaugh commanded.

"I'm not in the room with her . . . " Gilles paused for a moment and added, "Obviously. I'll have someone call you later. Now I'd like you to answer some questions."

"Really?" Dr. Kavanaugh said. "Don't you think it's more important that I get back to Montreal as soon as possible?"

"At the moment I don't have a lot of questions but I want them answered and then you can worry about getting back here." Gilles did not give Dr. Kavanaugh the opportunity to interrupt again. "When did you leave for Toronto?"

"I was on the two-thirty from Trudeau."

Gilles made a note. "And you've been in Toronto ever since?"

"Where the hell else would I be?" Dr. Kavanaugh made no attempt to hide his impatience.

"One more question," Gilles said. "What have you been doing since arriving in Toronto?"

"You mean my alibi," Dr. Kavanaugh wanted to add the words "you idiot" but thought better of it. "I met with colleagues; I checked into my room and went out to dinner with friends. All the normal things one does at a conference."

Gilles made a note in his notebook and said, "Thank you. I'll want to speak to you again when you're back." Gilles disconnected the call. He was not about to give Dr. Kavanaugh an opportunity to hang up on him.

Gilles found Steve in the ambulance bay chatting with a nurse. "I'm done, thanks," he said. "Can you page Annie for me?"

"Yeah," Steve said. He picked up a phone, punched some numbers into the keypad and asked Nurse Linton to come to registration. He hung up, and the message was broadcast throughout the hospital.

Gilles and Steve returned to his office and a couple of minutes later Annie came in through the door that led from the hallway.

She was about to say something to Steve about not actually being on duty when she noticed Gilles was in the office with them. She came over and stood close to him. Their fingers touched. "How's Claire?" Gilles asked.

"She'll be okay," Annie told him. "She was lucky; the wound wasn't deep. She's been stitched and she's resting. She's back in a room in the ER."

"That's great," Gilles said, relieved that Claire was not badly hurt. "Can I talk to her?"

"I don't see why not," she replied. "But I should warn you that she's been given some drugs and she may be a little wonky from them."

"I'll be brief," Gilles promised. "I have the basic information. I just want some clarification on a few points."

The areas of the emergency department where the patients' rooms were situated were divided by colour: green, yellow and orange. Claire was in a room in the green area, the area for the most seriously ill patients.

Claire's eyes were closed and she was breathing evenly. She was attached to a heart monitor and a medicine drip. Gilles could see the lines of the heart monitor moving evenly across the screen, which he took to be a good sign. Marjorie was seated in a visitor's chair in the corner of the room. She'd managed to place her chair in such a way that her head rested against the wall, and she was dozing. She jerked awake when Gilles and Annie came into the room. It took her a second or two to focus, then she held a finger to her lips.

Looking at Claire, Gilles decided that his questions weren't all that important and could wait. He whispered to Annie that he would leave Claire in peace and question her the next day when he hoped she would be feeling better. Annie nodded and they were about to leave Claire's pod when she opened her eyes and said, "Oh, hi."

"I'm sorry," Gilles said, "I didn't mean to wake you."

Annie walked over to Claire and made some minor adjustments to her pillows and took a close look at the heart monitor. "Are you comfortable?" she asked. Marjorie got out of her chair and put a protective hand on her friend's shoulder.

Claire turned to Annie and nodded and then turned her attention back to Gilles. "Is there something you want?"

"I had a question, but it can wait. It's more important that you get your rest." He spoke softly.

"It's okay," Claire said sleepily. "It's only one question."

"I just wanted to know if anything else occurred to you. Some detail that came to you."

Marjorie glared at Gilles, as if to say: you idiot, you're disturbing her for this. It can wait.

Claire smiled but said nothing for a moment or two as she considered the question. "No, nothing." She closed her eyes and Gilles, Annie, and Marjorie thought that she had fallen back to sleep. Gilles and Annie were about to leave when Claire opened her eyes and said, "You know, it was odd. When I replay events in my mind I realize that I heard him coming up behind me. At the time I thought it was a jogger. But now I remember the sound of his shoes. He was wearing hard shoes, not sneakers, and I could hear them on the sidewalk. I just didn't think anything of it. Stupid, eh?"

Marjorie stroked her friend's hair and said, "Not at all. Why would you think that?"

Gilles agreed. "Nothing stupid about it. Why would you think you were in danger? But the information could prove useful. We won't disturb you any longer."

"Hmmm," Claire said and closed her eyes again. Marjorie returned to the visitor's chair, and Annie made certain that the patient was sleeping comfortably. She accompanied Gilles out of the room using the door to the hallway.

"Is that information really of any use?" she asked her boyfriend.

"Yeah, it is. It won't help us to find the assailant, but if we do arrest someone his footwear may help us to determine the likelihood of his involvement," he explained.

He and Annie walked toward the exit that led to the waiting room. "Let's get back to enjoying your evening off," he said.

"Right. But I have to be back here first thing tomorrow and I'm tired."

"Yeah, me too," Gilles agreed.

They returned to Gilles's condo and without much conversation undressed and got ready for bed. They fell asleep; Gilles curled behind Annie, his arms wrapped around her.

Dr. Eric Kavanaugh was able to get a seat on the first plane out of Toronto, the 7:15 morning flight from the Billy Bishop Airport. He arrived at Montreal's Trudeau Airport an hour or so later and got an Uber to the Gursky Memorial Hospital. He headed to the ER and got the unit agent to tell him where his wife was; he also demanded her chart. He stashed his overnight bag under the unit agent's desk and strode to Claire's room. He barely broke his pace as the door slid open at his approach. He made no effort to be silent.

Marjorie had awoken a minute or so before Eric came into the room and she was on her feet, stretching the kinks out of her body after a night sleeping in a chair. Eric did not notice her immediately.

Marjorie cleared her throat. Dr. Kavanaugh looked up and said, "Oh, hi, Marjorie. What are you doing here?"

"Really?" she asked. "Surely you didn't expect me to leave Claire alone, did you?"

Dr. Kavanaugh sighed and mumbled, "I suppose not." He turned back to Claire's chart and flipped through it. "There's no medical reason to keep her here any longer. I'm going to get the resident to sign her release and take her home."

Neither Dr. Kavanaugh nor Marjorie was whispering and the conversation woke Claire. Her eyelids fluttered a few times as she brought the hospital room and her reason for being in it into focus. "Oh, Eric, hi," she said sleepily when she noticed her husband. Marjorie took a pace closer to Claire's bed and put a protective hand on her shoulder. Claire turned to her and said, "Marjorie, my god, did you spend the night?"

Eric Kavanaugh didn't wait for a response. He repeated what he had just said for Claire's benefit. "I'll have you signed out and I'll take you home."

"I have a better idea," Marjorie asserted. "Why don't I take Claire out for breakfast and then get her settled at home, or if she prefers she can come to my place. I'll stay with her." She turned to Eric and added, "I'm sure you have a busy day ahead of you and I don't think Claire should be left alone."

"Well, yes, I'd have to return to the office. There are things I have to attend to," Kavanaugh agreed.

"Then it's settled. I'll take care of Claire for at least the rest of today and then we'll see."

Claire patted Marjorie's hand and said, "You're a good friend. Thank you. I feel fine, but, you know, not fully myself."

Eric left the room to get Claire's release signed. It wasn't long before a nurse came into the room to disconnect Claire from the heart monitor and infusion pump. Marjorie helped her get dressed.

Eric returned just as Claire finished dressing and said, "You're good to go. I'll walk you to the taxi stand." He turned to Marjorie and said, "I'm sure a breakfast will be okay, but don't keep her out too long. I'd like her to be at home, where I can monitor her."

CHAPTER NINETEEN

"Some new evidence has come to my attention and I think it is best if we continued this conversation at my office."

An hour or so after having breakfast together, Annie was on duty in the ER and Gilles was at a long table in the interrogation room at the Major Crimes Division. Arrayed before him were all the reports, notes, and statements that he had gathered from his investigation of the two murders, two attempted murders, plus the recent attack on Claire. Gilles was, at that particular moment, uncertain how it fit in with the other crimes.

Gilles was struggling to understand the connection between all the crimes. He had gathered up all the material he had and planned to spend the morning, or however long it took, reviewing the material and then re-reviewing it until the pattern of connections was made manifest.

In order to facilitate his analysis, Gilles had dragged the whiteboard from the squad room to the interrogation room so he could diagram his research in quiet. After an hour and a half of reading and drawing names in boxes on the whiteboard with different colour lines connecting the names, Gilles sat at the boardroom table and examined his handiwork. He stared at the whiteboard, lost in thought, pursing his lips out and then in, out and in, out and in.

◉

The cubicles in the ER were full that morning and Annie spent a hectic half day caring for her patients. When noon rolled around and the charge nurse told Annie that she could finally take a break she decided to grab a coffee and a sandwich at the café in the main building, far away from the ER. She feared that if she remained too close to the ER she would be asked if she could help out if things got crazy. She wanted to recharge her batteries undisturbed.

She took a shortcut to the main building; instead of following the labyrinth of hallways that led from the ER to the main building she walked outside and, because the weather was good, enjoyed the walk to the front entrance of the Gursky, the equivalent of three city blocks.

As she stepped out of the revolving door into the lobby she almost bumped up against Dr. Kavanaugh who had just exited and stopped to talk to someone and naturally assumed that everyone else would walk around him. Annie was about to make a pointed remark but, uncharacteristically, held her tongue. She noticed that Dr. Kavanaugh was neatly turned out in a blue blazer, grey slacks and a grey chalk-striped shirt with a white collar. He wore a silk tie with an abstract peach-and-blue pattern. She remembered that Gaston was looking for a blue blazer with a missing brass button, so she took special notice of Dr. Kavanaugh's blazer and its sleeves. All the buttons were in place.

She slipped around him keeping her eyes downcast to get another look at his sleeves and crossed the lobby to the café.

She got in line to order her coffee and sandwich and while she waited her mind wandered. It did not take long for an idea to penetrate her casual musings. She was certain that there was something wrong with what she saw of Dr. Kavanaugh's clothing. She could not put her finger on what that something was. It was nothing obvious such as a missing button or a button sewn on with a different colour thread, nothing like that. But something.

She paid for her coffee and sandwich, left the building and found a place at one of the picnic tables on the Gursky campus. While she ate she reviewed in her mind all that she had seen, and still could not put words to what was bothering her. After lunch, on her way back to the emergency department, she decided to call Gilles and share the little information she had with him.

She called but he did not answer. She disconnected and tried again . . . and again.

Gilles had lost track of time. He snapped out of his deep concentration when Detective Sergeant Gaston Lemieux came into the interrogation room. "Gilles, voilà. Je te cherchais."

Gilles looked at his superior and said, "Crisse, I'm sorry. I should have told someone where I was. I wanted a quiet place to think." Gilles indicated all the paperwork on the table and the whiteboard against the wall opposite. "Do you need the room?" Gilles began to organize his reports into some kind of order.

Gaston looked over Gilles's work, smiled and said, "Non, nothing like that. Your cellphone is ringing. I thought you'd want to know."

Gilles gave Gaston a confused look and reached into the inner pocket of his sports jacket, which he had hung on the back of the chair next to him. How was it possible that Gaston could hear his cellphone and he could not? The phone was not where it was supposed to be.

"It's on your desk," Gaston pointed out.

"I'm an idiot," Gilles said. He looked at his watch and saw that it was almost one in the afternoon. He got up from the table, put on his jacket. He and Gaston walked out of the interrogation room. Gilles picked up his cellphone and noticed that he had missed several calls from Annie.

Annie would only call so many times if she had something important to tell him.

Gilles called Annie, hoping she would not be with a patient. She answered on the second ring.

"I'm sorry, chérie, I left the phone on my desk," he explained as soon as Annie answered. "Is everything okay?"

"Yeah, fine," she replied. "I thought I would tell you that I almost bumped into Dr. Kavanaugh in the lobby—literally. He was wearing a blue blazer and I knew that you were interested in them and people who were wearing them."

"It would be too much to hope that he was missing a button, I suppose?"

"No, no, his jacket was fully intact. But here's the thing, there is something not right about it. I don't know what it is, but something," Annie explained.

"You mean something like different coloured thread?"

"No, I thought of that. It's something else. Something struck me as not being right."

Gilles didn't say anything for a minute while he thought about Annie's reply. "Well," he finally said, "I think it's time Dr. Kavanaugh and I had another chat. Is there any way you can tell me how long he'll be at the hospital? I'm going to try and get the authorization to send a car for him, to bring him to me."

"Not a clue," Annie told him. "And you know that we don't work in the same part of the hospital so I have no idea what he does or when he comes or goes. Running into him was pure coincidence."

"Okay, sweetie, thanks," Gilles told her. "I appreciate the heads-up."

Gilles slid the phone into his jacket pocket. He faced Gaston, who was leaning against Gilles's desk, and asked, "Do you think the captain will authorize picking up a material witness?"

Gaston avoided answering the question directly. He walked to his work area, which was an enclosed inner office. There was no view but there was a certain amount of privacy. There were windows in the wall that looked into the squad room so Gaston could see the bullpen and the officers could see who, if anyone, was in his office. But conversations were private. Gaston indicated that Gilles was to follow him.

Gaston slid into the chair behind his desk, which held a computer monitor and keyboard and, in the lower left corner, a telephone. There was only one file folder on the desk. Gilles occupied the visitor's chair.

"What've you got?" Gaston asked.

"A person of interest wearing a blue blazer that may not be kosher," Gilles explained. "The husband of the last vic —Dr. Kavanaugh."

"And . . ." Gaston prompted.

"That's it," Gilles told him.

Gaston said nothing for a moment. He appreciated Gilles's eagerness to get anything he could from anyone at all. But getting someone in a blue blazer that might not have been kosher, whatever that meant, to voluntarily come in for questioning was a stretch.

"Look," Gaston leaned forward and looked straight at Gilles, "that's not enough for a material witness warrant, much less an arrest warrant. You can ask the person to come in, but if he says no then it's no. You have no way to force him. You can go to the captain if you like, and I'll come with you if you want, but he'll not do anything more than tell you to request that the subject come in for an interview. Trust me."

Gilles's shoulders slumped and he sighed in exasperation. He wanted the home-court advantage when he questioned Dr. Kavanaugh.

Gilles got up from his chair and thanked Gaston for his advice. "I'll question him at the hospital and hope I learn something." He turned to leave when Gaston asked him to sit down again. "I don't understand how the doctor fits into your thinking. I thought he was almost a victim and that he was away when his wife was attacked."

"You're right on both counts," Gilles agreed. "But there's something not right about the guy. A certain arrogance. Yeah, he was stabbed, but not like the others. It was a surface wound, more like a deep cut, and the other stabbings were done by someone who meant business."

"He was in Toronto when his wife was attacked," Gaston repeated.

"Yeah. But if he somehow knew about his wife's affair then he would have motive."

"Did he know about it?"

"Not so far as I know."

"Just be careful not to accuse him of anything," Gaston said. "People like him have lawyers."

Gilles arrived at the Gursky Memorial Hospital at about two fifteen. He parked his car near the main entrance. A security guard came rushing up to Gilles as he exited his vehicle and was about to tell him that he couldn't park there when Gilles flashed his badge. The security guard nodded, shrugged and turned back to the security desk in the lobby. Gilles strolled into the lobby, asked the security guard where he could find

Dr. Kavanaugh, and was directed to his office, a couple of doors down the hallway that ran to the eastern entrance of the hospital.

Gilles walked in without knocking. He found himself in the secretary's office.

"May I help you?" she asked.

Gilles looked at her and said, "I'd like to see Dr. Kavanaugh."

"He's in a meeting in another part of the hospital," the secretary reported. "Do you have an appointment?"

Gilles showed the secretary his badge and stated, "Please call him and tell him that I'd like to talk to him. I'm Detective Sergeant Gilles Bellechasse. I'll wait."

Without waiting for an invitation, Gilles occupied one of the chairs in the waiting area. He could hear the secretary whispering tensely into the telephone, and five or so minutes later Dr. Kavanaugh strode into the office. He was not in a good mood. Annie had been right, he was wearing a blue blazer, a gold pocket handkerchief in his breast pocket. Annie was also right that nothing about the way Dr. Kavanaugh was dressed was out of order or even slightly askew. He could have posed for a fashion magazine.

"What's the meaning of this interruption?" he demanded. He stood over Gilles and did not extend his hand for a shake. The way he hovered made it difficult for Gilles to get up without forcing the doctor to back up a step or two; he got up quickly, almost throwing Dr. Kavanaugh off balance.

"I wouldn't have bothered you if it wasn't important," Gilles said. "Is there somewhere we can talk privately?"

Without a word, Dr. Kavanaugh circled around Gilles, opened the door to his private office, and walked in. Gilles followed him, closing the door behind him.

Dr. Kavanaugh's office was elegantly appointed. It was big enough to contain a large dark wood desk and a sofa, coffee tables and a couple of chairs to the left. There were windows on both sides of the desk and bookshelves on the wall behind it. There was a round table and four chairs to the right of the door, an area used for informal meetings. Everything in the office was neat and tidy, no dust on the desk, not a book out of place. The desk itself held a telephone and a computer terminal and keyboard. Separating them was a desk blotter. A cup with pens and pencils, a stapler and other work implements formed a semicircle around the top of the blotter.

Gilles knew from comments from Annie and her friends that money was tight at the Gursky and luxuries few. He wondered how Kavanaugh had managed to get himself an office worthy of the CEO of a large corporation.

Dr. Kavanaugh had marched to his desk and sat down. Gilles sat in one of the three visitors' chairs, the one in the centre, which directly faced the doctor.

"You called me out of a meeting," Dr. Kavanaugh stated. "Why?"

Gilles had decided on his drive to the hospital that he would take an oblique approach in questioning Dr. Kavanaugh, as there was nothing to be gained by being more direct. "Yes, I'm sorry to have disturbed you," Gilles said. "I wanted to ask you some questions about the attack on your wife while events were still fresh in your mind."

Dr. Kavanaugh tilted his chair back a couple of inches so that he was looking down his nose at Gilles. "What can you possibly mean, fresh in my mind? I was in Toronto. I told you anything that could possibly be helpful when I spoke to you."

"Yes, I'm sorry, I haven't made myself clear." Gilles maintained a conciliatory tone. "Now that you've had some time to reflect, can you think of anyone who would want to harm your wife?"

"No, of course not," came the predictable answer.

"Well, let me ask the question in another way," Gilles said. "Is it possible that someone connected with the people in her art class might have wanted to . . .?" He let the question trail off.

"Are you out of your mind?" Kavanaugh asked. "Those people . . . well, other than her friend Marjorie, I didn't know any of those people."

"None of them?" Gilles asked. "You are aware that one of them was murdered, non?"

"You mean one of those kids from the park? What's that got to do with Claire?" Dr. Kavanaugh rocked forward in his chair, placed his fists on his desk and got to his feet. He stared icily at Gilles.

Up to this point Gilles had been sitting back in his chair in a relaxed pose with his legs crossed. Now he uncrossed his legs and sat up straight, his back not touching the chair back. He held up one hand palm out and said, "Sit down, Dr. Kavanaugh. I'm not done." Eric Kavanaugh sat back down, a corner of his upper lip raised in the beginning of a snarl. He maintained a stony silence. "Well, one of them, Esperanza, was in her art class, and I have it on good authority that she knew him rather well."

A vein throbbed in Dr. Kavanaugh's neck as his face became flushed with anger. He got up from his desk, placed both fists on it, and leaned forward so that he was looking down at Gilles. "How dare you!" he exclaimed. "This meeting is at an end. If you have any more questions you can call my lawyer. Do I make myself clear?"

Gilles knew that this was the typical bluff of those with something to hide, and did not take it seriously. From where he sat he had a clear view of the shiny brass buttons on the sleeves of Dr. Kavanaugh's blazer, and after a moment or so of gazing at them he understood what Annie meant when she said that something was not right. Annie would have known what it was if she had seen it for more than a couple of seconds. There were four brass buttons on each sleeve of Dr. Kavanaugh's blazer, seven with lions rampant and one with a lion recumbent.

Gilles got to his feet and looked Dr. Kavanaugh straight in the eyes. In a calm voice, only a couple of decibels above a whisper, he said, "You know, I don't normally take threats about lawyers seriously. But some new evidence has come to my attention and I think it is best if we continued this conversation at my office."

Dr. Kavanaugh snorted a laugh. "You think so, do you? How about you fuck yourself? I'm not going anywhere. Now, get the fuck out of here and leave me alone."

Gilles took his phone out of his inside jacket pocket and started to make a call. Before he hit the call button, he said, "We can do this the easy way or the hard way. I can call my office," Gilles showed Kavanaugh his cellphone for emphasis, "and have them send a squad car, and have you taken out of here in handcuffs. Or you can walk out with me. My car is parked in front."

"What about a third option," Kavanaugh said. "You get in your car and drive off without me."

"There is no third option," Gilles said.

As Gilles waited for Dr. Kavanaugh to accept the inevitable, an idea occurred to him. Had he been alone or with Annie, he would have slapped his forehead, feeling stupid for not having seen the possibility before. He called his office and asked for one of the constables who was on duty. Gilles turned his back to Kavanaugh, walked a couple of feet from his desk and cupped the phone with his free hand so that the doctor would not hear him. "J'ai besoin que vous vérifiez les horaires des compagnies aériennes," Gilles said. He gave the constable the date that the doctor had been in Toronto and asked the cop to check *all* airlines that flew the Montreal-Toronto route for the twenty-four-hour period starting the day Kavanaugh left Montreal, to see which flights he had been on. "I'll be in soon," Gilles said. He again turned his attention to Dr. Kavanaugh. "Which is it going to be?"

Dr. Eric Kavanaugh sighed and said, "I'll go with you. But I want it clear that it is under protest. And I'll not answer another question unless my lawyer is present."

Dr. Kavanaugh strode around his desk and out of the office, acting as if going to the Major Crimes Division office was his idea. Gilles followed, doing his best not to smile. In the outer office, Dr. Kavanaugh stopped at his secretary's desk and said, "Please call Jay Berg. His phone number is in the contacts file and have him meet me at . . ." He paused and looked at Gilles. Gilles gave the secretary the location, although he was certain a lawyer, especially a criminal lawyer of Berg's stature, would know where the Major Crimes Division was.

Before his secretary could ask any questions Dr. Kavanaugh turned and walked out of his office with Gilles Bellechasse at his elbow.

Neither man talked on the drive to the office. The reasons for their silence were more or less the same. Gilles wanted anything that Eric Kavanaugh said to be on the record, and Kavanaugh did not want to say anything that might be mis-construed and used against him at a later date. Gilles guided Kavanaugh through the shopping centre to the elevators, pausing only to inquire if Dr. Kavanaugh wanted a coffee. The offer was refused. Gilles sighed inwardly; this meant that he couldn't stop to buy one and he did not want the sludge in the squad break room that would pass for coffee this late in the day. He hoped that he would be able to convince one of the constables or clerical workers to take pity on him and fetch him a coffee.

Before Gilles guided Dr. Kavanaugh through the door that connected the reception area to the squad and interrogation rooms, Gilles stopped and told the receptionist that he expected Maître Berg and to please "l'envoyer à la salle d'interrogation numéro un."

The receptionist checked to ensure that interrogation room number one was available and nodded.

Gilles led his quarry to the interrogation room and told him to sit down. The room itself reeked of the body odours of the hundreds of people who had been questioned in it. The walls had last been painted a dark green when the office space was rented, and had turned blackish over time. The ceiling had at one time been white, but over the many years when people were permitted to smoke in offices, had turned khaki brown. Other than the chairs and a table there was no furniture in the room. A shelf on the wall held recording equipment, and a microphone hung over the centre of the table. The wall opposite Dr. Kavanaugh held a two-way mirror.

Gilles sat down opposite Dr. Kavanaugh. Under the table edge there was a button that Gilles could use to summon someone from the squad room. As soon as Gilles was settled in his chair with his notebook open in front of him, Eric Kavanaugh stated, "I take it anything I say in this room is being recorded." He nodded in the direction of the mic. "So I am stating for the record that I'll not answer any questions until my lawyer gets here." With that he folded his arms across his chest and glared at Gilles.

"The recorder isn't on yet," Gilles pointed out.

"The people behind the glass heard me." Kavanaugh jutted his chin in the direction of the mirror.

Gilles wished he had stopped for a coffee so he would have something to do while they waited in silence. He often wondered what would happen if he brought a book in with him and read during the silent periods. Would the suspect break the silence and say something that could later be used? Gilles had no desire to risk the wrath of Captain Lacroix in order to find out.

After about ten minutes of being stared at by Dr. Kavanaugh, Gilles decided that silence would not intimidate Kavanaugh into saying anything. He pressed the buzzer and a minute or two later a uniformed cop, Constable Bélanger, Gilles's former partner, poked her head through the door.

"Can you watch our guest?" Gilles asked. "I want to go down for a coffee. Would you like one?"

Nicole came into the room and sat down in the chair Gilles had just vacated and said, "Oui, s'il te plaît." And then she added, "La recherche que tu a demandée . . ." She didn't finish her sentence because Gilles cut her off with a shake of his head.

Gilles went down to the food court in search of coffee and spotted Jay Berg coming in from the parking lot. The two men did not know one another but Gilles recognized him from the many times he had seen his photograph in the newspaper. Gilles caught up with the lawyer, introduced himself and asked him if he wanted a coffee. "Good idea," the lawyer said, "but I'll buy my own."

Jay Berg was couple of inches shorter than Gilles's six feet one inch, and a little paunchier. But his dynamic personality somehow made him seem taller. He had an oval-shaped head with thinning hair, brown going to grey at the temples. His intelligent eyes were hard to read, as they were shielded behind grey-tinted glasses. The set of his mouth indicated that his smiles were rare and hard-earned. Berg was dressed in a rumpled, dark grey suit and he carried a well-worn tan leather brief case that he must have had since the early days of his practice. He bought two coffees, one for himself and the other for his client.

They rode up the elevator without talking, and as they passed through the reception area Jay Berg stopped by the desk of the receptionist and said, "Bonjour, Hélène, ça va?" The receptionist smiled and returned the greeting.

Gilles led the lawyer to interrogation room one and opened the door. Constable Bélanger got to her feet. Berg parked himself in the chair next to his client and handed him a coffee. Gilles handed Nicole Bélanger her coffee and walked her to the door, thanked her, and whispered to her that when he next buzzed to please bring in the file of research he had requested.

On his way back to his chair, Gilles turned on the recording equipment. While Kavanaugh and his lawyer added milk to their coffees, Gilles stated, for the benefit of the recording equipment, the day, date, and time, and the names of those present.

"So, what've we got here?" Berg asked.

"I'll tell you what we've got," Kavanaugh said, "We've got bullshit and harassment!"

Berg put a restraining hand on his client's forearm and waited for Gilles to answer the question.

Gilles cleared his throat and answered, "Dr. Kavanaugh has been brought in for questioning in relation to two murders and two attempted murders."

"Is he a suspect or a witness, or neither?" Berg queried.

"At this point he's not a suspect, but that could change," Gilles replied.

"So, at worst he's a witness and can leave at any time?"

"Yes, but if he left before I had a chance to question him, that might change his status," Gilles explained.

"Okay," Berg said. "Ask your questions and I'll decide if my client will answer them. He has the right to remain silent."

Gilles started by asking where Dr. Kavanaugh was at the time that Mikel Esperanza was murdered?

"How do I know? Probably at work. I'd have to check my agenda," the doctor replied.

Gilles asked him for his whereabouts at the time that Ron Jardine was murdered and Hari Deshpande was attacked, and received the same answer.

"I would like to know how it is," Gilles asked, "that one of the brass buttons on Dr. Kavanaugh's blazer is different than the others?"

Berg was surprised by the question and did nothing to hide it. Dr. Kavanaugh did his best not to let his eyes betray any emotion other than arrogant indifference to Gilles's question, but the colour did drain out of his face. He recovered his composure quickly. "I'm a doctor, not a tailor, how the hell would I know?"

"I need some context in order to understand the question," Berg put in.

"We recovered a brass button with the image of a lion rampant embossed on it, very much like seven of the buttons on your client's blazer. One of the buttons has clearly been replaced. I know that because it has a lion recumbent on it."

"Or," Berg pointed out, "the manufacturer sewed the button on for whatever reason. Maybe it ran out of one kind and used the other."

"It's possible," Gilles agreed. "Further investigation will answer that question." He buzzed the squad room and waited the minute or two it took Constable Bélanger to bring the file folder.

Gilles opened it and slowly read through the information contained in it. Jay Berg was used to police interrogation tactics and understood that it was entirely possible that the detective was pretending to read an empty file in order to intimidate his client into thinking that he had some incriminating information. Jay held a whispered conversation with his client telling him, in effect, not to be taken in by the tactic.

Gilles closed the file folder and spoke directly to Dr. Kavanaugh. "I see that you flew to Toronto yesterday afternoon."

Dr. Kavanaugh sighed and said, "Yes, as I told you."

"I also see that you flew back to Montreal on a four o'clock flight, arriving at five. To be accurate it was the Porter Airlines flight leaving at 3:55 and arriving at 5:05. Giving you plenty of time to attack your wife and get the . . ." Gilles paused and opened the file, read for a second or two, closed the file and continued, ". . . and get the seven o'clock Porter flight to the island airport. You were back in Toronto when your wife called you and safely back at your hotel when I phoned you there."

From the island airport to the hotel by taxi was a matter of a maximum of thirty minutes. Kavanaugh was taking a risk, but a calculated one. Kavanaugh knew he had a couple of hours to get back to Toronto while his wife was being attended to. If he had succeeded in killing her, which was his plan, he would have had more than two hours to establish his alibi.

Gilles didn't say any of this to Dr. Kavanaugh, letting him work out for himself the nature of the evidence that he had. Kavanaugh's natural arrogance kept him from showing the nervousness he felt. But it was clear to Gilles from the way the suspect gripped his lawyer's forearm that he understood that he had a problem, a very serious problem.

Jay Berg didn't yet know the whole story concerning the crime his client was suspected of having committed, but he knew that the information that the detective had just provided was not good for his client. "I'm calling a time out," Berg stated. "I want to confer privately with my client."

Gilles got to his feet, picked up the file folder, and said, "I'll give you the room."

"Thank you," Berg stated. "I'm sure I don't have to remind you to turn that thing off." He pointed at the mic that hung over the table.

Gilles nodded, turned off the recording equipment, and walked out of the interrogation room.

Once they were alone, Jay Berg shifted his chair so that he was looking at his client. "Tell me," he stated. "Don't leave anything out. And remember, lying to the cops is dumb, but lying to me is beyond stupid."

"My wife was having an affair with some grotty little art student who was also a drug dealer. A total loser," Kavanaugh began. He didn't stop talking until he'd told his lawyer the whole story.

"Holy fuck," Berg said when Kavanaugh finished talking. Jay Berg was used to defending all kinds of criminals, including murderers. As bad as they were, the killers usually had some kind of bizarre reason for their crimes. He had never had a client who killed or attempted to kill completely innocent people in order to cover up the crime of murdering his intended victims—in this case, his wife and her lover.

After a short pause, Berg told his client, "I'm going to bring the detective back into the room. You are not to say one word. Get it? And if you're arrested, which is more than likely given the evidence I think they have, do not talk about your case to anyone in the jail. It's full of snitches."

It had never occurred to Kavanaugh that he would end up in jail. He went white and stopped breathing for a minute. He took a couple of deep breaths and nodded his agreement.

Berg went to the door of the interrogation room and called for Detective Bellechasse to return. Berg remained on his feet and when Gilles came into the room said, "I don't know what your next step will be, but I've advised my client to say nothing. You're not to ask him any questions unless I am in the room and I'll be the one answering them on his behalf—if I answer them at all."

"D'accord," Gilles responded. He then said to Eric Kavanaugh, "Stand up, please. Dr. Eric Kavanaugh, I am arresting you for the murder of Mikel Esperanza, Ron Jardine, Jr. and other crimes. Turn around."

Eric stood, but did not turn until his lawyer gently nudged him. Gilles tapped the buzzer under the table and came around and placed Kavanaugh's wrists in handcuffs. Constable Bélanger and another cop came into the room and Gilles said, "Take him and have him booked."

They led Dr. Eric Kavanaugh, now a prisoner, out of the room. "I'll catch up with you at the jail," Jay Berg called after him. "Remember, not one word to anyone."

CHAPTER TWENTY

"Mikel was a lovely person and did not deserve to die."

For what probably amounted to the first time in his adult life, Eric Kavanaugh took someone's advice. He kept silent. Part of the reason was that the experience of being jailed was terrifying. The cops and guards who processed him did so with bureaucratic indifference to him as a person, much less as a doctor and highly respected member of the medical community of Montreal. Jail was a cold, dank place that had been in need of improvements for decades, perhaps a century. To Eric it seemed positively Dickensian. His fellow inmates were people he would, under normal circumstances, cross the street to avoid. The constant noise and harsh neon light were unsettling. During his first twenty-four hours of incarceration he was certain he would lose his mind. He couldn't contemplate the rest of his life in such a place.

True to his word, Jay Berg came to see Eric the day following his arrest. Eric made a valiant effort to maintain his professional, detached demeanour. It took great effort and lasted about ten minutes. "When can you get me out of here?" Eric pleaded, near tears. "I can afford bail so long as it's not totally unreasonable."

Most of the people Jay Berg represented were career criminals who understood the justice system as well as any member of the criminal bar. They knew that once they were in, there was a good chance that they would not be getting out. Eric watched a lot of television and required a dose of Jay Berg's brand of reality. "There's a possibility that you won't get out," he said. Eric slumped in his chair and seemed to become smaller. "I'll talk to the crown prosecutor, Manon Tremblay, and see if she'll be reasonable when we appear before the judge. You have to understand that this is, or will be, a high-profile case, and she may want to make an example of you. We'll see."

"Oh, fuck!" Eric exclaimed.

"Exactly," Berg agreed. "There'll be a trial and I want to start working on your defense. We'll work backwards, starting with the attack on Claire. You say you were in Toronto, no?"

From his conversation with Gilles, Berg had a general idea of the charges that his client would be likely to face. The specifics would come in a day or two, but he wanted to start getting Eric's story organized as soon as possible. For the next two hours they talked about Eric's whereabouts when Claire was stabbed and they worked their way back to the first stabbing, of Mikel Esperanza. Eric claimed he was at work at the times of the stabbings and he was certain that there were any number of people who had seen him. Berg was less certain.

Eric cited the fact that he himself had been the victim of a stabbing in the same park as the other victims as proof that he had not done anything wrong. "I was a bloody victim for Christ's sake!" he shouted. Again, there were no witnesses.

Jay Berg was successful in getting bail for Dr. Eric Kavanaugh, but he had to pledge their house to the court. The doctor was at liberty to await his trial at home, but he could not leave except to see his lawyer or for medical emergencies. And of course he had to surrender his passport and all but one of his credit cards. Claire chose not to remain in the house with her husband as he waited for his trial to begin. Marjorie opened her home to her.

◎

Manon Tremblay had crossed swords with Jay Berg in court on many occasions, and was aware that he was able to magnify even the smallest flaw in her case. In order to ensure that there were no problems with the evidence she arranged a meeting with Gilles Bellechasse to evaluate it for herself.

Gilles explained how the button in Ron Jardine's hand was the first lead they got, and which, in the end, pointed to Dr. Kavanaugh. Manon informed the cop that if that was the only evidence the accused would very likely walk. It was even possible that Berg would have the evidence of the button excluded as there were too many blue blazers with brass buttons to be certain that this button identified the murderer.

Gilles outlined the rest of the evidence. First and foremost were the flights that Kavanaugh took to and from Toronto. This gave him ample time to attempt to murder his wife. Working backwards from this, Gilles investigated Kavanaugh's so-called alibis for the two murders and one attempted murder. In all cases the good doctor was scheduled to be at meetings, but the others in attendance remembered that he was late or that the meetings were held at a different time than Kavanaugh claimed.

Following Kavanaugh's arrest Gilles obtained a warrant to search the Kavanaugh home, and he took the extra precaution of getting Claire's permission as well. The search turned up two pieces of incriminating evidence. First there was an Amazon.ca invoice for half a dozen SOG Seal Pup hunting knives. The cops found one of the knives in Eric's tool box—a clever attempt to hide something in plain sight.

Finally, they found a Wusthof Tri-stone knife-sharpening kit in a desk drawer in Dr. Kavanaugh's study. Claire told the cops that she had never seen either the knives or the sharpening stones before.

Manon Tremblay was satisfied that the evidence was unassailable and that Jay Berg's client was done for.

A month after his arrest and a couple of months before his trial started, the Collège des médecins du Québec suspended Eric Kavanaugh's license to practice medicine. On the first day of his trial Eric pleaded not guilty to all the charges against him. Berg arranged for Eric to meet with Manon Tremblay to review her evidence. On the second day of his trial, Dr. Eric Kavanaugh changed his plea to guilty; to one count of premeditated murder, the killing of his wife's lover, Mikel Esperanza. Killing your wife's lover, Eric thought, was a manly—and excusable—thing to do. The court disagreed. Eric Kavanaugh was sentenced to life imprisonment with no possibility of parole for seventeen years.

Claire was neither in the court for the two days of Eric's trial, nor to hear the sentence delivered a week later. She read about it in the *Montreal Gazette*. The families of the murder victims, along with Hari Deshpande and his family, attended both days of the short trial and sentencing. The three families feared that Kavanaugh had made a deal that would allow him to gain his freedom after serving a short prison sentence. The Esperanzas and the Despandes were pleased that they would be spared a lengthy trial. The Esperanzas had no desire to relive the trauma of losing Mikel. The Deshpandes wanted to put the experience behind them. The Jardine family were unhappy that Eric would not stand trial for the death of their son and brother, but understood that his sentence would not have been any different had he been tried and found guilty.

Shared grief brought the families of the three victims together and during the short trial they sat in the same section of the courtroom and would chat in the corridor before court was in session and during breaks. The Esperanzas and the Jardines did their best to cope with the emptiness that would haunt their lives forever and did nothing to hide their impotent anger toward Kavanaugh.

The three families had their final conversation on the court house steps on rue St-Jacques. Members of the extended Jardine family had some experience with the justice system and, uncharitably but not without reason, expressed the opinion that they hoped Eric Kavanaugh would, one way or another, end his life in prison. The Esperanzas, (Mikel's father had returned to Montreal as soon as he could following the tragedy of his son's death) and the Deshpandes agreed.

The fact that Eric Kavanaugh had been stabbed was never mentioned. Both Tremblay and Bellechasse were certain that he did it to himself. Other than its location his wound was no more serious than a cut made while chopping vegetables.

Gilles was in court when the judge delivered his sentence. He congratulated Prosecutor Tremblay on the verdict. He was pleased to see Eric Kavanaugh being led out of the courtroom in handcuffs to begin his sentence.

On the morning that Claire read about her husband's prison sentence in the *Gazette* she was having breakfast with

Marjorie. Claire closed the newspaper and pushed it aside. She reached for a napkin to dry her eyes. "Surely you're not shedding a tear for that son of a bitch?" Marjorie said. Claire had been in a fragile state from the time that Eric was arrested, rarely going out and barely talking. Marjorie adjusted her schedule so that her friend was rarely alone. "Hardly," Claire replied, some of her character returning to her voice. "He deserves it." She wiped her eyes again. "I feel awful for the Esperanza family. Mikel was a lovely person and didn't deserve to die. Eric could have divorced me and got on with his life. He didn't have to become a murderer. And those other people. It is just so sad and I feel awful for my part in this mess."

Marjorie came around to the side of the table where Claire was sitting and pulled a chair in close to her friend. She put her arms around her and said, "Don't blame yourself. You didn't kill anyone and you aren't responsible for the acts of a deranged egomaniac. You're not the first woman to . . . well, you know. Eric had choices and he made the wrong ones. Let him rot in jail."

Claire sniffled and dabbed the corners of her eyes. She said nothing, but it was clear to Marjorie that she was on the way to becoming her old vivacious self.

CHAPTER TWENTY-ONE

"Your girlfriend has good observational skills."

To say that the hospital vibrated with gossip when Dr. Kavanaugh was arrested would be an understatement. Everyone who worked at the Gursky, from the newest hired member of the cleaning crew to senior medical staff, had an opinion on his guilt or innocence. With the exception of Dr. Kavanaugh's secretary, the consensus was that he was guilty. Most of the discussions concerning Kavanaugh and his crimes centered on motive. Very few people who worked at the hospital in any capacity knew of Claire's affair with Mikel Esperanza; in fact, they barely knew Claire. It was well known that Kavanaugh was married to a very beautiful former employee of the hospital, but not much more.

Those who worked in the emergency department and knew Gilles Bellechasse and Annie Linton had a much better handle on events. In the days following the arrest of the chief of medicine, Annie was unable to have a meal or a coffee break alone during her shifts at the hospital. Everyone, people who knew her well and those who barely knew who she was, wanted the inside dope on the murders and the arrest of Kavanaugh. Annie, not much of a gossip to begin with, put off most questions by telling the interlocutor that

Gilles did not discuss his cases with her. No one believed her, but that was her story and she stuck to it.

Claire spent the period following her husband's arrest at her friend Marjorie's and intended to return home as soon as the hubbub died down. Marjorie convinced her that that would be a bad idea and she was welcome to stay for as long as she liked. In the end, Claire stayed with Marjorie until her husband pleaded guilty and was sentenced. She started divorce proceedings as soon as she could. Eric agreed that she could have the house so long as she sold it and paid his legal fees with the proceeds. The rest would be hers to do with as she pleased, and it pleased her to buy a condo not far from where Marjorie lived.

Claire had to find a job and she chose not to return to working in a lab. Instead she got a job in an art gallery on Sherbrooke Street and discovered that she had a good eye for up-and-coming artists and, better, was really gifted at selling art to the gallery's wealthy clientele.

Over time, Claire was able to construct a meaningful and happy life for herself. But there was also a sadness, a feeling of guilt over what had happened to Mik Esperanza and the misery it caused his family. If she had not had an affair with him, he would still be alive. It was impossible to shake her sense of responsibility over the events that flowed from her decision to be with him. She met with Mikel's family to offer an apology to them for the unhappiness she had caused and they graciously accepted it. But Claire knew that their acceptance was only politeness. She knew they would never forgive her and that she would never forgive herself.

When the news of Eric Kavanaugh's guilty plea and sentence reached the hospital, it was greeted with I-told-you-so shrugs and not much else. As always in a high-pressure environment, present crises took precedence over past events.

Again, the exception was the emergency department. By the time Kavanaugh began his sentence, word had somehow leaked out that Annie had provided the clue that focused suspicion on him and which led to his arrest. Annie faced another round of questions for a day or so and then life in the ER returned to its normal day-to-day state of rushing from medical emergency to medical emergency.

◎

A couple of months following the final disposition of the case, Gilles ran into Manon Tremblay in the halls of the court house. After the normal exchange of pleasantries, Manon said, "Il y a quelque chose que je voulais te demander."

Gilles understood that she was referring to the Kavanaugh case and answered, "How can I help you?"

"The lion thing on the brass button tipped you off to the fact that Kavanaugh was likely the murderer?"

Gilles nodded and said, "Yes, absolutely."

"But I've always wondered how you knew about it? When you brought Kavanaugh in, the fact that the brass button came from his blazer had been established. So how did you spot it?"

Gilles smiled. "I wasn't the one who first observed the mismatch of the buttons. It was my girlfriend, Annie. She's a nurse in the emergency department at the hospital."

"A nurse," Manon repeated. "I see. That explains it."

ACKNOWLEDGEMENTS

It's one thing to write a novel but quite another to impose on your friends to read early drafts of it and have them suggest changes and improvements. I'm blessed that I have people I can turn to for just such advice and who offer it without complaint.

John Aylen took time from his busy work and gardening schedule to read the novel and made invaluable suggestions that I followed in order to remove a lot of back story that added nothing to the plot. Elise Moser, who I've known from the time she was an undergraduate at McGill University, served as the editor of the novel. Her editorial suggestions were excellent and I was pleased to follow them. Deirdre O'Donnell King lent me her years of experience in the field of literature, suggesting the addition of some further detail to give the novel a sense of place as well as further cuts to excess verbiage. I am indebted to her. Barbara Rudnicka proofread the manuscript and hunted down all the errors and typos that so annoy readers and writers. This is a difficult job and I appreciate her attention to detail.

Robin Philpot, the publisher of Baraka Books, shared my affection for Annie and Gilles and saw the merits of *A Stab at Life* in an early and unpolished version. It has been a delight working with him and I look forward to a long association with him and Baraka Books.

I am fortunate to call Montreal my home. It is a terrific city to use as a setting for a novel. I'm not the first writer to feel this way and I am indebted to those who have gone before me for making Montreal a character in their novels. I've changed the name of one of Montreal's parks and moved it a couple of blocks to the east and north to suit the plot. I've also added some restaurants that are not so far a part of culinary Montreal.

Mary Reinhold read a very early version of the novel and pointed out some obvious flaws in the manuscript. In addition to this she nourishes me in ways too numerous to list.

My brothers Joel and Norman and my son Nicholas fill my life with joy and I am thankful for their support.

I have been a volunteer in the emergency department of the Jewish General Hospital in Montreal since 2009. I have witnessed the nurses in that department perform miracles of compassion and diagnosis on a regular basis. They are truly amazing people and deserve the gratitude and appreciation of the public they so willingly serve. The character of Annie Linton is modeled on Margaret Quinsey one of the ER nurses at the Jewish General Hospital. Margaret, Maggie to her friends and colleagues, greets each patient with a warm and encouraging smile throughout the work day. She is tireless in her efforts to comfort the sick and to help them to heal. She is without question a very special person and I am pleased to count her as a friend and inspiration.

Notable Fiction from Baraka Books

Things Worth Burying, A Novel by Matt Mayr

Exile Blues by Douglas Gary Freeman

Fog by Rana Bose

The Daughters' Story by Murielle Cyr

Yasmeen Haddad Loves Joanasi Maqaittik by Carolyn Marie Souaid

Vic City Express by Yannis Tsirbas (translated from the Greek by Fred A. Reed)

A Beckoning War by Matt Murphy

The Nickel Range Trilogy by Mick Lowe
    The Raids
    The Insatiable Maw
    Wintersong

And from QC Fiction, an imprint of Baraka Books

Songs for the Cold of Heart by Eric Dupont (translated by Peter McCambridge) 2018 Giller Finalist

The Little Fox of Mayerville by Éric Mathieu (translated by Peter McCambridge)

Prague by Maude Veilleux (translated by Aleshia Jensen & Aimée Wall)

In the End They Told Them All to Get Lost by Laurence Leduc-Primeau (translated by Natalia Hero)

Notable Nonfiction

The Complete Muhammad Ali by Ishmael Reed

A Distinct Alien Race, The Untold Story of Franco-Americans by David Vermette

Through the Mill, Girls and Women in the Quebec Cotton Textile Industry, 1881-1951 by Gail Cuthbert Brandt

The Einstein File, The FBI's Secret War on the World's Most Famous Scientist by Fred Jerome

Montreal, City of Secrets, Confederate Operations in Montreal During the American Civil War by Barry Sheehy

Printed by Imprimerie Gauvin
Gatineau, Québec